UNDER ONE ROOF

SAMANTHA TONGE

B

Boldwood

First published in Great Britain in 2022 by Boldwood Books Ltd.

This paperback edition first published in 2023.

1

A CIP catalogue record for this book is available from the British Library.

Paperback ISBN: 978-1-83751-992-7

Ebook ISBN: 978-1-80415-402-1

Kindle ISBN: 978-1-80415-403-8

Audio CD ISBN: 978-1-80415-410-6

Digital audio download ISBN: 978-1-80415-401-4

Large Print ISBN: 978-1-80415-405-2

Boldwood Books Ltd.

23 Bowerdean Street, London, SW6 3TN

www.boldwoodbooks.com

For Martin, Immy and Jay.
There's nobody else I'd rather live under one roof with xxx

1

Robin walked along the corridor to Uncle Ralph's room, a journey she could have made with her eyes closed. Usually he would have been in the residents' lounge, beating his friends at cards. Instead, today her uncle sat on his bed by the window, combing his hair, minus his usual cordial smile.

She kissed his forehead when he stiffly stood up, and watched as he lowered himself into his armchair. Robin knew better than to offer to help. Instead she handed over a Tupperware box before sitting down opposite. He prised off the lid.

He savoured the first bite of one of his favourite biscuits and then sighed.

'Best get on with it.' He passed her the letter, the reason he'd texted last night.

Her eyes skimmed the page; it was from Faye's neighbour, Blanche. Robin remembered her kindness well. So Faye had slipped partway down... the loft ladder? A pang of longing shot through her chest. Robin had climbed those ladders numerous times a day in her teens, they always had been rickety. *Broken wrist... bruised ribs... won't accept any help...* What would she have been doing up there?

'How did Blanche know where you live?' Robin asked, not looking up from the letter.

'Faye's mentioned Moss Lodge to her.' He finished his biscuit and put down the box, then struggled to thread his watch strap through the keeper. Robin ignored the pursed lips as she leant over and did it for him. 'She's as stubborn as they come,' he continued. 'If you ask me, she won't have any problem convincing the hospital she can manage, once they've discharged her next week. I've tried ringing her mobile to make her see she has to involve the authorities, to get the necessary support, but she's not picking up.'

A sense of discomfort flickered inside her and Robin stared at the crumbs in her uncle's grey, bristly beard.

'Maybe this is fate – you've nothing else to do at the moment, what with being made redundant.' He gave her a look and she forced a bright smile, despite her stomach churning. Her payout wouldn't last forever and she'd already received several job rejection emails.

'Now don't you try to dress it up, Uncle Ralph, just go ahead and give it to me straight.'

'It's a chance to take a break in the Peak District, the autumn leaf fall there is outstanding.' He raised an eyebrow. 'Feel any better?'

Robin shook her head. Going back there, facing Faye's disapproving stares and comments once more, she'd feel like a child again.

'Imagine me living with Faye. We wouldn't last two seconds.'

'But it's down to us to look after her, she hasn't got anyone else and I promised your dad, brother to brother, that I'd always look out for her.'

Robin sat very still. 'You're serious, aren't you? And why haven't I ever known that?'

'I couldn't tell you when you were younger, you were so damn angry about everything. I didn't want you to run away from me as well.' His voice softened. 'When Alan died it was as if I'd inherited my very own family, a sister-in-law and a niece – who became so much more. I wouldn't change a thing, other than wanting my brother back – and wishing you and your mother had made it up. You're as pig-headed as each other.'

Robin winced. She was nothing like Faye. 'I can't go to Stonedale.'

'Can't or won't, Missy?'

He still spoke to her as if she wore dental braces and the centre of her world was the Sunday night Top 40 and *Girl Scene* magazine's Dear Debbie problem page, and for a split second she wanted to go back to her teenage years and be that young girl again. Robin shook her head. There was no going back. She helped herself to another biscuit and put the whole thing in at once.

Uncle Ralph reached into the box again too, but his fingers faltered. 'Please love, do it for me – I can't let Alan down.'

* * *

Back in her flat, that night, Robin tried to zone out in front of her favourite dance show but the slick, glitzy performances didn't captivate her. She forced down a salmon salad, her usual Saturday night meal. As eleven o'clock approached she laid out her gym kit; Sunday mornings always meant an hour on the treadmill. Rain was due tomorrow so she searched the small, square lounge looking for her umbrella, but despite the tidiness, she couldn't find it. After brushing her teeth for two minutes

Robin got undressed. Her wardrobe comprised of starched lines and taupes, with the discreet, executive look she'd honed over the years.

She climbed into bed and thought back to what Uncle Ralph was asking of her. Before leaving she'd wrapped both her hands around one of his – a hand that had helped her so much over the years, wiping away teenage tears of frustration, filling in forms with her as she learnt to open bank accounts, a hand that had held her arm firmly as he walked her up the aisle.

Robin had tried to pay him back as she got older, to clear the debt he never called in – in small ways at first, like making his evening meal occasionally and then, as time passed, more significant opportunities arose. She nursed him through bronchitis and, from time to time, he'd go on holiday with Robin, her husband, Todd, and their daughter, Amber, before their marriage ended. In the last year or two she'd cut his hair, although perhaps that wasn't much of a favour.

Robin hadn't seen her mother since Amber was born, eighteen years now. Uncle Ralph looked so tired these days; how would Faye have aged? Or would time have treated her more kindly, without a difficult daughter around? Robin had barely looked at her uncle when she'd first moved in with him, because he looked so like his brother, her dad, with the same cleft chin and gentle tone. A runaway teenager must have made his life much harder.

Robin turned onto her side and hugged her knees, squinting through the darkness at her bedside cactus.

'It's a good thing you don't need frequent watering,' she whispered. 'I'm taking a break in the Peak District, the autumn leaf fall there is outstanding.'

2

Robin sat in her car, outside number sixteen Parade Row, willing herself to get out. Maybe she should have rung to warn her mother she was coming. Blanche didn't want Faye to know that she'd written, so wouldn't have said a word. The plus side to all this was that if Robin left now, Faye would be none the wiser.

She opened the car door, then closed it again. The Sunday traffic hadn't been bad, but she felt exhausted. Robin sat there a few moments more, before flexing her hands and getting out. The front door was still bottle green. She gazed down the row of two up, two down, terraced houses that could have come from any other street in the village. She went up to the gate, opened it and walked across a small concrete yard and past two wheelie bins. Without front gardens the houses looked straight onto the street. Robin knocked on the door. She wanted to get back into her car and drive around the village but she'd already done that twice, both times reading the stone sign, in front of the bridge, that went over Sheepwash River, saying *Stonedale, a Thankful Village*.

A couple of barks answered as she knocked again, Faye

wouldn't have liked neighbours owning a dog. However, another louder bark sounded. Faye had a dog? Surely not? A sliding chain clanked on the other side. Her heart pounded as the door opened and a snuffly French bulldog with large bat ears stuck its wrinkled nose outside, paws pounding up and down in an important manner like a marching drummer.

'Heel, boy,' a voice said.

The slate-coloured dog retreated behind navy slippers with a sulky expression on his face. The two women looked up at the same time.

The sight of Faye almost winded Robin.

Her mother used to be taller. Now she was hunched, with brunette hair that had faded to grey and skin that concertinaed around her mouth. Her eyes looked huge behind rimless glasses, the only part of her that had grown in stature. Faye gasped and leant the arm without a sling against the wall. The burgundy cardigan matched the slacks but wasn't done up properly and half of her blouse's collar stood up. Her short hair was a mess.

'What are you doing here?' she asked, with heavy breaths.

'I heard about your accident.'

'I'm ship-shape,' she snapped and flinched as she moved to support her own weight again. 'It's you who looks as if they could do with a good meal.'

Too fat, too thin, never perfect. Not everything had changed. Robin waited, holding her gaze and Faye blinked rapidly for a moment before moving to one side. Reluctantly, Robin gestured for her to lead the way and closed the door behind them both as Faye shuffled into the lounge on the left. The proud air she always carried had disappeared. Before going in, she turned and gave Robin's feet a pointed look. As Faye disappeared Robin slipped off her shoes and dropped her car keys into one of them. She followed her mother in.

Robin hadn't been back to Stonedale since 1989 when she'd escaped. With Yul. Her first boyfriend. She wouldn't think of him now. She stopped in the lounge doorway and couldn't help feeling disappointed. It now had light beech furniture instead of dark mahogany and the coal fireplace had been replaced by an electric one. It was silly to have expected things to look the same. The walls were painted a delicate mint-green, a little faded, instead of the old bold, floral wallpaper, and pale laminate floor lay where chintz carpet once did. The comfy three-piece suite had gone, and now a smart chaise longue stretched out beneath the bay window, although it was fraying at the front. A wilted plant sat on the sill instead of the weekly bunch of carnations Dad would buy. There was a green armchair on the left as you walked in and another to the right, against the opposite wall, next to a beech cabinet with a neat pile of magazines on top, all called *Word Weekly*, and a remote control. Gingerly, Faye lowered herself into the right hand one and the dog sat patiently at her feet until she'd settled, then he jumped onto her lap.

Faye stroked his ears and patted his back. Robin forced herself not to stare.

The only traces of the life she once knew were the pictures on the walls – the painting of Sheepwash Bridge and a pretty watercolour of a vase of sweet pea flowers, she'd forgotten that. Above the beech cabinet was the photo of her parents outside All Saints Church, on their wedding day. And... oh... one of Robin in the last year of junior school, all freckles and curls.

'You aren't as gobby as you used to be,' said Faye. 'What's the matter? Cat got your tongue?'

The sharp voice, more like the one Robin remembered, cut

through her thoughts. But she still couldn't speak, words stifled by memories. To the far right, behind a dining room table and chairs, a large bookcase had replaced the old Welsh dresser that used to be filled with Dad's collection of small antique brass bells. On the top shelf was a seaside painting from the only holiday the three of them had taken abroad. She'd been so excited to go to Spain and even Faye enjoyed herself, splashing in the waves. Robin had hardly recognised the carefree woman in a bikini, strolling along the beach in Malaga. The painting featured a beachside restaurant that they'd often gone to.

She sat on the chaise longue and zipped her anorak up higher. 'This room is different.'

'Time doesn't stand still just because folk leave.'

Faye still wore her wedding ring, still pulled on her ear when she was thrown off balance. But her pink nail varnish was chipped and her eyebrows needed taming. Small details Faye used to consider significant.

'Uncle Ralph said that you'd broken your wrist and bruised a couple of ribs.'

'How did he know?'

She looked so small, as if the decades had sapped her strength, as if the dog might look after *her* instead of the other way around.

'Robin?'

'Um... is he written down as your next of kin somewhere? Perhaps the hospital...'

'They had no right,' Faye said, hotly. 'Why didn't he tell me you were passing through Stonedale?'

'He tried ringing but you didn't pick up.'

'This isn't very convenient,' she said brusquely. 'Why exactly *are* you here?'

Robin glanced at the wedding photo again. 'I'm here until you can manage on your own.'

'You think you're *staying* in Stonedale? Just like that?' The sallow cheeks coloured up. 'If you'd rung first I could have saved you the journey.'

'Well, you don't answer the phone. You'll need help with the shopping, making your bed, taking that dog for a walk.'

'He's called Hoover.'

Robin got up and went into the dining area and through to the small kitchen, ignoring Faye's voice, from the lounge, asking what she was doing. The cupboards were half empty, the few products in there being cheaper own brands. The blind hadn't been pulled up, it bore a couple of stains.

A few minutes later, she came back and turned on the lounge light. 'Your fridge is almost empty, the milk is off, and dog biscuits have spilt across the floor.'

Faye's nostrils flared. 'If the only reason you've turned up is to criticise, then you can just bog off. It's nothing to do with you. I'll sort out my own affairs, thank you very much.' She went to get up but flinched again.

Teenage Robin would have gladly slammed the door on the way out; instead she closed her eyes and just breathed for a second. 'No, it's not my business, you're right, but I don't imagine I'll have to stay longer than a couple of weeks. I'm not surprised you're finding things difficult.' The idea of Faye needing help was going to take some getting used to. 'Has the spare room still got a bed in it?'

'Pardon?'

'The spare room, has—'

'I heard you the first time, I'm not deaf. Now you want to move back into this house? It's not your home any more.'

And it hadn't been for a long time. It hadn't felt like home for Robin for weeks before she left, during the time after Dad died.

'What if there's an emergency in the night? Look, from what I can gather, it's either me or a complete stranger, it's up to you.' Robin crossed her arms, fingers wrapping around her waist.

'I don't need any favours,' Faye muttered.

Robin sat down opposite her again and rubbed the back of her neck. 'I know this is a bit of a surprise but I'll keep out of your way, tidy the house, cook, collect any prescriptions, look after... Hoover.'

The dog's ears pricked up and he gave a stretch before running into the hallway.

'Why are you really here, Robin? Money, is it? Somewhere free to stay?' Faye's tone sounded as cold as the sneer on her face.

Robin bit her lip.

'Oh, hit the nail on the head, have I?'

They needed Dad here, without him neither of them held back. They used to have outbursts but knowing he'd always be home at six somehow reined them both in, it helped them navigate their difficult relationship and for his sake, as much as they could, keep it civil. Unless he was away on a job, then Robin would do her best to keep out of the house.

'How's that husband of yours?'

'Look, think what you will. Once your arm is out of a sling I'll head back to London. Dad, he was a practical man and would agree this is the best solution, don't you think?'

Faye stared for a moment longer and then turned her attention to the fire. 'It's been thirty odd years since you lived here. You can't just wind back time.'

'I'm not trying to.'

'Just go, Robin.'

Hoover came back in, Robin's car keys hanging from his mouth. He went over to the chaise longue and dropped them at her feet. Faye's mouth twitched.

The last time they actually met, nearly two decades ago, was when Amber had just been born. Birth hormones must have made Robin agree to Uncle Ralph's idea that Faye see her granddaughter, hoping it might be a turning point. Instead, it only made her realise how much she wanted Dad to meet her little girl and it reminded her how, in the end, on the day of the funeral, Faye had let him down.

Robin perched on the edge of the seat, wishing she was anywhere but here, yet wondering how Faye would eat and wash if she disappeared. Had she lived in this state for longer than since the fall? Did anyone look out for her apart from Blanche? And then there was Uncle Ralph's worried face, the sense that Robin owed him such a lot...

'The spare room's bedding is in a box, up in the loft,' Faye said, without looking at Robin.

Robin's breath hitched at the thought of going up there. 'What were you doing when you fell?'

Faye shrugged. 'I go up twice a year to swap over the winter and summer duvets. I don't put the heating on at night and it's been chillier the last couple of weeks.'

Robin nodded and went outside to fetch in the cool box of essentials she'd brought. She made a pot of tea, leaving Faye's cup by her chair before going back outside. Faye called after her to close the lounge door to keep the heat in. Robin unpacked the car boot and carried her things up to the spare room. When she walked in, and turned on the light, her stomach contracted. Dad's collections from car boot sales had all disappeared, like the pocket watches, the display case of pencils and vintage model plane kits, oh, and that gorgeous ornamental robin. It was gold and red with detailed feathering but had a large chip on its beak. However, Dad said it deserved its place on show as robins were such beautiful birds with many unique characteristics that made them extra special. The two of them used to laugh over the fun facts, such as a baby robin could turn green if it ate too many caterpillars.

The room had been repainted pale lilac and every surface was naked. Despite the cold outside she opened the window and stood there for a while. The net curtains at the front of the house opposite twitched. Robin ran a hand over the sill. When she was little, Dad would lift her up just before bed, so that she could count the stars. Perhaps he thought it would make her tired.

Robin stared at the houses over the road with the slate roofs and low eaves, the narrow gables and small doors that opened onto the pavement, their straight, simple lines had mirrored their house exactly. Dad said their style was dominant solid to void, meaning the windows were small compared to the limestone walls. Her new life, in her tiny flat, without Todd and Amber, felt dominant void to solid, empty and without foundations. She'd tried to fill her time with work and hobbies since the divorce, the silence with humming and television. The rent was cheap due to it backing onto a railway line, but the location was priceless to her as the vibration of passing trains felt reassuring.

She leant forwards to gaze down Parade Row. To the right, she'd passed the White Hart, a few doors down. It had been renovated, Tudor style and had a sandwich board outside advertising fancy Halloween cocktails. Dad used to love that pub just as it had been, with the paisley carpet that didn't match the striped wallpaper, and the booming juke box regulars often sang along to. She gazed down at her nails, painted with clear varnish, the beige tailored trousers. He also used to love her bright make-up, the New Romantic ruffles, the colourful ra-ra skirts. So many times she'd sit outside in his Ford Granada after he'd picked her up from Tara's house or they'd visited one of their favourite car boot sales. She'd think of excuses to stay outside in the car, talking and laughing with him.

Robin had been surprised to see the little library had closed, next to All Saints Church. Yet across Sheepwash River, past the wood and over the common, Stonedale Primary still thrived and had a new wing built. As she'd driven past Robin remembered the garish mustard school uniform. In the village centre she couldn't believe Tearoom 1960 was still in business, sitting next to a phone shop. The town hall still stood proud, set back from its simple ornamental garden and fountain, the two benches opposite each other. There was a new bookstore on the narrow high street, its windows full of pumpkins, and the vinyl record shop had disappeared, along with the video store and betting shop. Stonedale now had a swanky-looking hairdresser's and an outdoor clothes outlet, and a sweet shop as well, next to the town hall.

She and her friends used to get their pick 'n' mix from Woolies. That wasn't there either.

You couldn't call the village quaint, there was a practicality about it, almost an urban feel, despite the trees, the river and Peak District backdrop.

The patter of feet caught her attention. Hoover jumped onto the mattress. He cocked his head, those big ears moving like triangular satellite dishes. She went to leave the room and head into the loft – the sooner she could give the bedding a jolly good wash, the better. However, she stopped in front of the frame, the cut marks were still there, she ran her finger over the dents.

Each year, on her birthday, Dad had recorded how much she'd grown.

Robin pulled the ladder down from the loft, wincing at the screech of metal. Faye called up for Hoover and he skedaddled downstairs. Easily, she climbed up, as she'd done hundreds of times before. She felt for the switch, a tingling sensation ran through her, as if she'd been hit with electricity. As the darkness evaporated, Robin hauled herself up.

3

Robin stood on the loft's boarded floor and scrambled to her feet, studying the boxes that used to stand in alphabetical order, labelled by Dad, except now it all looked a mess. She walked around, straining to see if there was one marked Robin; she'd left so many possessions behind.

She couldn't find anything in her name, and unable to resist any longer, glanced over to the loft wall on the left and a section that looked slightly different to the rest. Builder Dad had created a cosy room for himself in the loft, a place they used to jokingly call his shed, with the little desk where he'd polish and fix collectibles they'd bought. You'd never know it was there unless someone told you. He'd even installed electricity for lighting and a heater. He'd taken her up there ever since she could remember and she used to like looking up at the night sky through the roof window. It made the power cuts of the 1970s even more exciting, the moon acting just as well as candles, her feeling very grown up as he'd let her stay up late.

When Robin started high school and things between her and Faye got worse, she longed for a place she could escape to and couldn't have been more thrilled when, one Christmas, Dad revealed her present – he'd converted that part of the loft into a bedroom for her. It was secret and hidden to everyone but the three of them and then, eventually, best friend, Tara, and Robin's first boyfriend, Yul. Dad was happy to move his shed down to the spare room. Robin wasn't surprised that Faye hadn't objected and suspected she preferred her daughter hidden away, up in the roof.

She had the faintest hope that if Faye had kept any of her stuff it might be boxed up in there. Robin had been too proud, after she'd left, to ask Faye to post her anything. As she pushed the section of wall that had a handle on the other side, a shiver ran across her shoulders, as if any minute she and Yul would settle down on her bed and make the most of being able to kiss, in private. Or she and Tara would stand under the roof window as if it were a spotlight, as they pretended to be pop stars and belted out the latest Culture Club release.

She pushed the door firmly closed behind her, and shivered again before pressing a switch to her right. It worked.

Robin felt a little dizzy.

Like a snapshot in time, her bedroom was stuck in the 1980s, just like a time capsule.

It didn't even look very dusty, colour and confidence still sprang out in every direction. She dropped onto the bed, the geometric patterned duvet cover feeling cold to touch. The poster at the end of her bed still showed Boy George, arms folded, nonchalantly looking her way in that bowler hat. She'd seen him in concert many times. More singers kept him company on posters across the other walls, like Alison Moyet and The Thompson Twins, a large one of Wham!

Shaking, she gazed around the room, ah yes, her wardrobe was opposite the side of her bed, just to the right as you walked in. The room's furniture was white and flat-pack; Dad had got it from MFI, same as the shelving, three rows of it across one wall. A big plus to the window being in the roof was that she'd had four whole walls to cover with knick-knacks. Robin stood to look at cuttings she'd stuck up, the kind of things teenagers these days would keep in their smartphones, such as a newspaper article about Band Aid and a magazine feature on Culture Club disbanding – she'd drawn sad faces across that one. On a sheet of lined A4 paper, torn out of an exercise book, she'd written all the lyrics to 'Lovecats' by The Cure. The line about being so wonderfully pretty was circled in red and she ran a trembling finger over it. Yul had drawn that. She smiled at the sheet of paper as if it were him, and for a second, she wished he were here.

And then, as she remembered what happened between them, she didn't.

Behind her bed, on the left, was the little dressing table she loved, with a star-shaped mirror she and Dad had found at a car boot sale. How could she have forgotten that? Robin went over and sat on the low stool, she looked in the glass and saw the woman she'd become who was a far cry from the girl who'd loved fashion and butties, and shopping in town at Affleck's Palace. Back in the flat she'd sometimes turn away from the hallway mirror because, when she was tired, Faye stared back at her.

On each of the mirror's five points she'd stuck a photo... Robin leant forward and studied a shot of her and Tara, at a disco, both dressed as Adam Ant, in their naval costumes – just a little more formal than the party outfits she wore these days. On the dressing table was a pile of colourful scrunchies and a stack of magazines – *Just Seventeen*, *Jackie* and tens of her favourite one, *Girl's Scene*. She picked one up and shook her head as she looked at the Dear Debbie page. She and Tara would secretly read Tara's cousin's copies, giggling as they pored over the letters. Then they were old enough to buy their own, and studied the problems about sex as if reading the advice gave them experience. Little did she know that at forty-eight, she still wouldn't have all the answers.

Robin hugged the magazine to her chest, it warmed her insides like a hot water bottle. Now and again, she used to leaf through one of Amber's magazines – teenagers still wanted to know about crushes and periods, but also about messaging nude pics, online bullying and transitioning. So much had changed since she'd lived in this room. Yet in some ways maybe it hadn't, teens would always struggle with their identity and the issue of fitting in.

As she put it back, Robin noticed, at the bottom of the pile, sheaves of lined paper, covered in biro. She pulled one half out, read a couple of lines and grinned. She used to love writing short stories, English had been her best subject at school. As she got older, she attempted steamy romances. Tara would critique them. They'd laugh so hard as they tried to think of creative ways to describe body parts. She tugged it out further and from underneath, a typewritten sheet of paper fell to the floor. Heart beating, Robin picked it up. One of the responses from Dear Debbie? Carefully she smoothed out the creases. She'd written many letters to this problem page and the personal replies had reassured her about so many things that any other teenage girl might have asked their mother. For a few moments she couldn't stop staring at it.

Robin stood up, wanting to stay in here for hours and flick through the books and pull out the drawers at the end of her old bed. She lifted a faded, red Toffos wrapper out of the bin, you couldn't buy those any more. She held it for a moment, as if it were precious. A lump formed in her throat. This bedroom, it was like meeting up with an old friend. Robin placed the wrapper carefully back in the bin. She stood on the bed, just as she always used to, and balancing on one foot reached up to open the window an inch. Like the rest of the room, it wasn't quite as dusty as she'd expected, not after more than thirty years. Then she lay down, put her hands behind her head and stared up at the glass and the first evening stars coming out. She closed her eyes for a second, pretending that Dad would shout up from the ladder any minute, tell her tea was nearly ready, and that afterwards they could polish up the latest brass bell they'd bought at the weekend. She felt as cosy as if she were under the covers and hummed 'Karma Chameleon', rocking her feet from side to side in time.

Robin Wilson,
16 Parade Row,
Stonedale,
Greater Manchester
October 1984

Dear Debbie,

MY HAIRCUT IS RUINING MY LIFE.

This may not seem like much of a problem, but it feels like the end of the world to me. As a treat, my best friend's mum took us to a fancy hair salon and I agreed to have a completely new style. It's way too short and I cried when I got home. Dad says it really suits me, but this girl at school who's always horrible burst out laughing.

And a boy I like saw me in jeans at the weekend, he said I don't look like a girl any more. He'll never ask me out now. It's going to take ages to grow back and this is really getting me down. Is there anything I can do? Please help.

Robin, age 12

Girl's Scene

41 Gover Street,

London

Dear Robin,

Oh, sympathies, every woman feels like this about her hair at least once in her lifetime, but fortunately there is an easy answer. You put on your best smile! The single most attractive thing about anyone is their self-confidence. In any case, I'm sure your dad is right and you look very smart. And if you don't get on with that unkind girl, she'd have probably laughed at any sort of haircut, even one you liked.

As for the boy, I've always thought a good relationship is

about a couple accepting each other for who they are. You might decide that wearing skirts at the weekend, until your hair grows back, is a small price to pay to keep him interested. Or maybe his reaction is a sign that he's not the right one for you!

Best wishes,

Debbie

4

With new energy, Robin sat up and swung her legs to the side of the bed. She left the room and pressed the door shut. After finding a box marked bedding, she emptied the contents onto the landing floor, then she lowered herself onto the ladder and turned off the light switch. Once down on the carpet, Robin smiled up at the loft for a few seconds.

'You took your time upstairs,' said Faye, when Robin eventually came out of the kitchen, having put the washing machine on and tidied.

'It took me a while to find the bedding. The boxes were a bit... jumbled up.'

'I make no apologies for not keeping a load of old paperwork spick and span,' Faye said, in an abrupt tone. 'I was trying to find something in the months after Alan passed and gave up in the end. I just never got around to sorting through all the old bank statements.'

'Perhaps I can help search, if you tell me what it is, I'll go back up and—'

'There's no point looking for it all these years later.'

It was pitch black outside now. Hoover was jumping around, as if trying to warn them of something.

'Does he need a walk? Something to eat?' asked Robin.

'I've fed him. Before I go to bed he can go out the back for twenty minutes. He's just excited, with all the commotion outdoors. Happens every Halloween.'

A rap sounded on the door and Robin heard laughing.

'Trick or treaters. There's a box of chocolates next to the hob. I got them in a few weeks ago.' Faye instructed.

They wouldn't have lasted a few days with Dad around.

Small witches and skeletons couldn't decide which was more appealing, the brightly coloured chocolates or the big-eared French bulldog. Robin closed the front door. She'd had her first proper slow dance at a Halloween party. Yul was dressed as Dracula. She'd been crying after an especially bad run-in with Faye. He hadn't tried to kiss her, he'd just held her tight. A Gothic monster saved the day.

'Have you turned off the hallway light? I don't waste electricity.'

Robin nodded. Faye never used to be so careful.

'Did they take all the runny caramels?' Faye asked. 'They usually go first.'

'You never used to like Halloween – said dressing up was for toddlers.'

Faye met Robin's gaze. 'Whereas you used to dress up every day of the year, in your polka dots and hats, but look at you now.'

Stiffly, Robin walked into the kitchen and busied herself making two omelettes. They sat up at the small marble-effect kitchen table with slices of bread and cups of tea. The kitchen had been modernised in grey and white, with elegant lines that were chipped in places. Hoover sat begging and when Faye said *lounge* in a stern voice, he disappeared out of the room, ears flat to his head. She ate quicker than Robin who, glad to escape, went to answer the door again. When she came back Faye had finished all the bread. Robin put a packet of biscuits on the table and left them open as she refreshed their cups. When she sat down again several had gone.

'How is the flower-arranging going at the cathedral?' asked Robin after three Digestives, not liking to eat so much sugar but needing to ease the silence. Dad used to give Faye a lift to St John's Cathedral; she'd never liked driving and always said God gave them two feet for a reason. For as long as Robin could remember, Faye went a couple of times a week, when she wasn't working at Lewis's department store in Manchester. Robin and Dad only went to church at Christmas.

'I haven't been since your father died,' she said, in a tight voice. 'With his salary gone I needed to increase my income. A full-time member of staff had just left so I managed to pick up extra hours.'

Robin had often thought about the financial practicalities of Faye's life after she left, especially when she got a job and her own income. But, eventually, like so much of her time before London, she'd locked those uncomfortable thoughts away.

'What does your husband think of you leaving him for a few days?'

'I've left him for a little longer than that,' said Robin and stirred her tea slowly.

'He's such a nice man, must be very understanding.'

Faye had only met Todd once.

Robin yanked the lid off the biro. *Focus on the basics.* 'I'll go shopping tomorrow, first off, toiletries, are there any essentials you've run out of?'

'I'll buy those myself.'

'Carrying a shopping bag will hurt your ribs.'

Faye stared into her teacup. 'Fine. By the end of the week I'll need some more pads.'

'Cotton wool?'

'No,' she snapped. 'Sometimes if I sneeze…'

Oh. Robin made a note and hastily changed the subject. 'Meals for this week, how about—'

'I haven't finished.' Her mother's face flushed and she stared at the biscuit packet. 'Look in the top drawer of my bedside table. I was due to buy new creams before I fell.'

Robin went upstairs and sat on Faye's bed. She pulled open the drawer and took out two tubes, feeling as if she was doing something she shouldn't. One was for athlete's foot, the other for haemorrhoids. She shifted awkwardly, feeling uncomfortable with this intimate information. They'd never had the kind of relationship where they told each other secrets, not like Tara and her mum. She didn't know about her mother's first boyfriend or how she coped with the menopause. Robin went downstairs and sat opposite her again. Despite the darkness she was gazing out of the window.

'Any other toiletries? I know it must be difficult to—'

'No,' Faye said in a clipped tone.

Robin rolled her lips together. 'Have you got enough detergent? I'll do the laundry tomorrow.'

'I can manage that. I'm very particular about my clothes.'

'You can't empty the linen basket and shouldn't bend over to load the machine. I'll iron them as well.' Robin shouldn't have felt surprised that every suggestion got knocked back. 'Which fruit do you like?'

'Tinned peaches, if pushed.'

She'd forgotten that. She used to get sick of them with Bird's custard.

'What about evening meals this week? What would you like to eat?'

Faye looked up. 'You mean *we*.'

'Yes, we'll eat together, of course.'

'I don't mean you, I was referring to Blanche. I cook enough for two every night, she suffers with arthritis now and doesn't have family around.'

Her husband, Dennis, must have died too. *Poor Blanche*. She'd always been kind, teaching Robin to bake, waving her off as she'd proudly take butterfly cakes or rock buns back to number sixteen. Faye never seemed to mind. From anyone else, involvement like that would have been seen as interference.

'She gives me an agreed sum of money every month, and we don't eat any of that modern guff – steak and kidney pudding and dumpling stews, we like them for tea. At weekends I do a rice pudding or jam roly poly.' Faye's mouth twitched and she sat more upright. 'If it's too much to ask perhaps you're not cut out for this do-gooder lark. One way or another you might get more than you bargained for, coming back to Stonedale.'

'What does that mean?'

'You'll find out.'

'For goodness' sake,' Robin threw her hands in the air, 'can't we at least have a straightforward chat?'

Faye glared. 'There's nothing straightforward about you turning up here expecting a red-carpet welcome.'

'No, but I'm trying. And I promised Uncle Ralph I would.'

'That's the only reason you're here, isn't it? Well, you can drop the dutiful daughter act, get back in the car and head back home, your home. This won't work,' she said in a voice that suddenly sounded tired. She looked at her watch. It was still the same one. Robin's dad had given it to her for her fiftieth birthday. She hadn't said much when she unwrapped it but cooked his favourite Lancashire hotpot the next day. It had a gold oblong face with a classic brown leather strap that looked worn now.

Tears pricked Robin's eyes. Fine. She'd done her best. She took a deep breath and walked into the lounge, banging into the kitchen door frame as she went. Hoover dashed up to her, tongue hanging out. He threw himself on his back, four legs in the air, and she couldn't resist crouching down to ruffle his stomach.

'Got to go, boy.' Stomach churning, she moved the phone closer to Faye's armchair and switched on the nearby lamp. It was getting late. If only she could ring Amber, if only they were still as close as before the split. It would remind Robin that whilst not perfect, she had one mother-daughter relationship that wasn't quite such a mess. Was Amber out for drinks with friends or working all hours to meet a deadline? She'd hardly heard from her since freshers' week and tried not to worry if she was eating properly or getting enough sleep, but some things weren't so different between parenting teenagers and babies. Only last week Robin had posted her a bundle of warm vests and vitamin tablets.

Her throat constricted. Perhaps Amber felt the same way about her as she felt about Faye.

You can't leave Stonedale. She won't manage.

Robin swayed on her feet as her dad's voice intruded. She looked out of the front window and half-expected his car to draw up outside, and him to wave madly like when he'd get out of the driving seat after a work trip. Since he died, she'd heard a voice in her head, like a conscience. It was the voice that had told the younger Robin to be nicer to Uncle Ralph and more recently, that it wasn't fair not to tell Todd the truth.

She wondered if it was Dad talking to her now, telling her to stay with Faye. Robin used to hate him going away on jobs, missing him even if it was only for a couple of days. He was the one to read to her before lights out and sit by her bed if she was sick, he helped her practise the recorder and taught her how to do headstands.

But even if it was his voice, this was too hard. Robin hurried upstairs, and went into the loft. Unlike thirty-two years ago, she wouldn't leave behind all her memories. For a start, she'd like to find her favourite old crossbody handbag, tiny and covered in red sequins and in the shape of a tape cassette. She and Dad had found it at a car boot sale and she'd worn it out every time she and Tara went clubbing. Robin could show it to Amber the next time she saw her, perhaps she'd want to borrow it, although a mobile phone wouldn't fit in it. Robin searched in the bottom of the wardrobe. Her hands felt a cardboard box and she slid it out. Bits of paper overflowed from the top – mainly receipts, Dad never liked to throw them away. She sifted through, pulling out an instruction booklet for a SodaStream and one for a Breville toastie maker. *Why's this box in here?*

Robin went to push it back but stopped. A whooshing noise rang in her ears as she realised exactly what she'd found. She couldn't take her eyes off it, oh so innocently lying in one corner of the box. She reached in and picked up the rolled-up sheet of tea-stained paper.

5

Robin sat on the bed, staring, afraid the scroll would suddenly disappear. Could this really be one of their treasure hunts? An old one? It would have to be, surely. But no, it was sealed. A new treasure hunt they'd never completed? One that had lay hidden for more than thirty years?

It used to be a Sunday treat. Dad would compile a list of cryptic clues that led the three of them around Stonedale, he'd write them on a tea-stained sheet of paper – for her benefit, she'd loved pirates when she was little – and roll that up into a scroll, sealing it with candle wax. Oh, the excitement when Robin would be allowed to open it, even when she became a teenager. Faye would then read out each clue that, when solved, produced a word. The first letter of each became part of an anagram, like S for school or N for newsagents. Dad was brilliant at crafting each clue's riddle. Each of his hunts was so different to the last and they never knew how long one would take to finish. The winner, between Robin and Faye, was the one who solved the anagram at the end, although Robin realised, as she got older, it wasn't really about that. It was more a way for Dad to make her and Faye spend 'good' time together.

Robin hurried downstairs, holding the scroll, and a cry caught her attention as she went into the lounge. She placed the scroll on the chaise longue before rushing into the kitchen. Faye was bent over, rubbing her side.

'What happened?'

'Caught my foot in the chair leg as I got up and slipped against the table,' she croaked.

Robin hesitated, then took her elbow, unable to remember the last time she'd touched her mother. Faye pulled away and gave another small cry. Robin waited until she righted herself and then guided her firmly back to the lounge, helped her sit down. She fetched a blanket and another cup of tea. They sat drinking, Faye's body looked more relaxed so Robin's thoughts turned to the scroll again, a fizz of excitement replacing the knots in her stomach. She picked it up just as Faye went for the remote control.

'Look what I found.' She held the scroll up as if it were about to be auctioned off for millions of pounds.

Faye lifted her head and her mouth fell open. Red blotches appeared around her eyes. 'Where did you find that?'

'In my old wardrobe. I wasn't expecting my old room to look just like it used to.' Robin waited for her mother to offer an explanation but she was still staring. 'Great, isn't it?' she prodded. Faye gave a tentative smile and her lips upturned – blink and Robin would have missed it. 'It came out of the box of Dad's paperwork you put in there. No wonder you couldn't find it amongst all the others.'

The red blotches left Faye's cheeks and she averted her gaze. She reached for one of the chocolates Robin had put down by her tea, having trouble undoing the wrapper.

'I don't know anything about a box in that room,' she said.

Robin felt like a child waiting to open birthday presents, itching to open the scroll to see her dad's writing again.

'It could be an old one, anyway,' Faye said and squashed the foil wrapper into a tight ball.

'But it's sealed, and we'd throw them away once we'd finished.' Robin ran her finger along the rolled-up paper. 'It was in with all his old receipts and instruction booklets.'

'Alan kept a load of rubbish in the spare room. The week before he died we'd decided to redecorate when he got back from the job in Sheffield, it had needed doing for ages. He promised to sort through all the junk. Why would he have put a separate box of paperwork in your room?'

Robin stood, studying the tea-stained paper and her breath hitched; she remembered now. 'Dad asked if I could sort through the receipts and throw out the old ones whilst he was away.' He was a terrible hoarder. A memory came back. He'd put that box in the bottom of her cupboard one day when she was at school. Robin had felt sick when she'd found out as she'd hidden something there that she didn't want him or Faye to discover. 'Dad must have known I'd find it and planted it for us two to do whilst he was gone.' She held it out, voice bubbling with excitement, her plans to leave momentarily forgotten. This scroll was one last link to him. 'Do you want to read it out?'

'Not especially,' she said. 'You may have found what I was looking for all those years ago. That doesn't mean I'm interested now.'

'*This* is what you were talking about?' Robin dropped into the other armchair.

'Just before your father went on that last trip, he did say he'd written one last scroll, for you and me to do whilst he was away.

He said solving it would change everything, that it would make our lives so much easier.'

Robin held the scroll to her chest. 'What could he have meant?'

Faye picked up the top copy of *Word Weekly*. 'I thought perhaps it was his fun way of letting us know he'd finally won on the bonds. Money was tight at the time.'

Of course. She remembered because Dad wasn't usually snappy, but in the run up to his death, he'd not been his usually cheerful self. A customer had gone bust and couldn't pay Dad for two weeks' work.

'But twelve months passed and any winnings could no longer be claimed anyway, as the owner of the bonds, your dad, was deceased. So I gave up. Life was busy, me working all hours. I went into the loft less and less.'

'But this is one last connection to him.'

Faye pressed the remote and picked up a pen. 'It's too late now.'

But she had to be curious. Robin's heart raced. The two of them doing this hunt together was effectively Dad's last wish. She gazed at the darning on her mother's sock. And maybe it really would reveal a hidden fortune.

Perhaps Faye would be more enthusiastic once she heard the clues. Robin gently broke the seal and unfurled the paper clumsily, rocked by the prospect of seeing words from him that had crossed decades without being read. Faye used to joke that doctors and builders had the worst handwriting and insisted he used only capital letters for the treasure hunt. And the writing was really small, as he'd squeeze all the clues onto one sheet of paper. Robin lifted the scroll in the air, one hand on top, the other at the bottom.

A note, set out like a riddle, had been scrawled across the top in his usual longhand. She narrowed her eyes and read it out.

'Here's a hunt for my favourite two,
Sheffield won't be fun without you.
Enjoy this hunt one Sunday I'm away,
Good luck to my own precious treasures, Robin and Faye.
Oh, and read Clue Two in advance,
That will give you a better chance!'

Faye didn't move an inch. Robin's throat felt scratchy. Dad called himself a sentimental old fool but she loved how he always made her feel special. She got to her feet and paced up and down the room, wanting to start the hunt right this minute. But they'd have to wait until Faye's ribs were less sore. Still, they could set a date now, it would be something to look forward to.

'When shall we do it?' she asked.

'So all of a sudden you're keen to stay, because of a stupid children's game?'

'No, of course—'

'Count me out, there's nothing about that scroll that, thirty years later, could possibly *change everything*, and the only reason we used to do those hunts was to keep you busy.'

Was it? Robin's hands dropped and she sat back down. But Faye enjoyed doing crosswords and word searches, and Dad's favourite TV shows were whodunits. 'How can you say that? You and Dad used to love our Sunday adventures around the village.'

'But Alan isn't here, is he?' she said curtly.

'I am.' Robin's voice sounded small, as if time had really turned back.

'Feel free to do it yourself, before you go, although I don't imagine the clues will work out, it's been so long.'

On her own? But that's not what Dad wanted. Robin rolled up the scroll again.

'No. I don't know what I was thinking,' she said. 'You're absolutely right.' At least there was one last thing she could do that Dad would have wished for. 'But I'm not leaving. You just slipping in the kitchen decides it. We don't have to like it, but I'm looking after you, no arguments. I'll happily cook for Blanche too, on the condition you take as much rest as possible. The quicker you heal, the quicker I'll be out of your hair.'

Faye exhaled with a resigned air. Robin left the lounge and climbed back up the ladder. She hauled herself into the loft, every limb feeling heavy. She couldn't bear reading the clues, not if they weren't going to try to solve them. Robin gulped and tossed the scroll back onto the top of the cardboard box, she closed the wardrobe doors and headed back downstairs.

6

Robin escaped into the tiny front yard and light November rain pitter-pattered onto her face. The fresh air felt good. She'd decided to stay in yesterday to clean the house, getting up bright and early like every Monday morning, but now the essentials she'd brought were running low and she needed to shop.

'So, how does this work?' Robin asked Hoover and pulled down either side of her grey woolly hat. He led her towards the pavement.

She held a couple of Faye's shopping bags, practical and floral, ones she might have bought herself. The common ground felt odd. Her voice was still ringing in Robin's ears about making sure she told her how much the shopping came to – she didn't need or want handouts, but instructed her to buy own brands and to look for discounts. This morning Robin had helped her dress again. Faye couldn't do up her bra and struggled with the zip on her trousers. She'd outright refused help in the bath. The old chintz patterns of the bedroom walls and floor had been replaced with a tasteful melange of cream and ice-blue. Faye didn't say a word whilst Robin did up her fastenings, trying not to focus on the loose skin and age spots on hands that used to wring washing and push the lawnmower, and leave red marks on little Robin's legs if she was naughty. The bruising, black and blue, across Faye's ribs, Dad would have hated seeing that. Faye had tripped over the garden hose once, years ago, and banged her forehead. He'd fussed over her until the bump went down, applying a cold flannel as the bruising appeared. Robin had expected her to snap at him for making a fuss, like she was with her now, but Faye hadn't seemed to mind him treating her like a patient.

Hoover yanked on the lead and Robin let him go ahead as they passed the White Hart's smell of stale beer. She continued along the line of uniform houses until he stopped by a lamppost and cocked his leg. Would she see anyone she knew in the village? They crossed a junction and neared the church at the top of the high street. Its grey brick and square lines contrasted with the unusual twisted spire, on top, that looked as if it was caught in a tornado. When she was little she'd stand as close as she could to the brickwork, click her heels, and wait to be whisked away for adventures in the Land of Oz.

They carried on past the new outdoor clothes shop, down the high street that simply looked like two more opposing rows of terraced houses, except for the colourful canopies and sandwich boards outside. Robin came to Brynner's Books. She could see now that it was a secondhand shop and looked well organised, a recycling bin by the inside of the front door for people to post their old reads into. She loved reading sagas these days, fond of the escapist idea that whole families stayed connected, that generation after generation became part of each other's story. Robin lingered for a moment whilst Hoover sniffed another lamppost. Several customers browsed through books, for a Tuesday it looked quite busy. She squinted; there was a room out the back, with tables, and she noticed a chalk-board on the wall, behind the till, listing types of coffee. The honey glow of the pine shelves and flooring compelled her to go in but dogs probably weren't welcome, whereas Tearoom 1960 opposite had a large silver water bowl outside. It was squashed in between the phone and betting shops, on trend with their minimalist, white plastic-framed fronts. The café showed a burst of character with the hanging baskets either side of the aubergine door and charcoal sign in the shape of a teacup.

Robin went towards the road and looked at Hoover.

'Sit,' she said, the word sounding more like a question. They waited until several cars and a tractor passed. Once on the opposite pavement he lunged towards the bowl, his strength taking her by surprise. She let him drink, finding comfort in the fact that this building had hardly changed. Its simple name referred to the year it first opened and suited the down-to-earth nature of the village. The ping of a bell caught her attention and a woman stood in the entrance, wearing an apron.

'And how's your mistress, Hoover?' she asked and looked up at Robin. 'I've been so worried. Are you a friend of Faye's? Can you tell me, is she... she...' The woman gasped. 'Well, I never. *Robin*? Is that you?'

Robin studied the ginger streak in the greying hair. 'Mrs Chapman?'

She darted forwards and wrapped Robin up in a tight hug, then stepped back and eyed her up and down, studying the duffle coat and plain loafers. 'You look so different, love, but those curls...'

The rain always did that, however much product she used.

'I heard about your mum's fall. I must pop around with a slice of her favourite cake. Is she on the mend?'

'She's doing better, thanks. I'm staying until she's back on her feet.'

Mrs Chapman put her hands on her hips and Robin admired the embroidered hem of her skirt, remembering now how she used to make her own clothes. In fact... yes, for her fourteenth birthday Dad commissioned her to make Robin a T-shirt dress covered in big numbers like her idol's.

'How are your mum and dad?' Robin asked. Mrs Chapman must have only been about thirty when Robin was last here. Back then, Mrs Chapman had been newly married and about to take over the teashop from her parents.

'You'd never know they were in their eighties. They still drop in now and then, and act as if they are undercover health and safety officers. But I'm always so busy. Going out for a coffee is such an everyday part of life now, not a treat like it used to be in the old days.' She jerked her head. 'Come on in, I want to hear all your news.'

'Thanks, Mrs Chapman, but I really must get on with my shopping. Perhaps another time?'

Her eyes twinkled. 'I think you're old enough to call me Maeve.' She bent down and gave Hoover a quick stroke. 'I bet you got a surprise, going into the bookshop.' She straightened up.

'I only arrived Sunday. I haven't been in there, yet.'

'Oh, right... you... you really should drop in.' She looked away. 'I mean, you always had your nose in a story.'

* * *

Having left Hoover outside, his lead tied to a post, Robin stocked up at the supermarket, thinking about Tearoom 1960 and how she and Dad would share knickerbocker glories. She half expected to see him appear in one of the aisles, or at least a friend from school, or teacher. Dragging her feet, she headed back to Parade Row, grateful she hadn't had to use one of the poop bags Faye told her to bring. Hoover walked more slowly now too, unless another dog loomed into view. Then Robin had to juggle the bags whilst he bounced up and down, his stocky shoulders making him look like a boxer in training.

Arms aching, Robin put down her shopping and let Hoover in, taking off the lead before he charged along the hallway. She followed him into the lounge and a twinge of guilt poked her in the chest. Faye wasn't in her chair, she must have got thirsty.

'You sit down,' she called ahead. 'Let me put the kettle on.' But Faye wasn't in the kitchen either. Robin hoisted the bags onto the table and hurried upstairs, almost tripping over the dog. Faye shouldn't have gone up there alone, but she wasn't in any of the bedrooms or the bathroom.

What if she'd taken a turn for the worse and been taken into hospital? No, the paramedics would have rung Robin, although Faye didn't have her mobile number. She went back into the kitchen where Hoover scrabbled at the back door. She opened it and expected him to rush straight to the end of the lawn, as he had early this morning, but instead he veered right.

Maybe Faye had gone to the outdoor loo. But she'd used the upstairs bathroom before they came down for breakfast, Robin had made sure of that as Faye's ribs hurt every time she had to climb the stairs. Robin had glanced into the outside toilet last night; the brickwork had been painted and a small sink put in, but it still felt draughty and rain had crept across the floor tiles.

'Are you in there?' She opened its door a little and heard jerky breaths as a roll of filthy toilet paper trundled out.

Robin Wilson,
16 Parade Row,
Stonedale,
Greater Manchester
March 1985

Dear Debbie,

I'M GOING TO MARRY ANDREW RIDGELEY.

I can't stop thinking about him. He looks like a movie star and I was so excited when Dad took me to see Wham! in concert last Christmas. It was the best night of my life. Andrew definitely looked at me in the audience when they waved goodbye after the last song. I love him and know we are meant to be together.

But my mum overheard me talking about how I'm going to marry him one day. She laughed and said it was a silly crush. How can it be? I like lots of pop stars, but this is different. I know we're just perfect for each other and not being with him really hurts. I lie in bed at night imagining how he will propose and what the wedding day will be like. How can I make Mum see that this is serious?

Robin, age 12

Girl's Scene
41 Gover Street,
London

Dear Robin,

Oh poor you, unrequited love is a painful thing – and I'm afraid that's all this will ever be. You've fallen for the pop star, not the person. No one knows what famous people are really like. Your mum wasn't very tactful when she laughed and I'm sure she won't have meant to hurt you, but she does have a point. This is a crush, you can't have true feelings for someone you've never even spoken to. But don't feel silly. We all have these fantasies at times, even grown women!

Go out, join clubs, and keep meeting new people, and I promise that, over time, you'll forget all about him and meet a real boy who fulfils all your dreams!

Best wishes,

Debbie

7

'Don't come in,' Faye said vehemently.

'What's happened? Are you okay?'

The creak of a toilet seat.

'The loo roll fell onto the floor.' Her voice sounded ragged. 'It was at a bad angle for me. It fell into a puddle and is dirty and wet.'

'Hold on. I bought a new pack.' Minutes later Robin passed one through the narrow gap. She shivered as she waited outside. Eventually, the toilet flushed and the taps ran. Faye shuffled out, wiping wet fingers on her cardigan.

Robin took her hand. 'How long were you in there, you're freezing?'

Faye yanked her hand back before slowly making her way inside, not even wiping her feet on the back door mat. As soon as she got in the lounge she leant on the back of her armchair, as if to recharge before lowering herself down onto the seat. Robin didn't know whether to help. She hadn't been in this position before – apart from that one time when she'd just started high school and Faye was off work with flu. On a whim, Robin skipped afternoon lessons, so that she could bring her hot drinks and cold flannels. She'd accused Robin of using her as an excuse to bunk off lessons.

Hoover lay down by Faye's feet as Robin turned up the fire and made a hot drink but Faye's hands shook too much to hold it steady. Robin stared, blinking for a moment. Once, a group of girls from the year above had followed her home. It had been snowing and they spotted her walking back from the village alone... yes, that was it, she'd met Tara in Tearoom 1960 and all along Parade Row they'd pummelled her back with snowballs. Robin's throat felt dry as she remembered how their baying got louder as they chased her until she fell over, but she'd refused to show she was scared. Faye heard the commotion and came out just as the girls crowded around her. Faye didn't help her up, didn't have it out with their parents, instead, she made Robin a mug of Bovril. However, Robin couldn't hold it still with her shaking hands and the brown liquid spilt, not because she'd been cornered by the gang but because Faye had actually paid her a compliment. She'd said Robin had done well to hide her feelings.

'Don't tell me, you ended up chatting in the bookshop?' Faye blurted out now.

First Maeve, now her, what was it with that place?

'Next time, I'll give you my mobile number and you must keep your phone on you at all times. I'm sorry, I should have thought...'

'Yes, you should,' Faye replied roughly.

In silence they ate lunch, ham sandwiches, farmhouse white bread for Faye, multi-grain for Robin, She made coffee and their milk cartons stood next to each other, hers with a green cap, Faye's with a blue. Robin washed up whilst Faye finished off with a couple of the fruity biscuits she'd just bought, along with healthy ingredients to bake her own. She hoped Uncle Ralph wouldn't miss her home bakes too much, but, at least, it was only for a few weeks and the catering staff at Moss Lodge made sure residents got their favourites.

Faye settled down and switched on the television. She flicked the channels until she found her usual game show. Hoover dozed in front of the fire, a back leg twitching now and again. Robin went outside and mopped the outside toilet's floor, she cleaned the sink and changed the towel. As darkness fell, fireworks went off, what with Bonfire Night approaching on Friday. Hoover hid under Faye's chair but crawled out at teatime. Faye had told Robin to put aside a small portion of raw minced beef, his favourite. A homely, savoury smell, rich with the carbs and red meat Robin would never normally use, filled the house as she reheated the cottage pie, reminding her of meals with Dad and Christmas dinner.

They ate at the kitchen table, and after they'd both finished, Robin got up and fetched the box of chocolates, now half empty. Faye offered it to her and, by force of habit, Robin shook her head.

'Suit yourself.' She reached in and took out a strawberry creme. 'You never used to worry about your weight.'

'And I don't,' she said, quickly, as Hoover's paws sounded, running downstairs, and he appeared in the kitchen, sliding to a halt on the tiled floor. Perhaps he heard the chocolate wrapper rustle.

'I don't care what I look like,' Robin babbled, 'it's about health.' She glanced at Hoover, parading around the kitchen, and perspiration broke out on her forehead. He'd been into her suitcase which wasn't completely emptied yet. Faye's eyes brightened as he showed off the bodyshaping pants.

Robin took out her phone and clicked into photos, chose a

shot and hesitated before sliding it across the table. Faye adjusted her glasses before lifting it up.

'She's got your dad's wide-set eyes. They first attracted me to Alan, made me feel I could trust him.'

'She's just started at Manchester University.' The best thing about coming up to Stonedale was the prospect of being nearer to Amber. Robin had already texted, hoping she'd want to meet for lunch.

Faye kept staring at the photo.

'Amber is studying economics.'

'She sounds like a sensible girl.'

Having to be sensible in your teens was overrated.

Faye pushed back the phone. It started ringing. Robin headed up to the spare room and swiped the phone icon. *Amber!*

'Mum…' The smallest of sobs came down the line and Robin's chest tightened. Immediately she pictured those beautiful hazel eyes swollen, her jaw set. Even as a little girl Amber would get cross with herself for crying.

'Love, what's happened?'

The line crackled.

'Where are you?'

'I slept on a friend's floor last night… well, someone off my course. George. My student house, it's flooded, a burst pipe.' She gulped. 'None of us noticed and the kitchen ceiling ended up collapsing. And I'd left my latest essay on the table. I'd printed it out, I find that helps, and had worked on it loads the last few days, with handwritten notes. It's got to be handed in next Monday, but now all that extra work is lost, I'll never catch up in time. And my Kindle with lots of course books was nearby, it's got ruined…'

'Oh, darling… What does student accommodation say?' Robin got off the bed and walked up and down.

'There's no space in the halls of residence, we're going to be put into a hotel that's not as near the university and has got horrible reviews on TripAdvisor. Our landlord doesn't know how long repairs will take, he's got to wait for the insurance payment to be agreed and...'

'We'll sort it. I'll come over and—'

'I've already looked at all the options,' Amber said tersely, 'there's no way out of this.'

'Of course there is, now don't you worry. I'll—'

'Mum. For God's sake. I can deal with this, it... it's just been a shock. I knew it was a bad idea to call.'

Robin bit her lip. 'Have you rung your father?'

'I didn't want to worry him.' She gulped again.

Robin asked her to go through exactly what had happened and said to keep her chin up, that she'd ring her again, later tonight. She lay on the bed again and closed her eyes. The mattress buckled and she opened them to see Hoover looming over her, shaking his head from side to side, her best bra covered in drool. Hardly noticing, she patted his head. If only she could wrap Amber in her arms and tell her everything would be all right. Todd had been so supportive when she first became a mother, seeming to understand Robin was worried she'd not be a good one. She'd often think back to the ornamental robin, with the chipped beak, that Dad bought, and how he told her another fun fact – that a robin's parental instinct was very strong and there had been many reports of them feeding the chicks of other species. Silly, but Robin always hoped this meant she'd be a more caring mother than Faye.

8

Robin kept herself busy the next morning. Despite ringing Amber again, who told her not to fuss, she called the university's accommodation office to, at least, try to get the hotel changed. However the man she spoke to wasn't any help, insisting that because Amber was over eighteen, he couldn't discuss it with Robin. After lunch she took Hoover into the village to walk off her frustration. She stopped to stare through the bookshop's window. It was Wednesday afternoon and all the shops still shut in Stonedale. On the wall on the left, in front of the till, was a mural of a big tree, green and lush, its trunk made out of a pile of books. She couldn't see any special reason as to why Maeve and Faye thought she might have already popped in.

After she'd dropped Hoover back at Faye's, Robin knocked at the door of number ten, three houses down. She'd made the evening meal, filling up a Tupperware container for Blanche. She was retired now from her care home assistant job and, like Faye, in her late seventies. A gust of wind lifted her hair and Robin knocked again. Eventually, a short woman with an angular face opened the front door. Blanche stooped slightly and swollen knuckles grasped the door frame. Spirals of white hair softened the prominent cheek bones. She wore baggy joggers and a hooded fleece, and a slash of red lipstick seeped into creases around her mouth. She looked so fragile compared to the solid woman Robin remembered, one who'd tie an apron around Robin's waist and let her lick the mixing bowl.

Robin put down the bag and gave her a hug. Faye had texted Blanche to say Robin would be cooking for her as well, from today.

Blanche beamed. 'Love a duck, look at you, all grown up now, and so smart, just like your mother.'

Robin gazed down at the starched line on her trousers and polished shoes.

'Lovely to see you after all this time, flower. It was such a relief to hear you're back in Stonedale.'

'Thanks for writing that letter to Uncle Ralph.'

'I wasn't sure what to do, didn't want to be seen as sticking my beak in...'

'You did the right thing.'

'I would ask you in, but I'm expecting a phone call at half past...' She beamed. 'From my Adopt-A-Grannie daughter, Susan.'

Robin raised an eyebrow.

'It's a local scheme for us oldies who might feel lonely. My end of the deal is that I pass on any supposed wisdom to the little ones.' She shook her head. 'Susan's got two kiddies at Millstone Primary but they already know far more about gadgets than me. I wish your mum had agreed to be adopted but she wouldn't even read the leaflet.'

Faye had never needed friends, why would Blanche think that had changed? And why would Faye want to adopt a daughter when she'd never had much interest in the one she already had?

'I'm just dropping off tea,' Robin said cheerily, despite once again feeling like the girl whose mum never came to the school play. She passed Blanche the bag. 'Lamb hotpot and peach crumble.'

Blanche's face broke into a smile. 'I've missed Faye and her home cooking. That woman's a diamond.'

Colleagues would call her efficient. Neighbours used to think her house-proud. Tara's mum said she was private and that there was nothing wrong with that.

Blanche and Faye always got on, but *diamond*?

* * *

Robin had hurried back as the doctor was due to visit. He said he was reassured to see her there, and despite Faye rolling her eyes, reiterated that her mother's recovery would take a good six weeks. Robin would be back in London by the middle of December. What if she found a job before then? Robin wouldn't think about that now. After he left, Faye switched on her gameshow so Robin went into the loft, hoping to find Dad's car boot bits and bobs. None of the boxes were marked with an A for Alan so she opened them discriminately. She found Christmas decorations, old glassware and a couple of lamps... Robin searched through nearly half until she could no longer resist the pull of her secret room. The heater still worked and she jumped onto the bed and pulled shut the roof window she'd left open, spotting her Sony Walkman on top of the wardrobe. Robin grabbed it and sat down on the mattress. She brushed off the dust and stroked the front before pressing play; she shouldn't have felt so disappointed that it didn't still work. She removed the cassette. Why would she have been listening to Bananarama? Tara was a fan of theirs, Robin must have borrowed the album. She took out her phone and Googled the playlist. Ah yes. That song. Feet in the air, she lay on her front, clicked on Spotify and downloaded the track.

Cruel Summer. Quickly, she turned it off.

Robin had run away that July morning, with Yul, just after her exams, after her dad had died before she could tell him her news. It was still dark and the train driver had shot her an odd look as she'd climbed aboard wearing a rucksack stuffed to the seams. She buried her face in the covers, sixteen years old again. However lonely she'd felt the last year or two, she'd never forget the sense of isolation of 1989.

She pulled open a drawer and sifted through a tangle of leg warmers. The one below was full of T-shirts. She'd forgotten that bright pink one with a boombox motif across the front and hesitated before pulling off her brown jumper, mussing up her hair in the process. She slipped on the top and glanced in the star-shaped mirror, turning from side to side. On the dressing table a beer-bottle-shaped, green container with a silver top caught her eye and she went over and sank onto the stool that wobbled sideways. Robin blew dust off the lid before tugging it off. She pressed the spray head and a splash of Brut landed on her skin. It smelt more like vinegar after all this time. Smarting, she wiped her eyes. Just seeing the bottle took her back to the hospital, with Dad. She'd been dreading his trip away to Sheffield but would have wished him anywhere in the world but there, wired up in that bed. He was slipping away but the smell of Brut held on as long as it could and embraced her when he couldn't as she'd bent forwards to give him one last hug. In the days running up to leaving for London she would smell this bottle even though it made her cry.

Robin sniffed and gazed around the room, loath to move a single thing. It didn't seem right after thirty-two years. She felt invested in keeping the room exactly as she'd left it – that way it felt like a connection to the life she'd led with Dad around.

She opened a wooden box on the table's right side. A lucky dip of lipsticks – and eyeshadows, she picked up the white one from the top and stared into the mirror, then prised open the plastic lid and applied a stripe across her nose. To complete the look she went to the wardrobe and searched for her Adam Ant frock coat. Robin got halfway through all the jumpers and jackets when she felt an urge to speak to Tara. Was she still up north, what was she doing now? Robin picked up her phone and went into Facebook. Before looking for Tara she checked to see if Amber had sent a message, but she hadn't even read the last two Robin had sent her. Then she put Tara's name into the search bar. Two Tara Dankworths immediately came up. She ran a finger over the photo of the one that had familiar-looking blue hair, not needing to check the other profile out. If only circumstances hadn't torn them apart. She still lived in Manchester but had kept other personal details private. Robin leant against the wall and hesitated before pressing the Add Friend icon. She should have looked her up years ago. It was strange to think Tara had only been one click away all this time. However, once Robin had felt ready to make contact again, she'd never been able to push away the concern that Tara might not want to know. Not after the way Robin had left things. But being here, in her old room, amongst the memories... the risk of rejection felt worth it.

Hello Tara! How are you these days? I know it's been a while. I'm up in Stonedale for a few weeks, it would be great to meet.

What was the best way to sign off?

Love Robin x

She wrote her phone number on the bottom and felt a rush of excitement when she pressed send. Just then, the doorbell sounded loud and clear, even up here, like it always used to. Faye mustn't try to get up. Robin switched off the heater and light and closed the door behind her, feeling half her age as she slid down the ladder.

'I'll get the door,' she hollered and looked at her watch, chiding herself, she should have made Faye another drink by now and seen if she needed the loo. She chased a barking Hoover back into the lounge. A chilly draught whooshed in as she pulled on the front door and clocked who it was, a girl from her schooldays, all grown-up now, standing in the darkness in a sensible raincoat.

'Just here to collect the Avon magazine,' the woman said and leant forwards, eyes bulging. 'Robin Wilson?'

'Um, hello. Yes. My mother's had a fall. I'm staying whilst she recovers.'

'Oh, the poor thing. I do hope she isn't in too much pain.' She tilted her head. 'You haven't changed a bit.'

Robin squeezed the door handle. With her brown jumper and smooth blonde bob, they both knew she looked nothing like she did years ago. She tried to remember the woman's name.

'You neither,' Robin said politely. It was almost true, with her petite figure, although she'd embraced going grey, it looked stylish in a layered cut.

'Must be weird for you, being back here.' A smile flickered across her face. 'Have you visited the bookshop?'

A third person mentioning that place? 'No, not yet,' Robin

said, brightly, and pushed the catalogue by the front door into her hands. The woman said goodbye to Robin and shot her a look over her shoulder before pulling out her phone. Robin closed the door firmly and Hoover ran up to her as she went in the lounge.

'That was a surprise. The Avon lady...'

'Stacey Evans.'

Ah, yes, that was her name. Faye carried on watching the television. Robin wondered what other surprises Stonedale had in store for her.

'Right, how about I make another brew and then I'll do a wash.'

Faye turned down the television and looked over at Robin. She sat bolt upright as her eyes widened.

'Did you explain to Stacey about your belongings in the loft?'

Why would she do that? And why couldn't Faye take her eyes off Robin's jumper? She glanced down and ran into the hallway and gazed into the mirror at the bottom of the stairs. The bold white stripe across her nose stood out even more than the bright top and messed up hair.

Oh crap.

Robin went into the kitchen and made a brew and sat back down on the chaise longue. Halfway through her drink, she put down her cup.

'Why didn't you ever empty my room?'

Faye's jaw tightened. 'I believed you'd come back, at the beginning.'

'Even after you knew I'd got a job and wanted to stay in London?'

She took off her glasses and rubbed her eyes. 'In the weeks after your dad passed and you left, the days seemed longer, despite working extra hours, so I kept myself busy by focusing on his things. I sorted through them and took most to the charity shop, the rest I boxed up and put in the loft.'

It didn't surprise Robin that she'd packed the remnants of him away so quickly, not after the way she behaved at his send-off.

'So why not do the same with mine?'

'They were already up there – out of sight, out of mind.'

Of course, it had been a matter of convenience, as if there would have been a sentimental reason. When Robin had first arrived in London, Faye rang Uncle Ralph's a few times but Robin had refused to engage. Faye threatened to come down and fetch her – Robin threatened to run away again. So the calls stopped, and Faye never wrote. Occasionally Robin would hear him talk quietly on the phone, telling someone she was doing okay. She didn't hear from Faye personally until that first Christmas after she'd run away. She said it was time to stop all this nonsense and come back home, but by then Robin had got a job in a fancy clothes shop, money in her pocket and a few new friends. Uncle Ralph had given up encouraging her to go to a sixth form college so told her about a job ad he'd seen in the window of a boutique. The owner started her off filling shelves, said she had an eye for fashion even though she insisted Robin wear nothing but muted shades to fit in with her customer base. Slowly, her New Romantic clothes got pushed to the back of her wardrobe. She'd started to build a new life to fill the dad-shaped hole that her mother didn't fit into.

Hoover yawned and jumped off Faye's navy slacks. He stretched out before the fire, on his front, square head nestled between his paws.

'I was surprised to see you'd got a dog. How long have you had Hoover?'

She put her glasses back on and glared. 'What is this, Twenty Questions?'

'No, Faye. It's called conversation.'

'There's no need to be rude. And why should you care? We've established you're only here to please Ralph. I hadn't heard a single word from you since I visited to see Amber.'

'Yes, well, you could have called.' Robin took their cups into the kitchen and washed them out, then came back through.

'Hoover belonged to Mrs Taylor next door.'

What? Robin sat down again. 'I didn't think you and her got on.'

'Because life stopped moving forwards without you in it?'

Stung, Robin picked up the newspaper.

'You're right, Robin, nothing's different since you left.' Faye reached out for the paper. 'Everything is.'

Robin got up to hand over the paper and leave the room when Faye spoke again.

'We were never best friends but came to an understanding. Now and then Sheila would drop by with her latest bake. Occasionally I'd give her a bunch of flowers from the back garden. But three years ago, she couldn't manage any more. Alzheimer's got her. The care home wouldn't accept pets and her children didn't want him. I found out Hoover was going to an animal shelter. I'd been taking him for walks as it was, so it made sense for me to take him on.' She took the lid off her pen. 'I didn't have to make many adjustments and he hates water so the pond could stay as it was.'

Who *was* this neighbourly person? And was Faye really trying to meet her halfway by telling her all this? It wasn't what Robin had expected.

* * *

Later, in the evening, Faye asleep in her chair, Robin took out her phone, the urge to talk with Tara growing stronger. Was her mum still alive? Was she in touch with anyone else from school? They used to know everything about each other and she couldn't help smiling as she recalled their paranoid teenage chats about hair removal cream and tampons. Robin had checked Facebook several times during the afternoon. Tara had been online, on and off all day, and the message was marked *seen*. In fact, the green dot showing she was active appeared again now, but she still didn't reply. Robin scrolled down her Facebook feed, without reading any of the posts. What if Tara never replied?

Amber wasn't replying to her texts either, so Robin called again, mentioned that she'd rung the university but they'd insisted they'd have to speak to Amber.

'Mum! I told you I'd sort it out myself. You just couldn't resist, could you? It's like that time you went in to see my A level maths teacher, without telling me. You told him I needed more time to revise for the final exam and asked him to move it. It was *so* embarrassing.' She hung up.

9

Robin woke up with a jolt. A tail batted her face, just as a pungent smell came from its direction. Hoover span around sharply, sniffed the air and gave Robin a disdainful look, backing away from her. He'd spent the night in Faye's room and normally stayed there until she got up. He pawed at the covers and barefoot, Robin hurried into the room opposite, the dog at her heels. Faye was still asleep, snoring contentedly.

The weather was mizzly and misty, and didn't bode well for Bonfire Night tomorrow. Robin sat at the kitchen table, elbows on the surface as the kettle boiled, and leafed through Faye's old handwritten recipe book, looking for inspiration. Blanche was calling after lunch, for coffee. Secretly, she was enjoying the comforting, stodgy meals her mother preferred and that Robin had deemed too unhealthy to cook for her own husband and daughter. Striking out on her own at sixteen, she'd cook from scratch for her uncle and make herself a lunchbox to take into work. After the chaos of running away to London she'd needed something solid to cling onto and concluded order, routine, discipline – they were the answer and that applied to food as well.

She'd rung him last night and kept things cheerful, glad they weren't face to face because he always saw right through her.

At two o'clock Robin spotted Blanche outside, moving slowly with her zimmer frame, and went out to meet her. Whilst she and Faye settled at the dining room table, Robin made their drinks. Hoover lay in the lounge with his collection of toys kept in the corner, behind the television, including a soft fluffy duck, a rope and a chewable plastic bone. A stab of jealousy had poked her the first time Robin had noticed them; Faye always used to be strict about her keeping her stuff upstairs, even when she was little. Perhaps it was just as well she'd never had a sibling if she saw a dog as a rival.

'Bless you, my throat's as dry as a bone,' said Blanche as Robin put down her cup. 'The doctor's trying me on new tablets.'

'My uncle has the same problem with his blood pressure pills. He swears by sucking on cough sweets. If you like, I'll pick some up for you.'

'You're a good lass!' she said, her slash of red lipstick widening.

Robin fetched Faye's old silver tea stand and set up the scones that she'd baked that morning, grateful to keep busy. Faye would use it if someone important came around, like the vicar in the run up to Dad's funeral. That day she'd put on her Sunday best and provided him with a full spread of sandwiches and homemade fruit cake, plus Battenberg, her favourite, whereas Robin could hardly pull her T-shirt on the right way or tip cereal into a bowl without making a mess.

'That's a smart blazer,' said Blanche. 'I used to have one that exact shade of turquoise. My Dennis, bless him, said it used to make me look like Lady Diana.'

'The colour's a change for me,' Robin said, her ears feeling hot. It had been hanging in her old wardrobe, the gold buttons had caught her eye. She used to wear it out shopping with Tara, with high-waisted jeans and a black bowler hat, a look so different to Amber's ripped jeans and woollen beanies. She couldn't resist fitting the blazer on with a casual ruched white blouse that suited curls better, maybe tomorrow she wouldn't straighten her hair.

'Right, I'll leave you to it.'

'Aren't you joining us?' asked Blanche.

Before Robin had time to think, Faye told her to bring in another plate. At the clink of a knife, Hoover ran over. Stumpy tail wagging, he sat at Faye's feet, head cocked expectantly.

'No,' Faye said sharply.

He wandered off and collapsed by the television.

'Good boy,' she called.

He turned his back to her. Robin couldn't help laughing and as Faye caught her eye a smile crossed her face for a fleeting moment. Robin looked away, unsure how to react. Blanche asked about her job in London. Robin talked about her career in marketing without mentioning she'd been made redundant. Blanche winced as she reached down to scratch her leg and Faye joined Robin in the kitchen as she boiled the kettle again. Faye filled a plate with shortbread fingers, moving more easily, bit by bit her recovery was showing hints of progress. She also pulled out a hot water bottle with a pink furry cover from one of the cupboards.

'This will help Blanche's arthritis.'

As they sat down again Robin looked at her phone a couple of times, willing Amber to let her know how things were going.

'Expecting someone to ring?' asked Blanche with a smile.

'Robin?' said Faye sharply.

She looked up. 'Sorry?'

Blanche leant forwards. 'Everything all right?'

'Yes, yes, it's nothing.'

'Come on, lass, spit it out,' said Blanche. 'Perhaps we can help.'

She sighed. 'It's my daughter, Amber. Her student accommodation has flooded.' Robin filled them in on the details.

'These things always resolve themselves one way or another,' said Faye.

'That's little comfort to her at the moment,' she muttered. 'It's her first time away from home. She must feel so alone and desperate, away from her friends, carrying all that responsibility. And I looked up the hotel on TripAdvisor, reviewers spoke of dirty carpets and cracked toilet seats.'

'Can you ring this student accommodation yourself?' asked Blanche.

'I did but they wouldn't tell me anything. Amber didn't appreciate it and made it quite clear she doesn't want me to get involved.'

'And quite right too. I'd been in work and paying my own way for a while at her age,' said Faye.

'Me too, but just because I had it tough doesn't mean I don't want to make things easier for my own daughter.'

Blanche thought for a moment. 'There is an obvious answer, of course, staring you in the face.' Her eyes twinkled and she clasped her swollen hands. 'Young Amber could move in here.'

Robin put down her cup and Faye stopped chewing.

'Into Parade Row?' said Robin.

'Have you got a better idea?'

'There's no way she'd ever swap student life for Stonedale.'

'Why ever not? Free lodgings, your grub and this little fella here...' She jerked her head towards the floor. 'It's only a short commute into Manchester. Just think, you'd have two people looking after you then, Faye.'

Faye's expression didn't change. It had always been the way, even when she was cross with Robin for leaving food on her plate or staying up late, her voice revealed the anger, never her face.

'One person fussing unnecessarily is more than enough, thank you,' she replied eventually. 'But I suppose this could be a practical solution.'

Was she serious? Robin had hardly spoken to Amber about her childhood. Faye would be a complete stranger to her. Now and again, Amber had asked why they couldn't visit her grandmother. Robin would just say things were difficult. As she got older, Robin talked of a falling out after Dad's funeral and said that they had never got on anyway. She spoke to Amber mostly about him, about his hobbies, his job as a builder. However, she could never bring herself to badmouth Faye because that niggling voice in her head told her not to.

Yet she couldn't expose Amber to Faye's cruelty. What if she picked on her granddaughter? Although Robin would be there to put a stop to it and, at least, here, everything was clean...

The three of them, living together? Robin had played at Happy Families with Todd for far too long and would never do that again. Yet to have her daughter here tomorrow, where she could see she was okay, make her favourite meals, listen to stories about new friends...

'Where's the harm in suggesting it?' said Blanche and she bit on a shortbread finger.

Robin Wilson,
16 Parade Row,
Stonedale,
Greater Manchester
August 1985

Dear Debbie,

I HATE MY HAIRY LEGS.

Since starting secondary school last year the hairs on my legs have become really dark. I hate them. PE is the worst time of the week, I'm sure the whole class is looking. Secretly, I tried Dad's razor but it made my legs bleed. My best friend's hairs hardly show, but she says her mum uses hair removal cream and it really stinks. What's the best way to get rid of them? I'm thinking about wiping on kitchen bleach to lighten their colour. I'm sick of wearing jeans in this hot weather.

Robin, age 12

Girls Scene
41 Gover Street,
London

Dear Robin,

First off, please don't try bleach, that's very dangerous and will damage your skin. You aren't alone in feeling like this and luckily, it's a problem that is easy to solve these days. Hair removal cream does smell but a shower afterwards should sort that out, or all you need is someone to show you tips on how to shave carefully. Why not ask your mum for some practical advice? I'm sure she'll help you sort this out a safe way, if she knows this is making you avoid summer clothes, because getting overheated isn't good for you either. Then you'll be able to enjoy wearing those shorts and skirts!

Best wishes,

Debbie

10

As the big windows of Brynner's came into view, Robin quickened her pace. She had decided, after all the comments, she should visit the bookshop, and left Blanche and Faye finishing the scones. The doorbell rang as she entered.

'I'll be there in a minute,' called a low voice. She heard the sound of chatter and clink of crockery from the café area at the back of the shop. Feeling at home with the aroma of coffee and jumble of books, she unzipped the top of her anorak and admired the tree mural. In fact, the whole shop had a green theme. On the far right wall were shelves bearing mini bonsai trees and the ceiling was sky-blue and covered with leaves that looked as if they were floating on a breeze. Each bore the title of a well-known book, ones by Jane Austen, Oscar Wilde, Bill Bryson and David Attenborough. She stood in front of the sagas, stuffing gloves into her pockets, and scanned the spines and the occasional cover that faced forwards, the browned pages and edges that curled. Robin wanted to flick through one and see if previous owners had made notes. Now and then she'd bought a secondhand book online if the original had gone out of print, and the first thing she'd do was lift it to her nose, finding the smell comforting. She reached out to take a historical novel.

'Sorry for the delay, can I help? Are you looking for something specific?'

She turned around and was faced with a name badge.

Jason Brown,
Manager.

Robin gave a small gasp. She took in the black eyeliner and tight jeans, the black jacket, its collar and sleeves upturned, of course they were. And the curve of his mouth, the bold eyebrows...

It really was him, standing there, not looking much different.

'Yul? It's me, Robin.'

He stepped back, went to say something but changed his mind.

'I never expected to see you here,' she stuttered.

'I own the shop. I'm in here every day.'

They stared at each other.

'I didn't recognise you,' he said.

'It has been a while,' she replied, momentarily deflated. The thick chestnut hair was still slicked back, still had a kink in the front. The grey strands at the sides suited him. The dark eyes now had lines at the corners.

'How come you're still in Stonedale?' she asked.

'Shouldn't I be?'

'You always wanted to travel. I assumed you would have left.' She smiled nervously.

He didn't say anything. Robin didn't know what to do so she carried on asking more questions.

'Do you live in the village? Tearoom 1960 has hardly changed. Are your parents still here?'

Yul gave a deep sigh and didn't meet her eyes. 'I heard you'd come back.'

So he knew she was here, but hadn't reached out? Cheeks flushed, Robin looked towards the sagas again, not really seeing anything, then she turned back to face him.

'You won't believe it but Faye's got a dog, called Hoover, and I've found Tara on—'

The doorbell rang and a woman with a baby swaddled to her chest came in. He turned to go.

'Yul?'

He went behind the counter, leaving her there alone without an excuse or word of goodbye.

She stumbled out of the shop, her legs seeming to know where she wanted to go. Robin hurried down the high street and a car hooted as she crossed the road over to Sheepwash Bridge. Minutes later she was in the woods. Acorns crunched under her feet and she climbed over a log that had fallen across the narrow path. Bare tree canopies let through the last rays of afternoon sun, picking out bursts of scarlet hawthorn berries. She pulled her scarf tighter as a ramshackle treehouse came fully into view, in the branches of a big ash tree in the wood.

It was still there.

Robin cut through the mud and a blackbird launched itself out of a cluster of ferns, squawking as it flew away. She stopped by the ash tree's wide trunk and stared up at the rotting planks of wood. She and Yul had spent many weekends here that last spring, before Dad died, before they went to London. They never discovered who'd originally built it, preferring to believe it was the work of hobgoblins. She ran her hand over the rough ridges of bark, hardly noticing her fingers destroying spiders' lacework. Robin thought about Yul and their time down in London and the trip to Charing Cross hospital's A&E.

She was stupid, stupid, to think he'd be pleased to see her. The momentary elation she'd felt, when their eyes first locked, had evaporated into nothing, leaving her feeling empty. He would have his own life now, like her, his business and maybe a wife, children. She walked back out of the woods. The picnic tables and war memorial were still there, to her left, and the cricket pitch stretched out, further in the distance.

At least some things were still familiar.

She walked back over the stone bridge that arched over the river and looked down at a shoal of tiddlers as water gently splashed and frothed. An image popped into her head of Faye, Dad and her playing pooh sticks. They'd walked onto the bridge at the end of one of their Sunday treasure hunts, Faye had worked out the anagram. She'd searched for twigs and handed them out so that the three of them could play Winnie-The-Pooh's game. On the count of three they let the twigs fall into the current, on one side. Then Faye kept running to and fro, to see whose came through first, under the bridge, bobbing on the water. This had made Robin even happier than seeing her own stick sail through first and win.

It was almost dark by the time Robin got to the supermarket, still playing the scene in the bookshop over and over in her head. Tired-looking commuters picked up ready meals and cheap bottles of wine. She barely noticed the goods that filled her trolley as she rushed up and down the aisles not wanting to bump into anyone else. Was Yul angry with her? Disappointed? He had no right to be. Shopping bags banged against her legs as she went back to Parade Row, the lights were on in Blanche's front room. She walked through to the kitchen and dumped her bags and downed a glass of water.

Faye looked up from *Word Weekly* when she went back into the lounge.

'Why didn't you tell me? You should have said he was here.' Her voice trembled.

'You've been to the bookshop?'

She nodded.

'Because I thought you might have worked out the obvious before now.'

'What do you mean?'

'The shop's name.'

Brynner's. Of course. Yul was a nickname used affectionately by his family. When he'd been born his gran said he looked just like her favourite heartthrob, *The King and I*'s lead actor, bald Yul Brynner. Robin had never known him as Jason. They first met outside Tearoom 1960, when they were fourteen. He was new to the village and almost collided with her when he came out with his parents.

'Yul, you almost winded this lovely young lady,' his dad had protested. Yul had pulled down his baseball cap but not before she'd noted how cute he looked.

Robin crossed her arms. 'Don't you think it might have been a shock for me, seeing him without warning?'

'Like you turning up here unannounced?'

It... it wasn't the same.

'It's not as if you've ever spoken about him to me, not even when you two were courting.'

Robin folded her arms more tightly. 'But you weren't interested.'

'I didn't get a chance. I asked you what you liked about him more than once.'

'Yes, because you didn't think he was good enough.'

Faye put down her pen. 'That's not true. I'd hear you two

talking in the loft, I knew you both loved books. Jason seemed to be more than a crush.'

Robin gave a little shake of her head. 'More likely you were worried what we were up to.'

'Sometimes, but you've got a teenage daughter, surely you understand that.'

Robin collapsed onto the chaise longue and a tear welled at the corner of her eye. Quickly she wiped it away, hoping Faye hadn't seen. She was used to the distance between her and Faye, but not between her and Yul. They'd order drinks for each other in town without asking, pick out clothes in shops that would suit, they'd known each other so well. But in the bookshop, he'd felt like a complete stranger.

'Did you talk to him when he got back from London, all those years ago?' Robin asked.

'I went around to his house to find out what was going on.' Faye shrugged. 'His parents invited me in and forced him to apologise for his part in you both running away. He didn't say much. His parents were distraught.'

Robin shifted, unable to get comfortable. Amber's first year at high school, she was bullied by a girl in the year above. Robin had only found out from the father of one of Amber's friends, and he'd given her such a look as if she didn't know her daughter well enough. Robin had felt so humiliated. Had Faye felt like that?

'Jason came back to Stonedale again, last year. We nod at each other if our paths cross. I don't understand why you're so upset now. You were young. It was a long time ago.'

So Yul hadn't lived in the village all these years. Robin wondered where he'd been instead. She thought back to Dad's funeral, the service at the church with all of his friends and workmates, then the last farewell at the crematorium, just her,

Faye and Uncle Ralph. 'Not everyone finds it easy to cut off their feelings.' Hoover came over and jumped up. He pushed his nose against her arm. 'Why *is* he called Hoover?' she muttered, glad for the distraction.

'Sheila said he always used to hoover up scraps that fell on the floor whilst she cooked, it made him ill a couple of times as a puppy.'

'We used to call Dad a dustbin for the same reason – if I left anything on my plate he'd lean over and take it.'

Faye nodded. 'Despite me telling him off.'

For a second Robin felt like they were three again, Dad winking as he forked up a spare potato, Faye tutting loudly even though Robin and her dad knew she was glad not to see waste. Faye opened the door of the beech cabinet. With her good hand she lifted out a half full green bottle and handed it to Robin, wincing afterwards as she touched her ribs.

'The tonic water is behind the barley squash, in the cupboard next to the cooker. You need to toughen up.'

'You knew about the last scroll. Never told me about the bookshop. Is there anything else I need to know?' asked Robin.

'Yes, there are ice cubes in the freezer's top tray,' said Faye, turning back to her puzzle.

11

Tonight would be Bonfire Night, Robin registered, as she woke up in the spare room on Friday morning, the gin and tonic glass by her bed. She sat up and leant against the headboard, reaching straight for her phone. She went into Messenger. At seven-thirty, Amber was probably still asleep. A green dot was visible next to Tara's name so Robin decided to make one last attempt to connect and typed a few words. She sat bolt upright as Tara replied, before she typed back quickly, asking Tara about work, about her home life. Tara practised acupuncture and Reiki in Manchester city centre and she lived with her partner. Her words seemed stilted and she didn't give much away, but then Messenger always made things sound less natural. Robin told herself that was the reason, ignoring a sense that Tara might not be quite as keen as she was to hook up again. A couple of cocktails and it would just be like old times.

She hoped Tara might be free and willing to meet this weekend.

Tara: Okay. I'll only have an hour though, in my lunch break. Meet me at the Old Wellington on Sunday, at twelve. I'll book a table. See you then.

The little green dot went off. Robin showered and was about to rinse her hair one last time when her phone rang. She turned off the shower head and almost slipped as she stepped onto the bathroom floor. Dripping, she grabbed her phone up from the shelf above the sink.

'Darling, how are you? Wasn't it a great idea that you move in here? You'll have peace and quiet to study and—'

'Mum. Slow down, stop getting carried away. I don't need you to make decisions for me. Honestly, remember when you told my teacher at school parents' evening I'd love to take part in the Duke of Edinburgh youth award programme? You and I hadn't even discussed it and none of my friends had signed up.'

Robin flinched. But getting that award had been a necessity for any university application, everyone said so.

Amber sighed. 'Look, I'm not coming to Stonedale. Personally, I can't think of a worse idea.'

'But... but it's the perfect solution.' Robin could hear the uncertainty in her own voice, still concerned about how Faye would be with Amber, despite believing this was the best option for her daughter, given the circumstances.

'Perfect for you, you mean, interfering in my life more than you already do.'

Oh. 'Please don't speak to me like that.'

'And what does your mum think? How's everything with you two? You've only just turned up yourself.'

'She's fine with it. Everything's fine.' Robin would have a word with Faye. Set her straight.

'Wouldn't it be awkward?' Amber asked in a short voice. 'I

don't know her at all and it's not like you've ever told me what the fallout was really about.'

'I've just moved on, that's all, and so has she.'

'You're good at that.'

Robin sighed and took a deep breath. She wasn't going to get drawn into that again. Not today.

'In any case, the argument between me and my mother is our problem, not yours.'

'Things are stressful enough at the moment without me having to referee arguments or walk on eggshells. Right, I've got to go...'

'It wouldn't be like that.'

Amber paused. 'You're telling me you're genuinely happy for me to get to know her? It's what you want?'

Amber needed security at the moment.

'Of course.'

'And you promise to back off? To leave me to sort my own life out?'

Robin flinched again. 'There's no need to go on.'

'But there is. I don't want you ringing the university again, like one of those hovercraft parents the papers talk about.'

'Helicopter. Look, love, I promise, okay?'

After saying goodbye, Robin stood still for a moment and breathed. Amber was going to arrive tomorrow.

She got dressed and helped Faye out of bed, hardly noticing her grumble that she had the bedside manner of a vet. Robin had missed Amber so much. They'd never been apart this long, and the distance that had developed between them this last two years hadn't eased her departure for university. Phone calls were all well and good but Robin needed to see her in the flesh. Had she made good friends? Was she coping with her studies? She had so many questions.

Robin whistled her way into the village, and the supermarket. She avoided the bookshop, pulling Hoover away from the lamppost outside it, as they passed. She needed to focus on getting ready for her daughter's arrival. On the way back she mentally went through the list of treats she'd bought, such as Amber's favourite baked crisps and that expensive shampoo of Robin's she used to borrow without asking. She rarely bought it these days. Robin had been a silent partner in Todd's business for tax reasons and when he went bankrupt they'd both lost their home and their money.

'This fell out of your pocket.'

She stopped and turned around. Yul held out a scrap of paper. He was standing next to a bucket of water with a window wiper in it, a chamois leather in his other hand. He wore a brown velvet jacket today.

'My shopping list... thanks.' She took it back. Robin waited for him to speak, missing the easiness that used to exist between them. A woman with a buggy walked past, her baby waving a bright pink dummy.

'Maeve's tearoom is heaving, your café area at the back can't have stolen many of her coffee drinkers.' Why, oh why, did she say that?

Hoover strained at the lead and she let it go slack for a moment. She studied Yul's face, his eyes made more piercing by the eyeliner. She wanted to ask if he was married, if he'd had kids, but that would sound as if she was bothered. His eyes dropped and he shot Hoover a smile, looking as if he were smothering a laugh, before going back to washing the shop's front window and Robin continued up the high street. She'd forgotten how him finding something funny always used to lift her too.

Robin had forced away thoughts of him, over the years, but

now couldn't help wondering what life would have been like with him. They'd always talked about having at least four children and being the sort of parents to pull them out of school and take off in a campervan, teaching them stuff that mattered, like how to skim stones and build a den. They'd felt so grown-up talking about such things, but now, in his presence, she'd felt like a clumsy teenager who couldn't find the right words.

Parade Row loomed and a toddler came past walking unsteadily, holding his mum's hand. He waved at Hoover and pointed, laughing. As Robin approached number sixteen an elderly couple smiled at Hoover and the man tilted his hat. A woman behind them looked at Faye's dog too and grinned. Dogs were certainly popular in Stonedale. They arrived at the front porch and Robin unlocked the door, before bending down to check his paws.

Tail wagging, Hoover innocently stared up, a bright pink dummy in his mouth.

12

Robin glanced at her watch and looked out of the front window again. Perhaps Amber's train was late. The Saturday service wasn't as frequent. This gave her the opportunity to have a word with Faye. She couldn't put it off any longer and sat down on the chaise longue, opposite her.

'Can we have a chat? About Amber. How things should be whilst she's here.'

'What is it with your generation? Talk, talk, talk. Sometimes it's just better to go with the flow. What is there to discuss?'

'Just that.' Robin clenched her hands together. 'The way you are with me. I... I won't have you speak to Amber in that tone.'

A tide of red swept up Faye's neck. 'I don't know what you mean.'

'I'm serious, Faye. I appreciate Amber being allowed to move in, but I won't hesitate to move her out... me as well, if she finds things unpleasant.'

Faye's jaw tightened.

Robin stood up. 'I'll give her another ring.'

'For goodness' sake, stop being such a fussbucket.'

It's not that, thought Robin, *it's mothering*. Sometimes Todd used to accuse her of fussing too, in recent years when work took over his life more. That had made her feel as if she were back in the 1980s, a sense that her views and feelings weren't valued.

Faye picked fluff off her jumper and smoothed down her skirt. When she'd dressed, Robin had noticed patches of her bruising were now turning yellow. Faye turned back to studying a crossword in *Word Weekly* and simultaneously messaging on her phone. She caught Robin looking.

'Another mistake. Julian very much appreciates me pointing them out.'

'Who?' asked Robin.

'The editor.' She shook the magazine. 'Six across is wrong.'

'You email him every time?'

'Of course. Standards. Not that I can be doing with email. I texted the office the first time. Julian rang me back. I gave him short shrift but we ended up chatting about his garden. He gave me another number to text if I found anything else. We're usually in contact once a month.' Her eyes shone. 'The last one was a humdinger. The clue was the first name of the first child of a monarch to get divorced. *Word Weekly* said it was Anne, for Princess Anne – Julian said that was the answer because she was never a monarch. But that's not logical, the answer's Henry VIII, because even though he ruled, he was the child of a monarch too.'

'How long has this been going on for?' Robin asked, trying to make sense of the Anne-Henry conundrum.

She shrugged. 'Five or so years. He's always very grateful. Says I'm one of his most eagle-eyed readers. He asked if I came from a family of puzzlers and I explained that I live alone. It's nice to feel useful again, since retiring. The magazine's office sends me a Christmas card and a free festive edition every year.'

The doorbell rang. Hoover gave a bark and Faye summoned him back as he charged into the hallway. Robin's hands fumbled with the lock, still thinking about Faye, and how she spoke of the editor as if he was one of her friends. She yanked the door wide open.

Amber. Her precious, Amber.

Her earbuds were in and she had a tall rucksack on her back that she must have borrowed from a friend. She held onto the pull handle of her big suitcase. Her shoulder-length hair seemed to have grown an inch at least, apart from the fringe which looked a little uneven, and her jeans looked looser than before. Under her eyes were dark circles. Wholesome, home-cooked meals, that's what she needed.

'It's so good to see you.' Robin went forward to give her a hug. Amber didn't reciprocate. She hadn't since Robin and Todd had split, but that didn't matter, she was here, she was safe, even if she stood as stiff as a board. Robin understood, after the way things had ended with her father. 'Let me take that case.'

'Chill, Mum, I can manage.' She stared at Robin's chest. 'What's with the jumper? You never wear red, and talk about retro eighties with those shoulder pads. Is it new?'

'I've had it a while.'

Amber shrugged and put one foot on the doorstep, then hoisted her case into the house. She let her rucksack fall onto the carpet and shoved her earbuds into her tan faux fur coat.

'Slip off those boots. I'll give them a good polish, later.'

'No, thanks,' she said, in a strained voice, as she removed them.

Robin smiled and was about to step back when she noticed Amber's right ear.

'What's that? You've had a *second* piercing?'

'So?' She folded her arms and stared defiantly.

'Where did you get it done? Did they clean it properly before—'

'No, I did it myself with a safety pin, of course.' She rolled her eyes and started to put one of the boots back on. 'I knew this was a mistake.'

'Look, it's just a surprise, that's all. There's no need to be like that.' *Count to twenty, Robin*. She pointed to the lounge door and Amber walked straight past her and went in. Hoover ran up and sniffed her feet. Amber stood uncertainly, before darting forward in Faye's direction, one arm outstretched towards the wrist that wasn't in a sling. Robin gave Faye a pointed look.

'Nice to meet you. How are you feeling after your fall?'

They shook hands. 'On the mend, thank you. He won't leave you alone, you know, until he's had a proper welcome.'

Robin stared at them both. She'd never thought, one day, they'd be together.

Amber hesitated before dropping to her knees.

'What's his name?'

'Hoover,' said Faye.

He rolled onto his back and sent puppy eyes Amber's way. She picked up the rope toy and played tug of war, swiping her arm from side to side. 'Thanks for letting me stay. I didn't want to put George out even more.'

Robin watched Faye who couldn't take her eyes off her granddaughter.

'Have you known him long?' Robin asked. 'George is a nice name.'

'For God's sake, Mum, George is only a friend, not even that really, and a Georgina if you must know.'

'Why don't you show Amber to the spare room, Robin, and then we'll have lunch?' Faye cut in.

'Sounds like a plan, I haven't had breakfast and didn't even have time to grab a coffee at the station.'

'But breakfast is the most important meal of the day,' Robin said.

Amber glared and turned to Faye. 'It'll be great to stretch out in a nice bed again. I was due to move into the hotel today. Not much of a choice – George's floor or a bed that probably had bugs and broken springs.'

'I wouldn't stretch out too far, you might hit your mother.'

'We're sharing a double bed, in the spare room,' Robin said brightly, realising immediately that she'd kidded herself it wouldn't matter, in the hope that she could keep her old loft room as it was, just for a while longer

Amber dropped the rope. 'You never mentioned that.'

'It's a big bed and I'm hardly in that room during the day.'

'But sometimes I work late or scroll on my phone if I can't sleep.'

Faye waved her hand. 'I don't like shocks either.'

Robin carried the rucksack upstairs whilst Amber dragged the case and took out her laptop before lying on the bed, on her front.

'I should have known you'd trick me into agreeing that staying here was the solution, letting me think there was a third bedroom,' she said.

'I... I never said you'd have your own bedroom.' Robin hadn't told Amber about the loft room. She hadn't felt ready to share it with anyone, not even her daughter.

'This is the final straw,' snapped Amber.

'What do you mean?'

'Is there Wi-Fi? Can I have the password? I need to email someone,' she said, ignoring Robin's question. With an abrupt movement she lifted the lid, her eyes on the screen.

Robin Wilson,
16 Parade Row,
Stonedale,
Greater Manchester
November 1985

Dear Debbie,

I'M SCARED OF GETTING OLDER.

In September the brother of my neighbour, Blanche, died, and ever since then she hasn't been the same. Sometimes I go to her house to bake after school, but she just looks sad now and when I visit she hardly says anything.

I know it's babyish but I'm scared of getting older and losing people I care about, and facing all the problems grown-ups have. What if I never meet someone or get divorced, or fall out with friends? What if I never earn much money? I don't want to always be worrying about the future. What can I do about this?

Robin, age 13

Girl's Scene
41 Gover Street,
London

Dear Robin,

Well done, Robin, you've almost answered the question yourself! There is no point worrying about the future because you can't control it.

When you started at primary school, I bet you thought high school looked scary, but you're there now, coping with new challenges, and it's not so terrible, is it? That's what ageing is like for everyone. Getting older is far from all bad, you know! You gain confidence and with independence might travel or get an interesting job, or one day have a family of your own. There are many exciting times ahead of you. And life has a funny way of just making you get on with problems that arise.

It's natural that your neighbour will be out of sorts for a while. What she needs most is understanding company. Why don't you bake a cake next time before going around? You can just sit and read quietly at her house, or watch a television show she likes. I'm sure that would mean so much to her.

Best wishes,

Debbie

13

After a moment's hesitation, Robin pulled down the noisy ladder and climbed into the loft. She felt protective of her teenage room, all the memories she'd not yet had time to re-familiarise herself with. Yet perhaps it might be fun to watch Amber's face when she saw the past fashions and gadgets. Robin reached down to help her but Amber ignored the gesture and pushed herself up, off the top rung.

'Be careful, love.'

A loud sigh travelled upwards. Robin took her over to the wall on the left and the section that looked slightly different. She pushed against it gently and held the door open as Amber went in. She stopped dead and Robin had to squeeze past her to get in.

'Oh. My. God.'

'I know.'

'It hasn't been touched since you last lived here?' She made a noise like an explosion. 'Mind officially blown.' She sat on the bed and bounced up and down. 'That duvet cover's pattern is blinding.' Amber got up and went over to the wardrobe and cautiously opened its doors. She let out a low whistle. 'It's like a vintage charity shop rail.' Carefully, she took out a polka dot ra-ra skirt and held it against her legs. 'You actually went out in this?'

'With lime-green tights.' Robin went over to the drawers at the end of the bed, pulled the top one out and rummaged through. A pair of fishnets fell onto the floor, along with a gold bustier. Amber swooped down and picked them up.

'Whoa! Were you going through your Madonna phase?'

Robin loved the dimples in Amber's cheeks. She hadn't seen them for so long.

'Bustiers were all the rage with a skirt or pair of trousers. Tara, my best friend, and I wore them clubbing. You should have heard us singing loudly at the back of the bus with everyone else, on the way into town.'

'But you left here at sixteen, that was too young to get into clubs, right? You have to be eighteen and have ID these days.'

Robin explained that there weren't checks back then and with make-up they all looked older and always got past the bouncers. Dad was fine with it, even Faye, it was just the way things were. She and Tara both had birthdays in September so had a few months' clubbing before the summer she left. Amber actually made eye contact and mentioned the clubs she went to. Robin hadn't heard of either of them. She felt a flutter in her chest as she told Amber about Piccadilly 21, opposite Piccadilly Gardens; it was plush with everything covered in gold leaf, they'd thought it so swanky. She'd drink Southern Comfort and her clothes and hair used to stink of cigarettes the next day, even though neither she nor Tara smoked. They'd dance in the base-ment around their handbags on the floor.

'One girl from school always took a huge bag containing her cordless curling tongs, for emergencies.'

'That's hilarious. I just take my phone, its case has a card holder. I don't bother with make-up or a brush.'

'Lots of girls used to have perms back then, the spiral, the shaggy.'

'Guess you were lucky then, yours being natural.'

Robin fingered her hair. She'd never thought about it like that before.

Amber went back to the wardrobe, every now and then pulling out an item of clothing, like the Choose Life Wham! T-shirt. It took Robin back to when Amber was little, spoilt for choice with the plastic scoops at the cinema's pick 'n' mix. Robin could hardly bear to look as she thought about the last treasure hunt she'd put back in there, and the clues that Dad had wanted her and Faye to fathom out.

'Look at this biker jacket.' Amber took it off the hanger.

Robin had begged Faye and Dad to buy it for her fifteenth birthday. Amber stood in front of the dressing table mirror, straining to look at it from the back, the jacket easily fitted her.

'This is unbelievably cool,' Amber mumbled.

Her words felt as comforting as a slice of cheesecake, as a heated blanket, as the hug she wouldn't give Robin.

She looked down at the pile of magazines. A half-empty tube of spot-cream lay next to them. 'How can these have only cost forty-seven pence? I knew you were old, but that's ridiculous.'

There were those dimples again. Robin couldn't remember the last time her daughter had joked with her like this. Amber perched on the stool and crossed her legs underneath just like Robin used to, flicking through several copies until she ended up on the problem page of *Girl's Scene*.

'Dear Debbie, my best friend says you can turn a period off if you want to go swimming. Is this true because I can't work out how to do it?' She put her hand on her heart. 'That's priceless. Thank God for the internet these days.'

'I read an article about the magazine years later. The editors were very proud of the fact they used to send a personal reply to every single letter that didn't get published. I doubt that happens these days.'

Amber shrugged. 'I wonder why she didn't just ask her mum.'

'Not all mums and daughters had that kind of relationship,' said Robin in a flat voice. 'I... I used to write to the Dear Debbie page a lot. Faye and I didn't talk about... private stuff. Whereas I knew Debbie would listen, wouldn't make fun of me.'

Amber shuffled to face her more directly. 'What about when you first got your period?'

'I hid the dirty sheets when I started and stuffed toilet paper in my pants, but Faye used to vacuum my room and check for laundry.' Robin used to call her Mum in those days. She consciously stopped after her dad's funeral, angry and resentful, wanting to put distance between them before she actually moved to London. 'I was still sleeping in the second bedroom downstairs at that point, where I am now. She found the sheets under my bed. When I got home from school she'd left a packet of pads on my pillow.'

'She didn't mention it?'

'No. I talked to Tara's mum about it.'

They fell silent for a moment.

'This room, it's so colourful, so... full of life.'

Robin looked around. Yes, it had always been so different to the muted colours Faye wore.

Amber looked down and took off the jacket. 'Why don't you put this on?' She held it out, avoiding Robin's gaze.

Robin put on the jacket, went over to the wardrobe and

rummaged at the bottom, doing her best to ignore the scroll on top of the box. Eventually she surfaced, holding a bowler hat. She brushed the dust off and put it on.

'It goes with your curly hair. All of this stuff, it's so *not you*.'

Robin felt an ache inside for the girl she used to be, the girl who was happy to close her eyes, wearing her Walkman and T-shirt dress, and dance under the roof window as if the sky was her audience.

'We'd better get back to Faye, we've been twenty minutes,' said Robin, looking at her watch. 'She'll be wondering what we've been up to.'

'Yeah, right, like she got curious for twenty years.'

Robin took a deep breath. 'I know.'

'Has she asked about your old job, about Dad... about me? Anything?'

'A little.' Hardly.

'It's weird. You've always been the opposite as a mum, wanting to know every detail about me. My school friends used to find it funny that you'd always remind me my period was due.'

They did? Robin busied herself, slipping off the hat and biker jacket and putting them away.

'Can I come up for another look, later?'

Robin touched the wall behind her.

Amber pursed her lips. 'I won't pry, if that's what you're worried about.'

'I'm still getting used to all my old belongings being here.'

Robin closed the wardrobe doors and they headed to the loft ladder. 'Why don't we come up together, after we've eaten?' she said as she climbed down, jumping the last few steps like she did when she was a teenager. She moved out the way and Amber stepped onto the landing.

'Nah, you're all right,' she said in a bored tone, the magic disappearing as she entered the spare room. 'I'll be down in a minute, I need to write that email.'

Robin stayed on the landing and peered at her lying on the bed, tapping into her laptop. She'd missed seeing that determined expression, the way Amber's mouth went lopsided as she concentrated. Robin was just about to leave when she heard Amber sniffing loudly. Robin rushed in and Amber snapped her laptop shut, wiping her eyes with her arm, as she sat up.

'Love, what's the matter?'

'None of your business.'

She rubbed Amber's shoulders but she pulled away. 'I want to be on my own for a few minutes.'

'Okay... if you're sure...' she said gently. 'I'll... I'll call you down when lunch is ready. Just remember I'm always here for a chat. Or maybe you could call a friend if you don't want to talk to me.'

Amber's body shuddered. 'I haven't got any friends. I hate my housemates. I'm emailing my personal tutor to let him know I'm dropping out of university.'

Robin hoped she'd misheard.

Amber's chin jutted forwards. 'And you can't change my mind.'

'But... but you've been having a great time, partying, freshers' week...' Robin sat on the bed, her legs feeling weak.

'I ended up going home early from all those events.' She sniffed again. 'I was an idiot to insist on private accommodation in the first year. It's off campus, away from the Students' Union, so it's always a hassle getting back at night, and there are only four of us and we're all so different. Most of the students in my classes live in the halls and have become part of big groups of friends.' Her voice broke.

'Oh love... what about the course?'

'That's the only reason I've stuck it out this long, it's everything I expected, I love it.'

'That's a good thing, isn't it? You can't throw away your dreams just because of a difficult few weeks, I'm sure if you contact the university accommodation office again and explain—'

'And this is why I didn't want you to know.' She threw her hands in the air. 'I knew you wouldn't understand. I don't want to discuss it any more.' She went over to the window, her back to Robin. 'I'll collect the rest of my stuff tomorrow and go back to London on Monday. It's my choice, my decision, and there's nothing you can do about it.'

14

'Did I hear the loft ladders?' Faye raised an eyebrow, as Robin put down a plate of sandwiches on the table.

Robin nodded as Amber came into the room, those dark circles under her eyes deeper.

'I imagine you'll have fun looking through your mother's old clothes,' said Faye, as she sat down and took a sip of squash.

'I won't be staying here that long, after all. This whole university thing has been a disaster.'

Faye adjusted her glasses and looked at the pair of them.

'But what will you do instead? You can't leave only a few weeks into the first term,' Robin said, aware of a pleading note in her voice.

'No point racking up huge loans if it's not what she wants,' said Faye.

'Amber, would you mind going up to the spare room and fetching the striped cardigan that's hanging in the wardrobe,' said Robin stiffly. 'I can't shake off a chill today.'

Amber frowned but went upstairs.

'Stay out of this, Faye,' said Robin sharply. 'I'm glad you're being pleasant with her, but I don't want you interfering. You know nothing about Amber.'

'That may well be true, but I know plenty about daughters determined to do the opposite of what they think their mothers want them to.'

'Really? Well, that knowledge didn't help you solve anything between us, did it?'

Without looking at Faye, Robin disappeared into the kitchen, hands trembling as she sliced up sticks of cucumber. How could she have not known Amber was struggling? If only she could make everything better. And who did Faye think she was, encouraging Amber to give up her chance of getting a degree, when she'd only known her for a matter of minutes? It was everything her daughter had worked for since getting straight As for her GCSEs.

She put down the knife, took a minute.

The reason Robin didn't go back to Stonedale in 1989 wasn't because Faye told her to stop all her nonsense, it wasn't because it was what Faye wanted.

It wasn't.

She carried the cucumber sticks into the dining room. The other two were at the table, chatting, Amber's tone more animated as Faye tilted her head and listened. It was good to hear Amber sounding more cheerful, yet strange that Faye was the reason.

'... and Tom comes in at three every morning, wakes us all up. He's set the smoke alarm off more than once, burning toast.'

'Isn't there anyone you can complain to?' Robin asked, as she sat down.

Amber shrugged. 'The others don't seem to care as much as I do.' She bent down to scratch Hoover's head. For some reason Faye was allowing him to sit under Amber's chair.

'It's a shame you can't stay for a while, but I completely understand,' said Faye, focusing on her sandwich. 'This Tom sounds as if he's still in baby rompers and has never put himself to bed.'

Amber actually smiled and looked down at Hoover again.

'I just need my own space.' She straightened up. 'I suppose... I mean, I could hang around for a few days if... I slept in the loft.' Amber's eyes slid towards Robin and quickly darted back to Faye.

'But you can't, it... it hasn't been lived in for over thirty years. It's not like the spare room that's been kept clean, and who knows there could be dry rot up there, it may not be safe and...' Robin swallowed.

Amber removed a slice of tomato from her cheese sandwich. 'Whatever. It's no biggie.'

Faye turned towards Robin, 'But that's the perfect solution. Or why don't you sleep in the loft and give Amber the spare room?'

'Because I ought to be near you in the night, in case of an emergency,' said Robin, heat flooding up her neck. 'As for the loft, it's just... I... I've only just found that room myself.'

'Oh, I see.' Faye waved her good hand around the lounge. 'You expected me to let you into my house, unannounced, and yet you can't let *your* daughter into a room you managed quite well without all this time.' She tutted. 'It's a pity you aren't as pragmatic as your daughter, it could save her a lot of bother, give her time to think.'

Amber's eyebrows shot into her hairline and she looked at the two of them.

'Just move your things downstairs if they mean that much,' said Faye. 'In fact, why don't you have a good sort out?' She got up and fetched the local newspaper from the pile of magazines on the cabinet next to her armchair. She sat down again and passed it to Robin. 'You'll find the tip's opening hours in there.'

The silence felt full of expectancy, waiting for Robin's reply.

'You're right,' she blurted out and picked up the paper. 'It was just a knee-jerk reaction. Stay here, Amber, in the loft, it will work out well after a good tidy, you could study and—'

'It would only be for a few days before I go back down south. I've decided now, so don't get carried away,' said Amber, with energy. 'It'll give me time to inform all of my tutors I'm leaving but...' She looked between the two of them. 'Only if you're sure.'

'It's fine. Honestly. As Faye says, it's only bricks and mortar.' Robin walked into the kitchen and cut herself a thick slice of cheese, pushing it into her mouth before putting on the kettle.

Looking a little brighter, Amber was standing in front of her grandparents' wedding photo as Robin carried the teapot in.

'I love the high collar of the dress,' she said and joined the other two at the dining table. 'You don't see ones like that these days. Mum wore a huge one for her wedding, she sold it straight after the divorce. Bo Peep style they called it.'

'Really?' said Faye, in a measured tone. 'You learn something new every day.'

Robin's neck flushed.

'When did you and my granddad get married?'

Faye poured before answering. 'July 19th, 1969. I was twenty-six, Alan was twenty-seven.'

Amber pointed to a woman in the photo, standing next to Faye.

'That's some hat,' she said. 'Wasn't your dad around?'

'He died in the trenches, I never met him. My mother passed a few months after Robin was born. She used to come over for Sunday lunch when we first got married.'

Robin barely knew anything about her grandparents, Dot

and Arthur, names without stories.

Robin told Amber how quiet Sundays used to be before shops and leisure centres opened seven days a week, and how a roast was the big event. Nervous excitement infused her body as she mentioned the treasure hunts and how Dad would spend weekday evenings making up the clues and riddles. She wanted to tell her about the scroll she'd found but didn't want to risk a fallout with Faye that might upset Amber further. Yet Faye laughed when Robin reminded her of the time Dad swore he'd do the dishes for a week if they solved an especially hard anagram he was proud of.

'You should have seen him in Faye's pink rubber gloves and flowery apron,' said Robin and she chuckled, Amber and Faye both smiling at her. This was... nice. She'd forgotten how Faye tilted her head back when she found things funny, scrunching up her nose, like during her favourite television show, *Are You Being Served*? and when Dad did his silly dance whenever Stockport County won.

'What would the treasure be at the end?'

'Just the satisfaction of solving the anagram,' said Faye.

'Dad would write the clues onto tea-stained paper and roll them into scrolls.'

'Didn't he run out of places in Stonedale to put into the clues?'

'No,' chipped in Faye. 'There are lots of oddities in the village and he could re-use them at any time, just making sure the new riddle for them was different.'

'It sounds like fun, I wish I'd been there.'

Robin passed Amber a bag of her favourite baked crisps, pleased to see her daughter just like her old self.

'I don't eat these any more. Have we got any proper ones?'

Amber scooted into the kitchen and was back in seconds,

with a different packet, munching already, crumbs going every-where. Robin stole a look at Faye who didn't seem bothered.

'How did you meet my granddad... if you don't mind me asking?'

Faye folded up her napkin. 'Bowling. His friends and mine played against each other one night. Our team all worked in Lewis's and my supervisor recognised one of his crowd as a regular customer of the men's department.'

'Lewis's?' asked Amber.

'The department store,' said Robin.

Faye spoke about the full-size ballroom on the fifth floor that had a beautiful glass dome and how the owners had once flooded the basement and filled it with gondolas so that customers could take rides. She tried to remember a time Faye had spoken to *her* with such an open, friendly tone.

'But where is it?' asked Amber.

'You can't have gone shopping very often if you haven't noticed it,' Robin said and pushed her arm gently. Amber leant away. 'It's at the top of Market Street, opposite Piccadilly Gardens, you must have been wearing blinkers today.'

Amber and Faye looked at each other.

'I've shopped loads in that building since starting uni – it's a Primark now.'

'Lewis's has closed? When did that happen?'

'It went into administration a couple of years after... you left. I applied for other jobs, so did my friends, we'd been worried for ages that we were going to lose ours there, rumours had been circling for a long time. As it was, Lewis's was bought out. The new owners didn't close it until about a decade later.' said Faye.

'So where was your new job?' Robin asked. She'd assumed so much about the way Faye's life had panned out. Robin would never have guessed that Faye lost the job she loved.

'I accepted a position in a small clothes shop in Stockport. The bus there was frequent and the owner was nice enough. But going off to work never felt the same, I missed my friends, the excitement and the perks. But things happen. You just have to get on with your lot.'

No Dad. No work friends. No flower arranging any more. Robin gone, although that wouldn't have bothered her... Faye's life really had changed as much as hers, after she escaped down to London.

'Why don't you tell me about this economics course?' Faye said swiftly to Amber.

Amber explained about mathematical modelling and econometric techniques.

'Slow down, love, you'll get indigestion,' Robin said.

Abruptly she got to her feet. 'Can I go upstairs and take another look at your old room? I could rearrange a few things, get it ready to move into tomorrow, perhaps, after you've had a sort-through and decided what you want to take out.'

'Of course you can,' said Faye. 'There's a duster and cleaning materials in the kitchen.'

Amber pushed her chair back and soon footsteps thumped up the stairs. Robin piled up the plates, took them into the kitchen and leant against the cooker. Poor Amber. She still couldn't believe it. Leaving university? She'd only just started. Perhaps Todd could help her see sense, stop her throwing away her future. Robin hadn't had the chance to go to college. She'd wanted to study English and was determined Amber wouldn't miss out like she had.

Robin walked out of the kitchen, drying her hands on a tea towel, just as Amber charged in.

She lifted her arm in the air, waving the last scroll.

15

Amber turned to Faye. 'Look, one of the Sunday treasure hunts you used to do.'

'Yes. Robin found it,' Faye said and carried on reading her magazine.

'Dad made it before he went away to Sheffield... that last trip, when he fell ill. He wanted me and Faye to do it whilst he was away.' He'd still want that.

Amber stared at the brown paper. 'You should open it.'

'I did. It was sealed with wax. There's a little rhyming note Dad wrote at the top for us.' Robin dropped the tea towel onto the dining table and headed for the chaise longue.

Amber passed her the scroll and sat, cross legged, on the carpet. 'Can you read the note out to me?'

Robin glanced at Faye who gave the smallest of nods.

'Here's a hunt for my favourite two,
Sheffield won't be fun without you.
Enjoy this hunt one Sunday I'm away,
Good luck to my own precious treasures, Robin and Faye.

Oh, and read Clue Two in advance,
That will give you a better chance!'

Hearing the words, once more, made Robin's longing to do the hunt even stronger. Amber took a hair bobble from her wrist, tied her hair back into a ponytail and tentatively reached out a hand. She scanned the page.

'These riddles are awesome with...' She re-read a bit. 'Fun instructions.'

'Why read Clue Two first?' Robin asked.

She tilted her head. 'You used to do this hunt all in one day?'

Faye nodded, watching Amber now.

'Ah, I understand what Granddad means. You could start it tomorrow. I suppose I could... tag along... see a bit of Stonedale before I leave.'

Granddad. It was almost too much.

'Faye couldn't manage all six clues in one day, not at the moment, it's a fair bit of walking.'

'I won't be doing it at all,' said Faye abruptly. 'As I've told your mother, there's no point. It's thirty years old.'

Amber's face fell. 'But this is the most exciting thing to happen since I started university.'

Oh, love. Much as Robin wanted to complete the hunt for herself, she now had an even stronger motive to fulfil her dad's last wish.

'It takes long enough to get warm *inside* the house these days,' said Faye. 'The clues' answers might have been built over or removed and Alan's not here to find out if we solve it or not.'

'But it would mean we might discover Dad's secret,' said Robin.

Amber leant forwards. 'What do you mean?'

Robin explained about how he'd said the anagram would change everything, that it would make life much easier.

'Wow. So Granddad could have won the lottery.'

'That wasn't around in those days,' said Faye dryly.

'Still, he could have hidden a stash of money somewhere, or what if he bought an antique at one of those car boot sales you used to talk about, Mum, and found out it was actually worth thousands?'

Faye readjusted her glasses.

That was a possibility.

Robin watched as Amber rambled, hands gesticulating, suggesting to Faye that he could have stumbled across a necklace full of real gems or a unique telescope. Her daughter's lighter mood would be reward enough, even if they never solved the anagram.

And what if doing this treasure hunt intrigued Amber enough to help her stick it out just a few more weeks up north, kept her in Manchester doing her studies, living in Stonedale for moral support until maybe, just maybe, her situation improved?

'You'd have the internet to help you with riddles,' said Amber.

'There's helping and there's cheating,' said Faye, who'd let her magazine slide onto the floor.

Amber hadn't been this keen to spend any time with her since she and Todd split. It had left a gaping hole in Robin's life; she missed her daughter. She'd suggested cinema trips, meals out, things they used to do as a threesome or without Todd if he was working, which in recent years he often had been. She'd even proposed a spa weekend now that Amber was older, but all ideas had been met with disinterest. Yet Amber took pleasure in telling her about the occasional coffee out she had with him, the odd trip to the theatre, a movie the two of them had seen. Even though he'd instigated the divorce, even though Amber was angry at them both, she blamed Robin more than Todd, said she was to blame for him calling it quits. But Robin didn't want to think about that.

'I never got to meet my granddad,' said Amber. 'Seeing a bit of this hunt done would be a way of...'

The three of them looked at each other.

'Why don't you do the whole thing with us, love?' Robin's nails dug into her palms as she willed the other two to agree. 'Faye probably couldn't manage more than a couple of excursions a week, at the moment. You could stay in Stonedale and we'd do the clues gradually, whilst you keep going to uni and see how it goes.'

Her expression hardened. 'Right. I should have known you'd have some agenda. I told you. I'm going back to London.'

Robin forced herself not to reply straightaway.

'Darling, you can change your mind any time,' she said gently.

Amber snorted.

'I mean it. And I promise I'll support you either way.'

'I can manage on my own, I don't need support,' she snapped.

'Neither do I, but here we are,' said Faye and gave Amber an understanding nod.

'What if we did one or two clues a week, see how we go?' Robin suggested. 'The hunt will finish in the middle of December, I'm going back to London then anyway. We can make the journey together if you're still up here, and you decide that leaving your course is the right thing to do. And yes, we could start it tomorrow afternoon, after I get back from seeing Tara,' she said, keeping her voice light.

'I didn't know you'd kept in touch with anyone from Stonedale all these years,' said Faye, her eyes narrowing.

'I haven't. I found her on Facebook last week and contacted her on the off chance.'

Perhaps it wouldn't have worked anyway, with just Faye and her. Dad had always been there to soften frustration due to dead ends and wrong answers. But what if they did it in a three after all? Solving this anagram had been Dad's last wish because he'd never really come round in the hospital. The last word she'd heard from him was *bye* as he'd shouted upstairs before leaving to drive over to Sheffield. Robin looked down at her lap for a moment, as the memory sprang into her mind of how she'd talked to him as he lay wired up to machines, crossing her fingers in the hope of getting a response. She wasn't religious but had even prayed, putting her hands together, closing her eyes tight. She told God if he saved Dad, she'd do everything she could to be a better daughter to Faye. Her mother went to church and the cathedral, and Robin had wondered if God might be angry with her for always fighting with one of his believers.

A minute passed.

'I can stay in the loft room?' Amber met Robin's gaze. 'Without any hassle about uni? Without you trying to change my mind if I choose to leave before you? Agreeing to do this hunt wouldn't be a promise that I'm staying until December.'

'Yes,' said Faye, before Robin could answer.

'Well...' She shrugged. 'My Sundays are free and I don't have lectures on a Thursday, and it's not like I've anything better to do. I could be the one to read the clues, that way it will be a surprise for you two. You haven't read them already, have you?'

Robin shook her head.

'I guess I could help...' Faye folded her arms and glanced at Amber. 'However, I'm only doing it if we *all* do it.'

Robin stared at Faye whose face remained expressionless.

'I'm prepared to have a stab at the first clue,' said Faye, airily, 'but only because it was an unwritten rule that number one would be as easy as pie.'

Hoover pricked up his ears, twitched his nose and scampered into the kitchen.

Robin Wilson,
16 Parade Row,
Stonedale,
Greater Manchester
February 1986

Dear Debbie,

MY SPOTS ARE EMBARRASSING

My skin looks horrible at the moment. I've got spots on my chin and forehead. I try to hide them with foundation but Mum says that will only make it worse. I'm sure the real reason she's saying that is because she thinks I'm too young to wear make-up every day, so I sneak it into school. A friend said cutting out chocolate makes spots better so I've tried giving that up for a month, but it hasn't worked. I try to tell myself it's a small problem but I feel so depressed when I look in the mirror. Please help.

Robin, age 13

Girl's Scene
41 Gover Street,
London

Dear Robin,

Most teenagers suffer from spots at some point and if you look around your school you'll see lots of other pupils with them as well. It's not just you. They are caused by your hormones going into overdrive, during puberty, and will most likely disappear as you pass through your teens. Your mum's absolutely right, wearing make-up all the time will only make them worse, but I'm sure she'd agree to you wearing it at the weekend or for special occasions.

And instead of covering up your spots, follow these tips: wash with a mild soap and warm water, twice a day, keep your hair tied back, try not to touch your face and DO NOT squeeze those spots! If you do, the skin will take longer to heal. If you think they are getting worse, have another chat with your mum and go with her to the chemist or your doctor. Spots can be genetic and she probably had them too, at your age, so I'm sure she will understand!

Best wishes,

Debbie

16

The train pulled into the station, Robin boarded and wandered through the carriages trying to find one that was empty. As it moved off she sat down on a navy seat by the window and gazed outside. A passenger came in, out of breath, and sat on the berth right opposite her.

Of course they would.

Tara would have told her to stop being such a grump. Robin used to call her the brightest berry in Stonedale. She'd be sure, along with Amber, to make the coming weeks much more bearable, once they'd got over any initial awkwardness. Even though it had been more than thirty years, Robin couldn't help hoping it would be just like the old times, within minutes... Surely not both her ex-boyfriend, and best friend, would be unwelcoming? Robin imagined Tara's face when they met, inquisitive, happy, her smile still so wide. Yes, that's how it'd be, she wouldn't allow herself to think otherwise.

Robin had woken up early and spent precious moments alone, in her old room. It smelt fresh after she'd helped Amber clean. The biker jacket was still on the bed and she couldn't resist wearing it. She'd rummaged in the bottom of the wardrobe where she used to stash accessories, unlike Faye, who'd always had a place for everything in her bedroom, still did. The rucksack she'd taken to London just hadn't enough space for her to cram in her favourite pixie boots. She found them, right at the back, under a bag full of colourful belts that she used to wear loosely around long shirts, but the rubber soles had dry rotted.

Doing her best to ignore the passenger, Robin took out her phone to go on Google Maps and remind herself where the Old Wellington pub was, but it slipped out of her woolly gloves, fell onto the floor and slid to the base of the berth opposite. She bent down to pick it up at the same time as the passenger who passed it to her. Thank goodness the screen hadn't cracked. She looked up at a dark grey beanie with chestnut hair sticking out from underneath.

'Oh. Hi,' she said.

Her pulse raced faster than the train. Yul stared at her jacket.

'I found it my bedroom. I'm just off to meet Tara,' she blurted out.

He sat back against the seat. 'She agreed to meet you?'

The hairs on the back of her neck prickled, why did he ask that? 'Of course she did. We were best friends.' She didn't know what to say next. Being with Yul always used to feel so natural, ever since he'd joined her class in the third year at high school and sat next to her in science. But then the last time they'd sat next to each other Margaret Thatcher was Prime Minister.

'Are you out for lunch too?

He simply shook his head. She turned to the side and stared out of the window.

'I'm checking out a couple of bookstores,' he said. 'Always pays to keep an eye on the competition.'

'Your shop looked great. I'd love to come back, I need something new to read – if that's all right.'

'Up to you,' he muttered.

Robin watched in surprise as Yul abruptly stood up to leave the carriage. She smarted but wouldn't let him ruin her afternoon with Tara. Robin put in her earbuds.

As the train pulled in Robin was already standing by the doors. She got off and speed-walked towards the barrier. The attendant nodded at her ticket and she strode through the station, past the food kiosks and escalators and out into the fresh air. What right had Yul to act the injured party? He'd been the one to leave her in London, all those years ago.

Robin walked down Station Approach, past trams and buses. The blue sky above geed her up. She crossed narrow streets, their names Ducie, Paton and Newton suddenly familiar, and as a vintage record shop blasted out music by The Clash, just for a second it was as if she'd never left. She reached the top of Market Street and turned around, gazing over to Piccadilly Gardens. Fountains danced that hadn't been there before. People sat chatting and drinking from takeout cups. Robin walked onto the pedestrianised area and glanced at Primark as she passed the central tram stop, looking for shops that had disappeared, spotting new ones. A busker caught her attention and she continued past a bench and litter bin, and a man with one leg sat on the ground playing an accordion. Further on, street dancers performed to Michael Jackson and outside Boots, opposite one of the entrances to the Arndale, three youngsters played violins, they looked like students.

She turned right when she got to New Cathedral Street and walked towards Harvey Nichols. *Posh or what*, said a sixteen-year-old voice inside her head. At the end was Shambles Square, she'd always loved that name and used to wish she lived in a street that was more her, unlike Parade Row – that sounded suited to army families. The Old Wellington came into view, in a sunken part of the ground, with wooden tables out front. What a stunning Tudor building. She'd read about it after the IRA bomb in 1996, it had been badly damaged but was restored. As part of the city centre rebuilding plan it was moved, brick by brick, and reconstructed here, nearer to the cathedral. Over the years she'd kidded herself she wasn't interested in anything Mancunian but had scrutinised the news when her home city popped up in the headlines, like in 2002 when it hosted the Commonwealth Games.

Arriving, she walked past the outdoor tables. Two minutes to twelve and she pushed open the door. People sat drinking, in front of laptops or friends. She climbed the winding staircase into another bar laid out with small dining tables, all occupied apart from one for two by the window. She gave Tara's name and was shown over. Five minutes passed and she still wasn't there. Robin peered outside, hoping to spot her, tapping her feet, studying the oyster bar outside, as other customers chatted and appetising smells drifted her way. As a teenager she'd watched movies where glamorous people knocked them back with champagne. She'd expected them to taste more sophisticated than a mouthful of sea.

'Robin?'

Robin scraped her chair back and got to her feet, darting forwards to give Tara a hug. She was taller than she remembered. The arms that always used to link with hers stayed by their sides.

'It's great to see you again, and your hair's still blue!' Robin touched the lapel of her jacket and grinned. 'Recognise this?'

Tara took off her scarf and felt coat, and hung them on the back of her chair. 'Your parents gave it to you for your birthday.'

'That's right! You borrowed it and your mum went mad, she thought you had a secret boyfriend with a motorbike.' The waiter came over. 'Wine?' Robin asked Tara, aware she was beaming. 'Unless you're wanting a Cinzano for old times' sake.'

'Sparkling water for me, please.'

Robin ordered a spritzer and the waiter left. At least they'd both be drinking bubbles. 'So tell me everything, this partner of yours, where did you meet him?'

'Prisha's a nurse. She moved in with me eighteen months ago.'

'Oh, right... that's brilliant.' She never knew. Or perhaps she did. Robin raised her glass. 'Here's to us being in touch again.'

Tara lifted her glass up, without meeting Robin's eye, without asking how things were going, back in Parade Row. Robin had forgotten the small gap in between her friend's front teeth. She didn't often see it clearly, what with the way Tara used to chatter.

Tara opened the menu and studied the dishes; at least the silence was filled with activity. 'We'd better order, I haven't got long.'

Robin suggested fish and chips, expecting her to grin. They used to go to the chippy every Friday night before youth club, thinking themselves grown-up as they were eating out. It used to help sober them up a little after sneaking some alcohol from home. But Tara simply ordered a veggie burger.

They talked about work, or rather Robin did. Tara was a lot quieter than she used to be and Robin's appetite gradually disappeared. They had so many years to catch up on yet ended up discussing how the city centre had changed. Robin told her about the upcoming treasure hunt that afternoon, and briefly Tara gave Robin full eye contact and smiled. Years ago, when Faye and Robin got really stuck, sometimes Alan would allow her to scoot off to Yul or Tara's house to see if they could help. Her friends would be just as excited to solve the riddles and then they'd dissect the whole hunt, on Monday, back at school.

Tara consulted her phone after the coffees arrived. 'I'll have to get going soon. At least it's nice outside for once, we've had so much rain lately.'

Robin put down her cup. 'Seriously, we're going to talk about the weather?' She tried to keep her tone cheerful. 'Tara, I'm sorry. I had hoped today would be different... is anything the matter?'

'Stop it, Robin,' she said softly and reached down for her mini rucksack. She took out her purse and left a couple of notes on the table.

'Stop what?'

'Acting as if we're teenagers again, as if we've just not seen each other for a few weeks.'

Robin's cheeks were burning.

'As if you never ran off without telling me why, without calling to let me know you were okay. Not even Yul would tell me exactly what happened in London. He was in bits when he got back.'

He was?

'And he acted like a bit of a jerk for a while.'

'What do you mean?'

She looked flustered. 'Drinking too much in the park at night... you know, typical teenage stuff.'

'Oh...'

'I thought we were best friends and told each other every-thing? We had all those plans for flat-sharing.' Tara looked at her properly.

'We were, I...' Robin's voice wavered. 'I missed you so much and thought about you often.'

'Not enough to write or phone.' She fastened up her purse. 'You know, Mum cried when she found out you'd gone – said she'd miss you coming round.'

Robin took a large mouthful of spritzer but felt no better. She'd never really thought about it from her best friend's point of view. She'd have been devastated if Tara had suddenly disappeared. They'd always been each other's cheerleaders. 'I... I'm sorry, Tara. Truly. It was all such a mess, but looking back, I should have reached out.'

Tara didn't reply.

'How is your mum these days?' Robin asked.

'Okay. I see her when I can. Not as often as I'd like.' She pursed her lips.

'Why not?'

She hesitated. 'Dad doesn't approve of my girlfriend, calls it a lifestyle, as if being with the person I love is like following a fashion.' Tara put her purse back in her bag and checked the time again.

'I'm so sorry, I had no idea.' Robin had always liked him. He used to give Tara and her change for sweets and would help both of them with homework. 'I... I should have been there for you.'

'How could you, you broke all contact before I'd even worked out properly who I was?' Tara slipped into her coat and held her scarf. 'I understood you wanting to run away from everything, I got it – I just didn't realise that *everything* included me. But, you know, we're grown women now, Robin, it was a long time ago.'

'It wasn't like that,' she said, her voice coming out higher and louder. The table next to them turned to stare.

Tara pushed her chair backwards. 'Look, I'm glad things have worked out for you, honestly. I know your dad dying must have seemed like the end of the world and you never had it easy with your mum.' She shrugged. 'But that all happened a lifetime ago with nothing between us since, so there's nothing to build upon, apart from the memories of two girls.' She stood up to leave.

17

A bark floated upstairs. Robin sat up and pulled a tissue from the box on the bedside table. When she walked into the lounge Faye was in her armchair, Hoover at her feet, Amber playing with him.

'We've been to the White Hart,' said Faye.

'I told Gran, why should Mum have all the fun?' said Amber, without looking at Robin.

Gran? Robin started. How easily that rolled off her tongue. Robin should have felt pleased, her argument with Faye was nothing to do with Amber, yet she couldn't help thinking a name like that should be earned over years.

'Did you manage the walking okay?' she asked Faye.

'It was hardly a marathon, in fact I don't know why I've been staying in. My ribs were fine once I got going. It's time I went out more. Amber's just going to make a cuppa before we do the treasure hunt.' She talked about the Sunday roast they'd just eaten and Amber chipped in that Hoover had been allowed in too. Robin had to take a breath; it was as if they were a proper family unit. Faye even asked about her meeting with Tara.

Robin sat on her hands. 'We went to the Old Wellington. It was... pleasant. And great to walk through Manchester after all this time. I couldn't believe how much it had changed and yet in many ways it hasn't.' Robin listened to herself rambling – even Amber stared at her, before going into the kitchen to put the kettle on.

Robin reached down as Hoover carried over his rope toy. His playful growls filled the quiet as she pulled it from side to side.

'That bad, was it?' asked Faye.

'I don't know what you mean.'

'You and Tara together, there are many words I could use to describe it, certainly in terms of the old days – noisy, boisterous, vivacious, high-spirited...'

'Years of doing crosswords have clearly paid off.'

'But *pleasant*,' she continued, 'that word was never applicable to the time you two spent together.'

'Times change, people do too.'

'Glad you realise that now, because you thought you could come back and *nothing* would have changed, as if Stonedale was some backwater, unlike your glitzy London. Foolish girl.'

Amber stood by the kitchen doorway, eyes widening. Robin caught sight of her and cleared her throat.

'How about we take our tea upstairs?' Robin asked Amber quickly. 'The sooner we finish sorting out my old room, the sooner you can move up there. It won't take long and then we can get on with the hunt.' Robin grabbed a couple of bin bags from the kitchen and climbed the stairs and loft ladder. Out of breath, she pulled open the wardrobe doors and yanked out clothes, stuffing the frills, the denim, the rainbow of colours into one of the bags.

Amber appeared. 'I've left our drinks in the spare... what are you doing?'

Robin's face tightened.

'There's no need to be like that, honestly, if it's that big a deal I'd rather book a ticket back to London today than have you resent me staying up here.' Amber took out her phone and with gusto punched her finger on the front of it.

'It's not that,' Robin mumbled.

Amber looked up, finger poised mid-air. 'What then?'

Robin swallowed. Yul first, now Tara... Coming back hadn't been how she'd expected, apart from Faye's cutting comments. It was one week ago today that she'd arrived in Stonedale and if anything, things were getting harder, not easier.

'Look, you don't need to empty the room. I can leave my suitcase downstairs and just take out stuff for a few days at a time.'

'It's okay. I'll clear the decks,' she said, turning her face away. 'This lot could do with going to a charity shop.'

'Just make me some space on the dressing table and maybe tidy out the bottom of the wardrobe for my shoes,' Amber said firmly. She picked up a pair of John Lennon sunglasses that had fallen onto the floor, put them on and looked at herself in the star-shaped mirror.

Robin hesitated and faced her. 'Be careful, love. Don't get too close, too quickly. Faye... she may not turn out to be what you expect. I know she's your grandmother but... I don't want to see you hurt.'

Her body stiffened. 'I'm perfectly capable of judging people for myself.'

Robin rolled her eyes. 'Okay. Forget I said anything. What do I know?'

They didn't speak as Robin sorted the wardrobe. Amber sat by the dressing table.

'Why does Gran give you such a hard time?'

Robin sank onto the bed and sighed. 'I don't know, to be

honest. Even though Dad loved me, I often wondered if I was lacking as a daughter. But Tara's mum liked me and Blanche too, she taught me everything I know about baking.'

'You've never asked her?'

Robin held the bag tighter. 'No. Why would I give her the satisfaction?'

Amber gave her a curious look and seemed about to ask another question but changed her mind. She stood up and took the bag. 'I'll put this lot back.'

Robin gathered herself as she watched Amber take over and then together they emptied the bottom of the wardrobe, which was crowded and dark.

Amber held up a pair of orange satin leggings. 'I'm going to need bigger sunglasses.'

They continued sorting through the musty-smelling belongings.

'What's with the empty bottles of hairspray?'

'Everyone used to backcomb. My hairstyle could have withstood a hurricane and on top had a height of about two inches.'

A mischievous grimace crossed Amber's face, just for a second. 'Thank God everyone's hair is straightened now.' She went down the ladder to fetch her stuff. Robin sifted through the drawers. The top one was full of socks and underwear. She grabbed the balls of socks, one by one, and tossed them into the bin bag before scrunching up a handful of bras, all padded. It had taken her a while to grow into her figure and having Amber had added inches to her bust. A pair of pants fell onto the carpet and she picked them up, soft, lacy and pastel, so different to the practical cotton underwear she bought these days, underwear similar to that Faye wore. The similarity between them felt strange. Robin stared at the pants again. Of course, she'd bought them from a market stall in Afflecks for the first time she and Yul slept together. She'd thought it would matter what she was wearing and that she'd better attempt to look grown-up and seductive. It never struck her he'd be nervous as well and probably wouldn't even notice. She rubbed the silk between her fingers. The wooden floor had felt so uncomfortable against her back, as Yul leant on top. It was Christmas, a few weeks after his birthday and freezing cold despite the blankets they'd packed in their sports bags.

'What are those?'

She hadn't heard Amber come back up. She put a pile of her clothes on top of the chest of drawers, along with a cosmetic bag.

'I don't even own knickers like that.' Amber sat at the other end of the bed and took off the sunglasses. 'Did you have a boyfriend?'

'Yes.'

'What was he called?'

'Yul – that was a nickname'

'Did you and he... I mean...?' She took the pants. 'You were only sixteen.'

'Of course not!' Robin snatched the pants back and pushed them into the bin bag.

'All right, no need to lose it, I won't bother asking anything again.' With a stony face Amber marched over to the dresser, sat on the stool and looked in Robin's old make-up box. Robin had seen that stern face a lot in recent times, when Amber had asked her again why she'd gone off her dad. The silence felt as suffocating as it did with Faye.

'Okay, okay. Yes, we did. Our first time was in the middle of winter. In a treehouse,' she mumbled.

Amber swung around. 'What? *You* had sex at sixteen? Wow. That's so... so not what I expected. I thought you were all supposed to be virgins in those days, at least until you went to university. Did your parents find out?' Her eyebrows had disappeared under her fringe.

'Neither of them ever knew.'

'And what was it like?' She tilted her head.

'Well... it was cold.'

Amber nodded encouragingly.

'It meant a lot, taking the next step with Yul, but... it wasn't like in the movies.'

'This is too much, I can't take it in.' Amber looked at Robin as if she wasn't her mum at all.

Despite the discomfort she had fond memories of the tree-house, the sense of forbidden fruit, the innocence. Yul said it was special, their secret, and that neither of them should ever take anyone else there, not even a friend, and they didn't.

'And a few weeks later, the spring before the trip to London...' Before her whole life imploded. 'We booked a hotel in Stockport for the afternoon. I looked older with my make-up on and Yul... he always had a confident air. That time was much better.'

Amber continued to look at her in amazement.

Robin went over and picked up her teenage magazines. 'I may as well throw these out.'

'No, don't. They'll make great bedtime reading, especially the photo stories. Perhaps teenage life thirty years ago was more interesting than I imagined.'

Robin sat back on the bed and lay down. 'Depends on the issue. It was all rather innocent in the early eighties. The content changed a bit by the end of the decade.'

Amber put the pile back on the dressing table and selected one to read. 'Thanks for telling me – about that boy,' she said, without meeting her eye.

For the first time in a long time Robin felt like a good mum. Silly really, it wasn't as if Amber had just eaten one of her pasta dishes packed with fresh vegetables or allowed her to help her with studies. As Amber flicked through the magazine, every now and then smiling, it reminded Robin of when she was younger and they'd read together.

Robin gazed at her posters, the bright 1980s make-up blazoned across famous faces.

'Would you mind if I looked in your cosmetic bag?' Robin said. 'Could I borrow a lipstick?'

'I suppose so,' she said in that bored voice that Robin knew she reserved for her. Amber jerked her head to the drawers where it sat on the pile of her clothes. Robin applied an eye-catching shade. In the star-shaped mirror she could see Amber, behind her, on the bed now, discreetly watching whilst she put it on. Robin sat down next to her and shuffled up, until their elbows touched, a loud tut indicating that, in fact, they hadn't got any closer at all.

18

Faye stood in the hallway in a maroon bowl hat. She was layered up with baggy jumpers and a navy poncho cape. She couldn't get into any of her coats, with her arm in plaster. The cape was smart, she'd worn it to work in the 1970s and never liked to throw it out. It was most unlike her current Burberry print coats in beige and creams that Robin had spotted in her wardrobe. Clearly Faye still kept up with fashion trends. Lewis's department store must have stayed in her veins. Robin waited for a sarcastic comment about the biker jacket. Day by day, memories of life in Stonedale were luring her into old ways, with the colourful comfy clothes, the comforting recipes in Faye's book, the easy-to-manage curls. At least those were the feel-good memories. Robin wouldn't want to go back to the unpleasant ones, like all the times Faye had made her feel stupid or unloved, and how she'd envied friends' relationships with their mums. Yet she'd been given a glimpse of how things might have been, watching Faye and Amber together.

Was it possible... surely not... but what if Faye had changed?

Robin gripped the bottom edge of the jacket and forced away

that confusing theory by thinking of her clothes again. When she and Amber had come down from the loft, Robin had nipped into the spare room and sifted through the clothes she'd brought from her flat, taking in the bland colours, the tailored pleats, the unobtrusive fasteners. It was as if they weren't hers any more, as if she'd been a personal shopper all these years, styling someone else.

Amber came downstairs, loudly chewing gum. She took a water bottle out of her coat pocket and stuck the gum on the side, before taking a swig. Then she peeled it off and popped it back in her mouth, before sitting on the steps and fastening her boots. Robin took Hoover's lead and quickly went outside, bracing herself for Faye's reaction, but instead she simply heard the two of them talking about the sticky toffee pudding they'd enjoyed for lunch. Puffs of white cloud skirted around each other in the crisp, blue sky. They all stopped by the gate.

'If we were doing all the clues in one day we'd need to prepare something for the second clue, before getting started,' said Amber, 'but as we're not, we don't need to worry about that. So, on with the first clue, here goes...

> *'Oyez! Oyez! Oyez!*
> *"What's that?" you say.*
> *It's a call to where I stand,*
> *On regimental land.*
> *I'm popular in the sun,*
> *My friends have larks and fun.*
> *In fact, at a first glance,*
> *You might see which country's dance?'*

Amber linked her arm with Faye's as they made their way onto the street. Robin couldn't take her eyes off them.

'This first one is supposed to be easy?' Amber said. 'Regimental land... is there some sort of military building or grave-yard here, Gran?'

Faye shook her head and gazed into Blanche's front window. Spotting her friend, she waved before making a sign in the shape of a 'C' with her gloved fingers. Blanche mouthed *please*.

'Don't let me forget to buy a chocolate bar before we come back,' Faye said as they moved on.

Apart from Blanche, Faye had barely spoken to the neighbours back in the day. Robin had heard three of them chatting together once, in a front garden, their backs to her as she stopped to untangle her Walkman's headphones. They reckoned Faye thought she was better than everyone else, with her co-ordinated outfits and distant air, said she acted as if working in Lewis's was like being employed by royalty. The women laughed and then one noticed Robin.

'Sorry, love, just our little joke.'

'Is it any wonder she keeps to herself, you lot are such bitches.'

They'd gasped and threatened to tell her parents but Robin knew they'd never do that as it would mean explaining. Her backchat had kicked in when she turned fourteen; there was no incentive to impress a mother who didn't seem to love her and if she was rude Faye would send her to her room to eat tea. A win-win. Yet as she'd sauntered away from those gossips, Robin couldn't work out why she'd defended her. She told herself it was because rebellious Robin showing her feelings, reacting in public, wouldn't have pleased Faye. However, deep down, she'd known there had to be another reason.

'Oyez, oyez, oyez are the words of a town crier,' said Faye. They came to the church. Robin was shocked by Faye's slow pace; it hadn't been as noticeable indoors. She also looked more hunched and the cape drowned her. She cut such a slight figure these days, as if a strong gust of wind might blow her over.

This wasn't the person she'd left behind all those years ago.

'A straightforward start, then, off to the town hall it is,' Robin said. They passed Brynner's and she couldn't help looking in. Yul stood behind the counter, serving a customer. He looked their way and the smile disappeared from his face.

'Who's that?' asked Amber.

'An... old friend.'

'Not Yul?' she joked.

Robin rolled her lips together.

'Oh my God, it is? What a mind fu— I mean...'

They continued down the high street and passed the sweet shop, arriving at the front of the town hall. Amber held up the scroll to read, reminding Robin and Faye not to peek at the other clues. Left to stand alone, Faye swayed unsteadily, so Robin moved closer and held the elbow of her arm that wasn't in a sling.

'The clue says it's in a regimental area...' Amber pointed at the squares of lawn edged with shrubs. 'The rows of grass fit that description, I suppose.'

They both nodded.

'So whatever it is must be in these ornamental gardens.' Amber consulted the scroll again. '*Popular in the sun.*' She looked around and squinted into the distance, pointing to the last row of squares of lawn, nearest the building. 'Is that a sun dial?' Amber took Hoover's lead and the two of them rushed off, past the town hall's fountain, and rows of shrubs with pretty crimson Camellias dotted amongst them.

Faye leant on Robin as they followed and the extra weight hardly registered. She used to be so sturdy. Robin stole a sideways glance; her mother's wrinkles were more pronounced in natural daylight. Were they a normal part of aging or had the deeper ones been caused by living on her own, having to suddenly work more hours when Dad went, or by little health worries? The pale face and puffy eyes could have been due to lack of sleep or... the old Faye didn't believe in tears, maybe things were different now. They caught Amber up and stood around the plinth, all three of them studying the circular iron plate.

'But who are a sundial's friends, and how could they have fun here?' Manically Amber chewed her gum. She brushed some soil off the plinth and it floated down towards the ground.

'If a phrase didn't make sense, then we studied the individual words instead,' Robin said.

'But that sometimes sent us on a long goose chase.' Faye's tone was sharp.

'Any other ideas of how to get out of a dead end?' Robin moved away so that they no longer touched.

Amber glanced at them. 'I bet the three of us can work it out?' Her words were said as a question and Faye gave a small nod.

Robin took the scroll. '*Have larks and fun*... larks, in that sense, is an unusual, dated choice of word, even for the eighties, so Dad used it for a special reason. A lark... it's a type of bird.'

'But why would birds be a sundial's friends?'

'Perhaps sundial isn't the answer,' said Faye and she gazed around the gardens.

Hoover's paw stepped on Robin's foot. She looked down and he winked.

'You could be right,' said Robin. 'Birds like trees, but there aren't any around here, it's all shrubs and grass.'

'But they like fountains, don't they?' said Amber.

Robin couldn't help looking down and Hoover winked again,

leaving her contemplating the possibility that the dog might be channelling Dad.

'That must be it,' she said, and Amber sped off again like a child on an Easter egg hunt. Faye and Robin smiled at each other, which would have been an unremarkable exchange for anyone else. As they approached the fountain and its tinkling water, Robin relaxed her fingers and slipped her hand around Faye's arm again. Except Faye pulled it away and leant over.

'Hoover, lad, what's with all the winking? Did that shower of soil get in your eyes?' She took a tissue out of her pocket and asked Amber for her water bottle, spilling a little onto it. Then she bent down and gently wiped his eyes.

When done, Hoover stared up at Robin, unblinking. Disappointment surged through her.

The grey concrete fountain was made up of two tiers. Of course, the figurines in it were birds. The bottom, bigger basin had six heads going around with water coming out of the beaks, whereas the top one was made up of doves circled together.

Amber peered into the water. 'Look at all those coins, lots of people have made wishes.'

'I threw in a penny once, after watching the film *ET*, because I badly wanted my own alien.' Robin gazed at the pennies – you didn't see so many of them these days. 'And if Dad and I ever said anything at the same time, the first to shout out *Jinx* made a wish. I once asked for a ticket to *Top of the Pops*. Dad said his wish was always exactly the same, but he'd never tell me what it was.'

Faye gave her an odd look and it made Robin think he'd confided in her.

'Remember how me and Dad would pull the wishbone from a roast chicken, when I was little?' asked Amber, in a voice that sounded much younger for a moment. 'I'd wish that you wouldn't make me eat the sprouts. Dad would really struggle if he won, said that he was happy with life exactly like it was.' She gave Robin a look. 'That he wouldn't change a thing.'

Robin had never understood that as she and Todd got older. They used to give each other spontaneous surprises during the first years of their marriage – little gifts, a trip out, perhaps a weekend away. But, as the years passed, Todd surprised her less. She told herself that was to be expected, once they became parents, both of them working hard, but couldn't help feeling taken for granted when, yet again, she was the one planning their holiday.

'What about you, Gran?' said Amber, turning away.

Faye looked tired, so Robin led them all over to a nearby bench.

'Wishes are nonsense, there's no magic wand in life, you have to work your socks off to get what you want.' She sat down and stretched out a leg, rubbing the knee.

'You've never made a single wish, not even as a child?' Amber stopped chewing. 'You must have.'

'Maybe I did... just once, after blowing out a candle. Alan and I had just got married. He was the first person to ever make me a birthday cake and insisted. I'd never even been given one before and he went to such an effort.' Her eyes looked shiny.

'Your mum never got you a cake?' asked Amber.

'Occasionally she bought me a present from the charity shop, that was about it. She always said banners and balloons and gifts were a waste of money, even though you could make ceiling decorations out of newspaper and a sponge only requires eggs, butter and flour.' She folded her good arm across her body, under her bosom. 'But it's just the way things were. I didn't know any different.'

Robin recalled an old photo Dad had shown of her once,

from Faye's childhood, a little girl, wavy hair in pigtails. Robin felt sorry for her, waking up to none of the surprises most children enjoyed on their special day.

'What did you wish for, then, when you blew out that candle?' Robin asked.

'For Alan to never leave me – and that proves my point. Wishes are nonsense.'

Over the years she'd always been so strong, in Robin's head, but as they made their way back to the fountain, Robin struggled to keep to her slow pace, full of anxious energy. She never knew about Faye's mother being quite that severe, nor about the birthday cake her dad had once made. Robin glanced at Amber. On their own, she and Faye would never have talked like this. They'd never have exchanged that special smile that took Robin by surprise.

Somehow Amber oiled the rub between them.

This treasure hunt could reveal more than Dad's anagram. Out of the house, away from painful memories, it could be a way of revealing more about Faye and… Robin wanted that. She did. Faye looked tired; she was slow, and now prone to falls. What if something happened to her, out of the blue, and Robin never discovered the truths she wanted… she *needed* to know? And a tiny part of Robin, deep inside, a part that she couldn't control, envied the warmth Faye showed Amber and wondered if Faye would ever show that to *her*.

She glanced at the scroll in Amber's hand. It had become even more important.

'So back to the hunt, dancing, how could that come into it?' asked Amber.

Faye stared at the birds on the top tier and her frown cleared. 'Lewis's had a Greek-themed party once with honey pastries, and wine that tasted…' She grimaced. 'Like paint stripper. We learnt Greek dancing. You stand in a circle with your arms outstretched, around the shoulders of the person next to you, moving faster and faster in a circle.' She pulled away and leant on the fountain. 'Us Ladieswear staff formed our own ring and danced all night. I fell asleep on the train back.' She touched the top basin. 'Now I think of it, we looked a little like this ring of doves, with their wings outstretched around each other.'

'So the letter is G, as *Greece is the word*!' said Robin and grinned. Neither of the other two got the joke and she couldn't help feeling deflated, until she looked down at Hoover who met her gaze and gave another wink.

Robin Wilson,
16 Parade Row,
Stonedale,
Greater Manchester
July 1986

Dear Debbie,

I'M WORRIED ABOUT MY BOOBS.

This is so embarrassing, but I don't think my boobs are normal. I can't stop looking at them in the mirror. One looks a bit wonky compared to the other and my friends' are all bigger. I've seen Page 3 girls in my friend's dad's newspaper and theirs all look perfect and both exactly the same. Why don't mine look like that? Anyone would laugh if they saw me naked.

Robin, age 13

Girl's Scene
41 Gover Street,
London

Dear Robin,

First of all, don't fret, every teenager feels like this about bits of their body. And stop obsessing in front of the mirror! Boobs aren't meant to look exactly the same and cameramen use all sorts of tricks to make models look perfect. Everyone's grow at a different rate, and they come in all sizes.

Some girls have red hair, others blonde, they may be curvy or have a more sporty figure… in other words we are all unique, thank goodness! It would be a boring old world if not.

Next time you're tempted to study your boobs, just remember they are sisters, not twins!

Best wishes,

Debbie

19

Blanche's kitchen was more homely than Faye's, with golden pine fittings and a colourful egg cup collection on the windowsill. A hanging rack stretched across patterned wall-paper with pots and pans dangling down. Faye's were all neatly stacked away. The small bin overflowed. Robin would make sure she emptied it before going back... back to Faye's. She wouldn't call it *home*.

'How about I brew up, flower, and you tell me all about how the treasure hunt went?'

Robin put down the boxed-up tuna salad she'd brought over, and the bar of chocolate from her mother.

'Guess it couldn't hurt. Faye seems to be up for dominoes when it's Amber who asks. They were on their second game when I left.'

Blanche put on the kettle and set out a plate of rock buns on her little table. Robin offered to help but Blanche waved her away. Robin chatted about the clues they'd solved and eventu-ally Blanche joined her and shuffled to get comfortable, rubbing her hip as she found the right position at her kitchen table.

'I can't remember the last time I had these,' Robin said. 'Dad used to call them rock bums.'

'His humour always was on my wavelength.' Blanche asked her to pour the tea. 'My hands have been bad this last week and cooking tea every night would have been a right to-do, but I can manage a baking session every so often. I'm determined not to give everything up just because of this flippin' arthritis.' Her eyes twinkled. 'I might even go dating, on that Tinker, it's such an appropriate name. I'm sure there'd be an adventurous modern man out there who'd be happy to fiddle around and get my old engine running again.'

'Just don't ask me for tips on what happens under the bonnet these days,' said Robin and Blanche laughed.

'I used to take batches of cakes into work,' said Blanche, 'and the residents loved them. It always surprised me how traditional bakes brought back memories from their childhoods. I made Parkin, once, and one chap shed a happy tear or two as he remembered his mother.'

'That's Uncle Ralph's favourite. I learnt such a lot from you about baking.' Faye had never spent time teaching Robin how to make the dishes from her recipe book.

'Oh, for the days when I could rustle up a tray of biscuits in minutes.'

'And when I could lick the bowl without feeling guilty.'

Blanche looked over the top of her mug as she slurped a large mouthful. Her glasses steamed up. She put down the tea, hands nursing the warmth.

'Earlier today, just after lunch, you passed my house on your own, coming from the direction of the village. You stopped outside my house to blow your nose... tell me to mind my own beeswax but you seemed upset.'

Robin picked up another rock bun.

'How's it been, coming back?' Blanche asked gently.

Where to start? Robin didn't trust herself to speak, not trusting her voice to sound as if she was holding everything together.

'Are you getting on all right with your mum?'

'It is what it is,' Robin said in as neutral a tone as she could muster.

'I know there was a falling out, all those years ago. She hasn't spoken much about it and shares very little about her past. But one thing I can tell you, lass… strangers, friends, family, there's always a reason for what they do and how they are. We think we fall into jobs or relationships or behaviours but there's always something underneath driving us. When we took on a new resident, I always liked to chat to them about their past, it told me so much.'

'What do you mean?'

Blanche picked up her half-eaten rock bun and shook it in the air. 'People are like plain dough when they're born but then life happens, adding salt or sugar, hard bits, soft bits, things that lift it up, things that don't. Take my Dennis. He was evacuated to the countryside during the war and lived with a family who owned their own shop. Keeping busy, helping out in the stock room and listening to chat about customers and profits, saw him through tough times and set his life on a particular course, into a sales career.'

'What about you, working in care homes?'

'That's down to my mum. She was ill when I was a teenager and died the day before I turned eighteen.'

'Oh, Blanche, I'm so sorry.'

'You understand how hard that must have been. And I nursed her, right to the end. My dad couldn't cope. I discovered a lot about myself, the dirty jobs didn't bother me. The one thing that made her death a little more bearable was knowing she'd been clean and comfortable.' Blanche took off her glasses and wiped them on her fleece. 'Caring, getting stuck in like that, gave me a purpose when my life seemed uncertain, as it did again a few years later when I discovered I couldn't have kiddies of my own. It made sense to give that love to strangers instead – strangers that became family.'

'That's lovely.'

Her pale cheeks flushed pink. 'But you know all this – you're not as long in the tooth as me but must have some inkling about your mum.'

Robin sighed and took a sip of tea. 'Not really. I know her dad died in the war, life was tough… that's about it.'

'Feelings from childhood never disappear, events that happen then leave their mark. She told me once that when she first started working at Lewis's it gave her a sense of family, all the staff events, the camaraderie… I'm not making much sense, am I? What I'm trying to say is… Faye's way is probably to do with her past.'

'Yes. I've suspected that from the little she's started to tell me.'

Blanche cocked her head. 'Then I hope you realise the significance – that your relationship, the friction, it's less to do with you and more to do with a history she had before you were even born.'

Robin stared at her. For so many years she'd thought that she might be to blame, she'd decided that *she*, Robin, might have failed, back then. So in some ways Blanche's explanation made her feel better, but in others it didn't. Faye's attitude to Robin may have been due to a rough childhood, but Robin hadn't had things easy as a little girl either, not with Faye, yet *she* hadn't taken that out on Amber. Although Robin did have the example of a great dad. Faye hadn't known hers. Even so...

Robin's eyebrows knitted together.

Blanche put her glasses back on. 'Tell me, flower... why did you come back to Stonedale?'

'To look after her.'

'But you didn't want to.'

Robin ran a finger around the top of her mug as she told Blanche about Uncle Ralph worrying, how she'd rung or at least messaged him, most days, since coming back to keep his mind at ease. He wasn't to know that contact was for her benefit as well. Robin missed him.

'But you could have talked him around, persuaded him it was better that you didn't get involved. Yet you convinced Faye to let you move in, you're sticking it out.' She reached across and patted Robin's hand. 'Ask yourself why that is. In fact, let me answer. It's because you've always had the heart of a good daughter.'

20

Amber headed off to lectures, grabbing a slice of toast as she left and Faye waved to her out of the front window. She'd never have approved of teenage Robin eating on the hoof. It hadn't taken long to get ready, Robin didn't miss the morning regimen of straighteners and styling products. She'd scrunched her curls and pulled on an oversized abstract print sweatshirt she'd found in her old room, loving the soft feel and lines so different to her usual executive look.

'Do you want to go into the village after lunch?' she asked Faye.

'With this rain? No. In any case, I'll get fresh air on the treasure hunt tomorrow – as long as it warms up. It was freezing when I let Hoover out back. I'm not going out in weather like that. And I've a busy day ahead with phone calls to make. I've got to ring the chemist to sort out having my prescriptions delivered and—'

'But I'm here, there's no need—'

'What about when you go back?'

Robin could stay in touch, perhaps. Come up if things got difficult.

She added a heaped spoon of sugar to her tea. Had she really just thought that?

Faye raised her eyebrows. 'This fall has made me realise I need to get organised in case anything like this happens again and I'm incapacitated, unable to get food in or type on my phone – contingency plans, to deal with the people who really matter. The doctor. The vet. Julian at *Word Weekly*.'

* * *

After lunch, Robin reached for her anorak hanging on the coat hooks in the hallway, but spotted her old biker jacket, she hesitated and then reached for it. She'd go to that outdoor clothing shop next to the bookshop and see if she could find thicker gloves and a decent scarf for Faye. There was too much riding on completing this hunt for Faye to drop out after just one clue.

She gazed at Brynner's glass front before going into the shop next door, where she found a lovely pair of thick navy gloves with flowers embroidered around the wrist. She picked up a checked scarf Faye would be able to wrap around twice. They also sold dog jumpers and the assistant helped her choose one that would fit a French bulldog. Dad would have loved browsing here; whenever he and Faye went hiking he'd look unusually smart, with his polished walking boots, red sports jacket and matching flat cap.

When she came out, Robin hovered for a second before veering right. She collapsed her umbrella as she went in. Yul was dealing with a customer. Robin felt glad to be in the warm, the smell of coffee at least feeling inviting. She pulled a saga from the shelf and sat down in an upholstered chair, near the window. Her mind drifted to the village library, and Robin wondered why it had closed down. Yul's mum once said that children were only lent to us and spoke as if they came from some sort of library too. Maybe Faye would have returned Robin – she wasn't what she'd expected.

The door pinged as the customer left and another one came in and went straight through to the café area. Yul had disappeared. She put the book down and went over to the till.

'Yul? Are you there?'

Dragging footsteps preceded his appearance. He wore a dark grey suit jacket today, sleeves rolled up.

'How can I help?' He stared. 'Is that *my* sweatshirt?'

She looked down. Shit.

'I lent it to you after... after that time in the tree house.' He broke eye contact.

Their special place. So he hadn't forgotten.

'You were so cold afterwards.'

'It was drizzling. You insisted I wear this on top of my jumper.'

'I liked to see you wear it.'

And now? she wanted to ask. Christ, this was ridiculous. Yul beckoned to her. She followed him into the back room café, and he had a quick word with his assistant. This part of the building looked out onto a small yard and there was an outhouse outside. Perhaps he stored stock in there. The wooden tables each had a literary quote carved across the middle. In the corner of the room was a vase of black roses – very Yul – and a painting of a desk bearing a stack of books and a skull hung on the far wall.

They turned left into the small kitchen and walked past the coffee machine and into the far end where there was a simple melamine table. He indicated for her to sit. She put down her bag and umbrella.

'Fancy a drink, on the house?' he asked politely.

'That would be... great.' She was so surprised she just said to get her what he was having. He returned, swiftly, with two cappuccinos.

They looked at each other.

'The name, Brynner's, I love it. Your gran was a lovely person. I'm assuming...'

'She passed away a few years ago, shortly after Mum died,' he said, in a tight voice. 'She never got over it.'

'Oh Yul, I'm so sorry, about both of them.'

His face softened. 'Dad and I were in bits, but Mum had a good last year and ticked off a few bucket list wishes. We even managed to take her to see the northern lights, and she flew in a hot air balloon. I was engaged at the time, prepared to give up my travels. That year helped me realise I'd only got engaged because everyone was doing it. And seeing Mum achieve her dreams, it made me realise I'd never be the settling kind.' He cleared his throat. 'So here I am, as free as a bird, back in Stonedale and mortgaged to the hilt.'

'This place really is wonderful. Where do you find your stock?' She wanted to keep the conversation going, to try to make things easier.

'I've got some collectables with magnificent covers. I find them online, like signed copies and first editions, but for the most part house clearances are a good source. I don't stock more than one copy of the same story but I refresh the choice regularly for my regular customers. I store ones I've pulled off the shelves with a note of the date they've last been on display.' His eyes had lit up.

'I... I couldn't help looking at your website, I hope you don't mind. There's nothing much on there about you... Customers love personal touches.' Her cheeks felt hot. 'I'm sure the story about your gran would really appeal. Sorry. I can't help it. I worked in marketing before I came back.'

'I'll think about it,' he muttered and a small smile crossed his lips. 'Thanks for stopping by. I... appreciate it.'

He went to get up but she touched his arm, speaking in a low voice.

'Tara said you went off the rails when you got back from London.'

He rubbed his forehead with the palm of his hand. He looked sixteen again. She wanted to lean forwards and hug him, tell him she understood, that everything got fucked up.

'Wouldn't you have?' he said.

'If I'd stayed here? One hundred per cent. But I went the opposite way, down in London. I threw myself into routine, into work, it felt safer that way, gave my life the structure I felt I had with Dad, with you, with the life we'd been planning. And...'

'What?'

'Maybe it was easier, not seeing you. That would only have reminded me of...' Her breath caught and he nodded.

'So you feel the same shock I do, now that you're back?' he asked.

Robin nodded, not trusting herself to speak.

Yul cleared his throat. 'How's it going with your mum?'

'Backwards, sideways, anywhere but forwards. And I don't think Tara and I will be meeting again.' She stood up, picked up her things and he followed her to the shop's front door. They moved aside as another customer came in. Outside the sky had cleared.

Lunch with Tara had made her realise that relationships *couldn't* pick up where they left off, not if the breaking point had been traumatic.

'She's still upset about me leaving, and I get it, we were best friends. You remember how it was, Yul, the... the drama, London... but I'm beginning to realise that's no excuse.'

'You never wrote to her either.'

'How do you know?'

'We... hung out together when I first got back, but eventually drifted apart without you. She was angry, Robin, and felt let down.'

'Did you tell her about the hospital and everything that happened?' she asked, her mouth dry.

'No. Not my place. Perhaps you should...'

They stood in strained silence.

'Tara wouldn't want to know, anyway, not now. It's too late. At least my daughter, Amber, has moved into Parade Row, that's one ray of light.' Robin told him about Amber's economics degree and how she was living in the loft bedroom, about the treasure hunt they'd found. Realising she was rambling, Robin went to leave.

She turned back, paused and then said, 'I tried to block out thoughts about you, over the years, and for the most part succeeded. But every now and again a memory would pop into my mind. I couldn't forget you completely, not after everything.' She started to walk away, wanting to say more but not sure how to.

'Same here. Looking good, Robin. Great taste in sweatshirts.'

21

Still in her fleeced hooded pyjama top and matching shorts, Amber yawned and stretched on the floor, for a second looking like the little girl who'd loll on the lounge carpet in front of weekend morning television. Robin was filling in a career questionnaire. Since coming back to Stonedale she'd grown despondent at the thought of simply falling into another position where she'd end up doing the same thing, year in, year out.

'How were lectures yesterday?' Robin asked.

'Fine,' she said and licked her fingers after polishing off a slice of cold pizza from a takeout she'd ordered for herself last night. Amber turned her head to Faye. 'We should get going with the hunt, Gran, especially as there's a special instruction at the beginning of the second clue. Let's just say we won't be eating up the table for lunch today.'

Robin got up to fetch the scroll from the dining room table and glanced into the kitchen and through the back window. It drizzled outside but the forecast predicted that, after shooting down rain all yesterday, heavy clouds would now retreat. She passed the scroll to Amber before sitting back on the chaise longue.

'Did Granddad read poetry?' asked Amber. 'How come he was so good at riddles?'

Faye looked at Robin and they both grinned. Robin couldn't remember when they had ever smiled quite so broadly at each other – apart from on the treasure hunts.

'Good Lord, no, my Alan didn't read fiction, and we went to a Shakespeare play once, he swore never again. But he always enjoyed a funny limerick and he took part in the pub quiz down the road, every week. We'd go together and sometimes my friend, Blanche, and her husband, Dennis, would join us.'

'I didn't appreciate, until I was much older, how selfless he'd been, helping me learn poetry over the years, for assemblies and English projects, and he always saw me in school plays. He didn't seem to mind that, as long as it wasn't Macbeth,' said Robin.

Amber held the scroll up in the air and, still lying on her back, unrolled it.

'A picnic is required to solve this clue,
Sandwiches, cake, I leave it up to you.
Take your packed lunch to help break the code,
And head to the anger of Stonedale's roads.
Walk all over that parlour game,
Your stomach will be glad you came.
Is the answer simply a patch of grass?
Nay! Nay! Nay! What a farce!
It's far more grand, even though related to a chore.
I don't need to tell you any more.'

'Ah, so Dad would have, of course, assumed we'd do this

hunt in one day,' said Robin, 'and that's why he wanted us to read the second clue first, so that we were prepared for him intending us to picnic outside.'

Faye tutted. 'A picnic is a damn silly idea at this time of year.'

'Dad planned for us doing it when he was away, in June.'

'Exactly. I'm not eating outside in this weather. The ground will be too wet if this clue does take us onto grass, after all that rain yesterday. Perhaps we should cancel or you two go without me.'

Amber pushed Hoover off and sat upright. 'But you were the reason we cracked clue one by saying maybe the answer wasn't the sundial.'

Robin hesitated. 'It's true. We can just make sure we wear suitable shoes.'

Amber shrugged. 'I'm going to run a bath, if we're not going out. Then I'll start looking at jobs in London, seeing as I might still go back. A school friend has sent me a link for an agency offering temporary office work.'

Faye watched Amber get up and her mouth made a chewing movement. 'If it starts to pour again, we come straight back.'

Amber hovered and then held out her hand and Faye allowed herself to be pulled to her feet by her good arm.

'That reminds me. Stay where you are,' said Amber. Her footsteps thudded upstairs and into the loft. A few moments later she reappeared, brandishing a thick black felt tip. 'I found this in a pencil pot. A cast isn't a cast unless someone has signed it, right?'

Robin waited for Faye to say what a stupid idea but instead she held out her arm.

'No bad language, mind,' she replied.

Amber signed her name with a love heart and doodled flower underneath.

'Get away with you now,' said Faye gruffly. 'I need to get my thick cords on and you need to change out of those pyjamas.' Amber shot upstairs again and left her staring at the cast as if it were a Picasso painting she were trying to figure out.

It made Robin wonder if she should have offered to sign it.

Half an hour later they stood outside on the pavement, sandwiches and cake in a rucksack, Faye staring down at Hoover in his new knitted jumper. It was royal blue with the image of a yellow crown.

'Will you be warm enough in that coat?' Robin asked Amber. It would keep off rain but was lightweight, for spring.

She rolled her eyes and didn't reply as she opened the scroll again and they started walking.

'So, we've packed our lunch and now we have to *head to the anger of Stonedale's roads*. Guess we may as well start in the village, then,' she said. 'Do you think he meant to write *angle*?'

'No,' said Faye. 'Your granddad's handwriting left a lot to be desired, but he was always very precise when it came to these scrolls.'

Faye hadn't called him that before. Robin imagined Dad being right here with them, defending his handwriting with jokey indignation. Hoover pulled her over to a lamppost. They'd come to Brynner's Books.

'Robin, wait!' Yul came over in tight white jeans. They showed off his muscular legs. He ran a hand through his hair.

'Good morning, Jason.'

'Mrs Wilson... Nice to see you out and about again.'

Amber stared at him. She'd quizzed Robin last night, wanted to know how she felt after seeing Yul again after so many years. Robin didn't know what to say, still wasn't sure herself. And she'd started to remember little things stored in that corner of her mind reserved for treasures such as Amber's first smile and Todd's face when she said she'd marry him. Like the tender way Yul would slip his arm around her and pat her back whilst Faye told her off, and how fully he'd pay attention when she talked. He'd put down a book or take off his headphones and sit like a child listening to a story. Robin had even imagined what it would be like to kiss him again.

'This is Amber.'

'Great to meet you. You look just like Robin's dad.'

'So I'm told.'

He looked back at Robin. 'Could we...? Would you mind...? Any chance you're free say... Saturday, just after closing?'

'Oh... okay, sure, I'll drop around,' Robin said, pulse racing, spirits buoyed by the suggestion, hoping his frostiness might be thawing.

Amber looked back over her shoulder as they passed the hairdresser's, whilst Faye shook her head at the Christmas tree already in the window. A cashier from the supermarket stopped and the young man asked Faye how she was. He couldn't take his eyes off Hoover's jumper.

'I couldn't resist buying it,' said Robin.

'She's from London,' said Faye and shot the man a mutually understanding look.

They came to the town hall's fountain.

'So, *the anger of Stonedale's roads*... let's try thinking of different words for anger, what about their wrath instead, or annoyance...?' Robin said.

'Or Mad. Furious. Raging,' said Amber. 'That's how I felt when our student house flooded, I couldn't believe none of us spotted the burst pipe.'

'Your landlord must have been angry,' said Faye.

Amber shrugged. 'I don't know how he kept so calm when we told him.' She bent over to look at the coins in the fountain.

'He's a nice bloke, it's a shame the damage is far more extensive than anyone imagined. He's making a decision in the next week or so as to whether he has to release us from our contracts and give our deposits back. I'm out of Manchester then. There's no way I'm going to risk another house with people I don't know, who might be even less like me.'

'*Mad* roads, *furious*, *raging*... hmm... doesn't help...' Robin frowned. 'Wait, what did you say? When did you learn all of this?'

'He emailed us all, last night.'

A sense of panic flickered through Robin's gut. 'You can't let a burst pipe also burst your dreams,' she said, in as light a tone as she could muster.

Amber folded her arms.

'I got *cross* with Hoover when he woke me up last night,' said Faye, swiftly. 'He collapsed, backside first, onto my face.' Hoover looked up with a sheepish expression. 'Very cross indeed,' she said, returning his stare.

'That's it, you've aced it again, Gran. This fountain could be your lucky charm. The clue must refer to this big *cross*roads at the end of the high street.' Amber pointed ahead and made a cross sign with her finger.

'No, you've done it, Amber! Well done!' Faye said loudly.

The three of them looked at each other and Amber gave Faye a hug.

Robin's mouth fell open, eyes widening at the sight of such affection between Faye and her granddaughter.

'Although, let's not get carried away,' said Faye and read-justed her glasses. 'We've solved nothing yet. What's the next line?'

They studied the sentence *walk all over that parlour game,* and between them made various suggestions including chess, dominoes and charades.

'I've got it: Bridge, we have to cross over the bridge,' Robin said.

Slowly they crossed the road, passing the clusters of hawthorn bushes after Hoover had taken a good sniff. They made their way over to the other side of the river, a fresh breeze building. Robin breathed in the smell of algae and the damp soil's earthiness, a familiar smell from the times Dad and her played hide and seek in the woods. She'd lie on carpets of leaves ever so still, thrilled when a squirrel or bird came close.

'We used to picnic here when you were little.'

Robin remembered. Dad would grin as he ate his favourite boiled eggs, whilst Robin would pinch her nose. As a treat, sometimes, Faye made lemonade from scratch, and it made Robin feel like a character out of her favourite Enid Blyton stories.

'We'd sit on a big tartan rug instead of a table, didn't we? Dad said it was more fun sitting on the grass because we could look at the ants and worms. We played pooh sticks too.'

'Happy times,' Faye said quietly, as if no one else could hear. 'I wished those innocent outings could have lasted forever.'

Robin's eyebrows shot up. She did?

'But the clue says that grass isn't the answer, it says *Nay! Nay! Nay!* to that. *It's far more grand, even though related to a chore...*'Amber stared at the scroll. 'And the word chore is emphasised, so I reckon that part of it must give us the letter for the anagram.' She pointed to the memorial around fifty metres away to the right, with the cricket pitch in the distance. 'What's that?'

They made their way over to the monument of a war horse with the numbers 1914–1918 engraved on one side, along with the words *With Gratitude*. It stood around three metres high, with patches of green rust, the solider sitting on it had the palm of his hand flat against the horse's flank.

'Chores...' Amber muttered. 'Washing, dusting, scrubbing...'

Faye and Robin looked at each other.

'This is known as The Iron Horse,' Robin said.

Amber's face broke into a smile. 'Ironing? So the second letter is I.'

'That's must be why Dad wrote *Nay! Nay! Nay!* It's a play on words for the sound a horse makes.'

'He was so clever. I'm determined to work out the next clue on Sunday, now I know the kind of hints and tricks Granddad would use – if you're up to it, Gran.'

Robin could have grabbed her hands and spun in a circle, like they used to when Amber was little. She was willing to stay a few more days, and then, hopefully, a few more after that.

Amber stepped forward and ran a finger over the engravings. 'Why would a village be grateful for losing men in a war, it doesn't make sense?'

Faye explained to Amber how not a single one had died, how Stonedale was a Thankful Village as written on the village sign. There were fifty-six thankful villages in the UK – places where all the soldiers came back from the Great War, and fourteen doubly thankful villages where no local men were killed in the Second World War either. Even so, when it was Remembrance week flowers were always laid and they admired the poppy wreaths propped up against the plinth.

Robin had never felt very thankful to live in Stonedale, she'd longed to live in town near the buzz of the nightlife and record shops, away from Faye, away from the cliques at school. She'd share a flat with Yul and Tara, and other school friends would come over for parties, in awe of their independence. They'd dress like their pop heroes, smoke pot, drink Asti Spumante and work at Afflecks whilst they followed their dreams, her studying English, Yul environmental science, and Tara learning all things New Age. Dad would visit and help them do DIY jobs around the flat. Everyone in the new neighbourhood would think them utterly cool and club owners would know them by their first names and let them into the VIP areas.

'Gawd knows how I used to eat off a rug,' said Faye.

'Dad used to love picnics, and always played Frisbee with me after we'd eaten, didn't he, Mum?' said Amber.

'Yes, I surprised him with one for our tenth anniversary, packed it with champagne and strawberries.'

'Where did you go?' asked Faye.

'Nowhere. Todd had to go into work. Apparently an emergency.'

Amber gazed at Robin for a second before turning away to take another look at the memorial. They approached the picnic area and Faye rested her good hand on the nearest table.

'Wait, the bench looks damp,' said Robin, 'I'll spread out the plastic bag I brought for our rubbish, the last thing you need is to catch a cold.' Quickly, Robin reached into the rucksack.

'Hurry up then,' Faye muttered and rubbed her ribs.

Robin glanced up. 'Look at that rabbit!' She pointed behind them, past the tables, near the edge of the thicket. However, Hoover had spotted it first; he gave a loud bark and raced off. Robin stared in horror as the lead trailed behind him. She must have let go for a second.

'Hoover! Come back this instant!' called Faye and the newly acquired ruddiness sapped out of her cheeks. 'He'll get lost, that mutt's got no sense of direction. How could you be so stupid, Robin?' she shouted.

Robin Wilson,
16 Parade Row,
Stonedale,
Greater Manchester
December 1986

Dear Debbie,

I'M DREADING MY FIRST KISS.

There's a boy who started at our school, at the beginning of term, and I really fancy him. He makes me laugh and we like the same music, and he's really caring, and different to everyone else. We've both been invited to a Christmas party and I'm wondering if we'll get off with each other there. The thing is, I've never kissed anyone properly. What if I make a fool of myself and do it all wrong? My best friend's never kissed a boy either, so I can't ask her for advice, and there's no point talking to Mum about dating, we argue so much.

I hold my thumb and first finger together and practise against that at night, and I watch the romantic scenes closely when Dallas is on the telly. Can you give me any other tips? I'm really nervous.

Robin, age 14

Girl's Scene
41 Gover Street,
London

Dear Robin,

Goodness, slow down, you haven't even got on the dance floor yet! It's normal to feel this way, everyone does that first time with a new boyfriend, even if they've had experience. It's part of the excitement. When your lips touch, relax and see what happens, trust your instincts, and just gently pull away if you want to stop. It sounds as if you and this boy already get on well and that's a great starting point. Honestly, he'll be as nervous as you.

As for your mum, why not ask her about when she was a teenager? You might be surprised and find common ground to talk about.

Best wishes,

Debbie

22

Amber charged off with Robin not far behind, instantly reminded of how she never really enjoyed her hours on the treadmill. She slipped on the sodden grass and almost tripped over a large twig. Hoover and the rabbit had both disappeared and the two of them ran through the thicket, calling his name. Eventually they met up.

'He's so small, how will we find him unless he's barking, there's hardly any light in here?' Robin caught her breath. 'Hoover, where are you?' she hollered.

'He's not answering to his name, why don't we try calling... I know, his favourite food instead?' said Amber.

'What?' Robin frowned.

She folded her arms. 'I suppose you think it's a stupid idea.'

'No... no, of course not, you're right, anything is worth trying... okay, well, he does love bacon. I cooked some for Faye the other morning and his ears pricked up as soon as he heard the word, before I'd even switched on the grill.' They walked further into the thicket, calling and dodging fallen branches and marshy black puddles, stopping every few metres to listen without the rustle of leaves under their feet. A bird flew up from a nearby bush, sounding its alarm.

'Perhaps he's gone back to her by now,' said Amber.

Going back to the picnic table empty-handed didn't appeal. Robin felt ten years old again, like when she'd lost her purse. Faye had shouted that she was spoilt and took pocket money for granted. At that age Robin didn't answer back, she'd just stood, head bowed.

'Bacon!' she called and Amber did the same, again and again. Then they tried calling Hoover by his name once more. With a shiver, Robin eventually turned to go back and almost bumped into a mossy log. At least, that's what she thought it was until she looked down to see two triangular ears, a wagging tail and a jaw clamped firmly around a plastic six-pack ring.

'Come here you little rascal!' She picked him up and buried her face in his coat before pulling at the plastic. He wouldn't let go and it tore in half, he started chewing and Amber managed to pull it out of his mouth before he swallowed. Then she took the lead and the two of them ran out into the open air, grass squelching as Robin joined them. By the time she caught up he was settled on Faye's lap eating a handful of treats she'd brought.

'I might have lost him forever,' she ranted. 'How could you let go of the lead, you stupid, stupid girl? And Hoover loves retrieving things, he might have found something dangerous.'

Robin caught Amber's eye.

'I don't know, my focus was on—'

'Well, it shouldn't have been. Owners put their dogs first.'

Robin leant against the picnic table.

'Gran. Everything's okay now,' said Amber.

If Faye shouted at her too, that was it, Robin would move them both out, tonight.

'Your mother's a fool,' she muttered, 'and can't even tell the difference between a rabbit and hare. That thing was huge.'

Before Robin could answer, Amber spoke.

'No, she's not, we all make mistakes,' she said quietly. 'Mum was trying her best to make you comfortable, putting down a plastic bag so that you wouldn't get cold. She was putting *you* first.'

Wow. Amber was so calm, so... in charge.

Robin hadn't noticed before, or perhaps she had but denied it; her treasure of a girl really had become an adult.

Faye pursed her lips. Robin knew all too well that her mother never had liked to lose an argument. 'I bet she's shouted at you many a time. It's what mothers do.'

Amber's expression looked blank. 'Do they? Not mine. Never has.'

Faye snorted.

'Sure, she'd get angry, ground me, send me to my room but Mum never shouted, not like that; she'd use this disappointed voice and that was almost worse.'

'What, not once?' she scoffed. 'I find that hard to believe.'

'It's true. I can only remember one time when I was little and—'

'It's all right, Amber, just leave it,' Robin mumbled.

'No, I want to hear this,' said Faye.

'I let go of her hand and went to cross the road to see a friend. She yelled that a car was coming. But it was to protect me, not to tell me off – that's a different kind of shouting, isn't it?'

Faye glowered as Robin unpacked the rucksack and handed out the ham sandwiches. She ate hers standing up. Every now and then, Amber threw down a pinch of bread for their feathered companions who chirped at each other and were the only ones talking. Faye wrapped hers up again after one bite and sat deep in thought.

'I didn't grow up in a Thankful Village,' she blurted out. 'Most of the men didn't come back from either war, my dad included. He never met me.'

Amber and Robin stopped eating as she explained that both her parents came from big families where there was little money and neither had wanted children. They'd had dreams of saving hard, buying their own house and travelling the world.

'But then my father got called up and my mother found out she was accidentally pregnant shortly after he left. She struggled bringing up a child on her own, her situation made worse by the fact she didn't feel remotely maternal. He was killed in the trenches along with all her dreams, as she never ceased to remind me, and I was told to get a job as soon as I could, even though I'd wanted to go to college.

'"You're nothing special, every mouth has two hands that can go out to work",' my mother would say.'

Robin sat down next to her.

'Perhaps I shouldn't have shouted, Robin.' Faye didn't look at her. 'But this dog, he's all I've got now. He loves me unconditionally, just like Alan did. I... I can't lose him, because I know what it's like to feel really alone.' Her voice shook. 'When Alan left, and then you...'

Why hadn't Faye told Robin any of this before? And she'd effectively given her an apology? And implied that... she might have *missed* Robin?

Robin stuffed in as much banana loaf as she could, hoping it would dull the confusion inside. Then she opened the flask and poured out three steaming cups of tea, and tuned into the birds' chirps again. After a while Faye ate her sandwich. A chunk accidentally fell onto the ground and a thrush pecked it up and flew away.

'That bird was just like you earlier,' said Faye as she looked at Hoover. 'Hare today, gone tomorrow.'

23

─────────

'Thanks for sticking up for me, today,' Robin said as she opened the wardrobe doors, to pick out more of her old clothes.

'Whatever.' Amber didn't look up from an issue of *Girl's Scene*. She was sitting on the geometric duvet cover.

'You shouldn't have to, though.'

She looked up. 'No need to go on. It's fine.'

'Faye had never told me all that about my grandmother before.'

Slowly Amber put down the magazine and her expression darkened. 'You two aren't so different. There's always been a part of you closed off.'

'What do you mean?' Robin joined her on the bed.

'I knew hardly anything about Gran before I came here,' she said and bristled. 'Even though I've only met her as a baby, you might, over the years, have told me snippets, for my benefit, but no, it's been one big mystery. I've only ever known that you two didn't get on and Dad told me not to quiz you.'

'It's... been difficult... Painful to remember. It was always easier to focus on the future.'

Amber tilted her head. 'Did your dad tell you not to question Gran?

'He did, as it happens.'

'Then her past must be as painful as yours. You mentally locked your mum away just like she did hers.'

The idea of being similar to her in such a profound way sent a shudder down Robin's spine.

The lines in between Amber's eyebrows disappeared. 'Why do you put up with the way she speaks to you?'

'I did stand up to her when I hit my teens. Once she called me the queen of backchat.'

Amber lifted up her legs and hugged her knees, nodding at Robin to go on.

'I'd storm out of rooms and slam doors, and once I turned sixteen I'd tell her I could do what I want. I'd try to tolerate her ways for Dad's sake, he hated seeing us fall out. But it had all built up, you see, the years of slights. Like when Tara and I did a charity walk, despite blisters I finished it and raised almost fifty pounds, but she never said well done, not once. And I spent ages painting a picture of our garden for an art project, I was so pleased with it. But Faye just gave it a cursory glance and said the daisies in the lawn were far too big. Tara's mum stuck hers to the fridge. Little things like that, day in, day out, niggled away.'

Amber's feet had slid to the floor. 'Whereas you brag about my achievements to anyone listening. Remember how you used to give me medals at primary school, on sports day, just for finishing a race?'

'I was always so proud and wanted you to know that.' Robin's cheeks flushed. 'Maybe I went over the top.'

'No... I liked it,' Amber mumbled. 'Didn't Granddad ever stick up for you?'

'Just occasionally he and Faye would argue, badly. I'd hear

from the loft but if I came down they'd stop.' Robin stared at the wall for a moment. 'Every time they'd talk afterwards. I never knew what they disagreed about, they were good at keeping fall-outs private, but during the following days Faye would make more effort with me, asking about school, suggesting we cooked together, but sooner or later her withheld snappiness would boil over and the tension between us would be worse than ever.' She shrugged and turned back to Amber. 'Looking back, Dad must have been trying to make things better between us.'

'I wish I'd met him. Granddad sounds brill.'

Robin could only nod, it wasn't easy to find words that truly expressed how amazing her father had been. 'I suppose I got used to the way Faye was and now... coming back... she seems so fragile. I wasn't expecting it. I'm only here for a few weeks and it's been almost easy, like falling into a well-worn groove, we both know the rules.'

'Easy doesn't mean it's right.'

When had Amber got so wise? Robin wanted to hug her but instead squeezed her arm. It was because of Amber Faye came out today. Oh, she'd gone back to her usual distant self tonight, with her puzzles and telly and indifferent reaction to tea, but today had proved that completing the treasure hunt could lead to so much more than solving an anagram.

'It's a shame you and Tara won't see each other again. You were really close?'

'We stuck together throughout primary and high school.' Robin couldn't help smiling. 'We got up to all sorts of high jinks.'

'Like what?'

Robin sat on the bed and told her about the time they'd secretly caught the bus into Manchester. Depeche Mode were playing at the Apollo. They'd gone to the Saturday gig as they weren't allowed out late during the week, but someone at school later told her that if you went round the side of the building, performers waved out of the dressing room window. It was a Tuesday and they sat giggling on the back seat of the bus, each of them clutching a disposable camera. Her mum and dad were both in bed when she got back.

Robin took out her phone and put on her 1980s Spotify list before searching for old bits of jewellery she and Tara would wear out clubbing.

Amber held up a neon pink, large, beaded necklace. 'At least the music was subtle,' she said as Sam Fox's 'Touch Me' started to play.

Whilst Robin pulled out a couple of tops from the wardrobe, Amber went back to the magazine, shaking her head every now and then.

'I'm reading an article about being a perfect size twelve, this girl is a size ten and hates it. Imagine that nowadays?' Amber scoffed. 'And there's a guide on how to keep your guy – tell all the other girls that he never cleans his teeth, no one else will want to date him. Ask him to explain the offside rule just one more time, it'll make him feel important. This is classic.'

'Yul used to like reading those magazines too. We'd do the quizzes together.'

Amber looked up. 'Did you dump him?'

Robin pictured Yul's face, in that hospital, him holding her hand so tightly it hurt. She turned off the music.

'No. He left me in London.'

'You ran away together? I thought you left Stonedale on your own.' She put down the *Girl's Scene* issue. 'Did Dad know?'

She nodded.

'Why did Yul leave you?'

'Things didn't turn out as we expected... we couldn't get jobs, the excitement soon wore off.' Robin wouldn't tell her the full story, not at the moment.

'Why did you keep that secret? Do you still love him?' Amber lifted her chin and frowned. 'I've heard you and Dad talking, how he felt you'd become distant from him, in recent years... is that why? Yul was your first love... have you been waiting for an opportunity to come up north?'

'What? No Amber, of course not, why would you think that?'

'Why do you think?' she asked in a sulky tone.

Robin gave a big sigh. 'How many times do I have to tell you that I wasn't having an affair with Greg? I hardly knew him, we'd only been working together for a month. Your dad misunderstood.'

'But misunderstood what, exactly? You've never fully explained it to me. Nor has Dad.'

Robin looked Amber in the eyes. Perhaps she hadn't. Maybe now was the time.

'I'd been having a problem with my phone and your dad offered to look at it. He noticed a message from Greg pop up with lots of laughing emojis. I grabbed the phone, making an excuse about Greg and I needing to talk about work.' She looked away. 'I suppose it must have looked suspicious. I'd spoken to Greg, in a low voice, at home, several times over the preceding weeks, you see, walking into a different room if your dad was present. Anyway, that day, he looked at the phone later and saw that I'd deleted the message and all the conversation history.' Robin met Amber's gaze again. 'That confirmed, for him, that I was cheating on him.'

'But why did you delete it? And what happened next?'

'You heard the rows – and I'm so sorry about that, love. Your

dad said it was the last straw after months, years of feeling I'd...
I'd gone off the marriage. He wouldn't listen to my explanation
that Greg was simply helping me choose a new set of clubs for
his birthday. I'd decided to make an effort for his fiftieth and
Greg was as keen on golf as him.'

'Hmm. Well, you can't blame Dad... you know what they
say... no smoke without fire.' Amber folded her arms.

'Darling... please, tell me... why won't you believe me? You
know that, finally, Dad agreed to meet Greg who told him the
truth.' Even though it was too late. Todd said he'd had enough
and still wanted a divorce; that his accusation proved that the
trust was gone.

'Because...' Amber's voice broke. 'I need a good reason. A big
one. There has to be, doesn't there, to end a marriage? Something dramatic? Not simply that you drifted apart.'

Robin had always thought so too. Until things had started,
slowly, bit by bit, to change, all the little negatives stacking up.
Perhaps that's why she hadn't taken the final step to call it quits,
and that had forced Todd to.

'So was it about Yul?' Amber persisted, chin trembling.

Robin dropped down onto the bed again. 'The memories
about what Yul and I had, they've mostly come back since I've
returned to Stonedale. I'd worked hard to lock Yul away
mentally when I first moved to London, you see, like you say I
did with Faye, Amber, ' she said, gently. 'Your dad and I splitting
up, it wasn't about Yul and I couldn't be more surprised that our
paths have crossed again.'

Amber gave a small smile. 'Did Dad ever tell you about any
of his past girlfriends?'

'Not when we first got together but in recent years he
connected with a load of school friends on Facebook, including

an ex. He met her for coffee and couldn't stop grinning when he got home. He kept going on about how well she'd aged, how glamorous she was.' Robin gave a wry smile. 'You know your dad, he didn't stop to think how that might make me feel.'

Amber raised one eyebrow and nodded, then went back to reading the old magazine.

24

Robin put down the newspaper, glanced outside. Did a woman with blue hair just walk past? She got up and looked out of the window, down the street.

Faye and Amber sat playing dominoes, laughing at the same moments, Faye congratulating Amber when she won, yet again. She was back early from lectures and on a high. Robin had surprised herself by managing not to punch the air when Amber cautiously mentioned a group from her course had asked if she'd like to go to a party, in their halls. After a few games she and Faye had agreed they'd watch *Mamma Mia!* which was on the television, Faye hadn't seen it. Robin tried not to feel like the odd one out, but was grateful neither of them noticed her quickly slip out of the room. She came back downstairs holding her bag, and as she put on her biker jacket she heard Faye talking.

'We never got to Greece but Spain was wonderful, I'd love to go back to the restaurant in the picture. Alan and I ate paella for the first time and drank Sangria. Robin always finished with these little fritters filled with custard. Her face was a picture.'

The affectionate tone caught her off guard and Robin felt a flutter in her stomach, wanting Faye to repeat the sentence, in case she'd misheard it. Faye had never given anything away when Robin was younger and the indifference was harder to bear than criticism. Todd used to give her all the clichés such as roses and chocolates, and they always gave her that flutter, but when the gifts slowly stopped, it felt as if he'd become indifferent to her as well.

Once out on the street Robin hurried into the village, studying every pedestrian. The supermarket was right at the end of the high street, its entrance opposite the river and the woods, just around to the left, and she stopped to go in, disappointed she hadn't spotted that woman again. Robin glanced up towards the station and was about to turn back to the shop front when a flash of blue caught her attention.

'Tara!' she called and ran, dodging villagers. Out of breath, she tapped her shoulder. Tara stopped but didn't turn round, so Robin took a few steps until they faced each other. Her cheeks were tear-stained.

'What's happened?' Robin caught her arm and reached into her trouser pocket. 'You can't go anywhere like this. Here, take this tissue, it's clean.'

'I don't mean to be rude, Robin, but I've got a train to catch.'

Robin stood back whilst she blew her nose. 'I thought I saw you walk past Faye's house.'

Tara's jaw looked clenched.

'Look... let me buy you a drink. How about Tearoom 1960? My shout?' she asked. 'Come on, just for half an hour.'

Robin didn't ask any questions as they went back up the high street and past the betting shop. The smiling faces of winter pansies in the hanging baskets welcomed them as they stopped outside the teashop. She opened the aubergine door and Tara entered first. Maeve looked up from the counter on the right. It was L-shaped inside with low mahogany beams, apricot curtains and colourful salt and pepper pots on each table. The sense of déjà vu felt comforting.

'Aren't you two a sight for sore eyes? How lovely!' Maeve smoothed down her apron.

'Could we have the table in the corner?' Robin asked and pointed to the furthest spot on the left.

She studied them both. 'You settle yourselves down wherever you want. Been visiting your mum and dad, Tara, or are you just after a slice of that fruit cake that your partner likes so much?'

Robin had forgotten how much they'd liked Maeve, despite her death stare. Her lights had been on late one Friday night, years ago. After youth club, Robin and Tara stumbled past, giggling. She stood outside, smoking a cigarette, clearing her head from doing her tax forms, she'd said. Maeve had eyed them keenly and said to come in for a black coffee before going home. Insisting they weren't fresh enough for the next day's trade, she also gave them a free scone each, with all the works.

'Both,' Tara mumbled.

'I'll bring a slice over in a takeout bag, then – along with your two usual orders.'

Tara actually met Robin's eye.

What was Maeve talking about?

'Didn't you bring any adult clothes with you?' Tara asked, in a flat voice. 'First the biker jacket, now that ruffled blouse.'

Robin glowed, she remembered it. 'I think I wore this to your mum's fortieth birthday party. You've been visiting your parents?'

She picked up the menu but Robin could tell she wasn't reading it. Silence fell, apart from Maeve's coffee machine and the chat of a dad and his two young sons, a couple of tables away. Robin gazed out of the window, just happy to be with her old friend.

'It's their golden wedding anniversary next month.'

'Fifty years? That's quite an achievement. How are they celebrating?'

'They're planning a party, that's why they wanted to see me. Mum rang a few days ago, as they'd seen a venue and have to book it this weekend to get a good price. She wanted to know what I thought. I managed to shift my Friday afternoon appointments.'

'What is it, a fancy hotel?'

'Yeah, they weren't sure as it's out at the airport and big and sterile looking, but inside it's got a vintage style jazz bar, a grand piano and a small podium with a retro silver microphone on a stand. The hotel provides a small band that plays all the classics by their favourite singers such as Ella Fitzgerald and Frank Sinatra. It's perfect.'

'I remember your dad had that framed photo of the Rat Pack.'

'Here you are, girls.' They leant back as Maeve set down two coke floats and passed Tara a takeout bag. 'Mint for you, Robin, vanilla for you, Tara.'

'Are you serious?' Tara's mouth curved upwards a tiny bit.

'Humour me. Just for a while I can look at you both and pretend I'm a young woman again.' She winked and went back to the counter.

Robin stared at the green ice cream melting into coke. 'You got off lightly.'

Tara lifted her tall, slim glass and hesitated before raising it in the air. Robin clinked hers against Tara's. They both sucked on the straws.

'This is disgusting. I can't believe we used to like these.'

'Just thinking about all those E numbers is enough to make me leave,' said Tara, sounding more like the friend Robin remembered. 'But I haven't the heart to ask Maeve if we can have two coffees instead.'

'I might need that cake bag, I think I'm going to be sick.'

There was that upwards curve again.

'Tell me to mind my own business, Tara, but... what's up? Can I help?'

She set down her glass and pushed it away. 'Dad.'

Robin waited, pretending to suck up more of the sickly drink.

'He said Prisha isn't invited. They've hardly told anyone about her, you see, none of their friends and not many of our relatives know. As I told you before, he doesn't approve...we've grown apart since I've got older and he can no longer deny to himself that I'm into women, hard as he's tried.'

Oh, Tara. Robin reached across and held her hand, half-expecting her to pull away. 'What about your mum?'

'She won't stand up to him over this. And what's the point? He's never going to change his mind.'

'What will you do?'

Slowly it came out, just how difficult it had been over the years, with those close to her, like her dad, like her mum's brother, like their childless next-door neighbour who used to say Tara was like a daughter to her. Not any more.

'Dad said it was just a phase when he first found out, I was twenty and he caught me kissing a girlfriend in my bedroom. He was convinced I'd grow out of it and Mum agreed. Then, as the decades passed, he implied I've just jumped onto some sort of fashionable LGBTQ+ bandwagon, even though Mum was coming around to it all, and told him it wasn't like that. These days we hardly talk about it at all, we veer around it like a puddle of oil that will send us all flying if we wade into it. I don't give a flying fuck about some stranger in the bar or passerby that can't cope with me and Prisha holding hands. Not that I often meet people like that living in Manchester, the city itself has always felt like a comfortable home. I live my life, no secrets. But Dad... he's supposed to care, supposed to offer support, supposed to try to understand me. We used to get on so well, when I was little, you remember that?' she asked, as if afraid her memories deceived her.

Robin nodded. 'I remember.'

'I wish it was still like that. But then you know all about having a parent who doesn't appear to approve.'

Robin squeezed her fingers and took a deep breath. 'I should have been there for you, all these years. I'm sorry, Tara. It's been a shock, coming back, seeing you and Yul... when I ran away to London I only ever thought about how terrible it was for me... and then London turned into a disaster. I was so self-absorbed, it never dawned on me that my leaving might have consequences back in Stonedale. I'm so sorry. Truly. Do you think you could ever forgive me?'

Tara took her hand away and sucked on her straw, taking her time, studying Robin's face, then she pushed the glass over to her side of the table.

'If you drink mine as well, I might consider it.'

'Gladly.' Robin went to pick it up.

She reached across and Tara stopped her.

'Sorry for how I was when we met up for lunch. I thought you'd never get in touch again. I've missed you, Robin.'

'I've missed you too.' It came out like a whisper.

'What happened in London? Why didn't it work out?'

Robin drank more of her float, sipping whilst she talked, the clinical mouthwash flavour reminding her of the hospital ward. She couldn't tell Tara everything. Not yet. So she talked about the plans she and Yul had had, and how exactly they all went wrong so quickly. They were both going to get jobs, they'd found a room that would do, how excited they were, how grown-up they felt... until their money rapidly started to run low. How scary it was, once, when two men accosted them on the street, one of them flashing the handle of knife in his inside pocket. They'd given them the cash they were carrying. And how they didn't have hot water to wash in for almost a week, and had to drop to eating just one meal a day. When the landlord threatened to throw them out, they'd faced the prospect of sleeping rough.

Then Tara told her about her job practising acupuncture and Reiki, and how hard she'd worked to build up a client list and get to the point where she could afford to rent business premises, as well as pay for a mortgage – how her parents had been supportive with that, helping her with all the legal tape. She asked about Amber and Robin explained how difficult things had been between them this last couple of years, how nice it was to have Amber living with her again, even if it meant giving up her loft room, even if they weren't getting on.

'And then there's the uneasiness between me and Faye,' Robin said. 'I was glad to get out of the house today. But one high point that's keeping me going is the last treasure hunt the three of us are doing.'

'Your dad was so creative thinking up those clues. I don't know how he found the time, working long hours.'

A lump formed in Robin's throat. Dad had always made the time.

'So... *did* you walk by, earlier on?' Robin asked.

Tara nodded.

'Why? Your parents don't live near Parade Row.'

'Force of habit, I guess, knowing you were there. Everything was a blur when I left their house and suddenly I found myself walking past your mum's.'

As they got up to leave, Maeve slipped Robin a bag of cake for Faye, refusing to let her pay. They fastened their coats and headed outside, where they said goodbye and hovered for a second. Tara held out her hand and when Robin grasped it, Tara pulled her close for a hug before dashing off. Robin blinked away tears before heading back to Faye's.

Robin Wilson,
16 Parade Row,
Stonedale,
Greater Manchester
March 1987

Dear Debbie,

FRIENDS ARE TEASING ME

My best friend and I are part of a small group at school but some of the other girls have started to tease me. Now that we're a bit older, on Sundays they like to hang around the park or go to each other's houses, Saturday's often busy with dance or sport clubs. But Sunday is the one day of the week I spend time with my family, it feels like the only day we all have fun together. They see me out with Mum and Dad and say it's babyish. Last week they all met up and drank cider. They aren't being mean and we get on really well, talking about music and fashion, but I don't see why I should do things I don't want to.

Yet I can't help thinking I'm being a bad friend. Am I?

Robin, age 14

Girl's Scene
41 Gover Street,
London

Dear Robin,

You're already confident enough to stick to your own principles and that's very important in life. And at your age you are quite right not to drink alcohol. It sounds as if your friends mean well, perhaps they just miss your company.

Why not suggest a board game evening at yours one week-end, with some tasty snacks, or what about a mocktail party? I'm sure your parents wouldn't mind, if you gave them plenty of warning.

Growing up can be a scary business and maybe you aren't quite as ready for change as these girls. And there's nothing wrong with that, but you wouldn't want to lose them, would you? Friends will be a great support in the future when you are dealing with boys and exams!

Best wishes,

Debbie

25

Robin finished the cappuccino Yul brought her from the coffee machine.

'Thanks. That was nice.' She waited for him to explain why he'd asked her to call by. It was dark outside now.

They'd talked about the shop and he'd explained how it used to be part of the hairdresser's next door, that when the video shop she remembered closed they took over the lease, starting big. However the salon didn't get enough custom. The landlord was friends with the owner and agreed to get builders in to halve the space, then Yul came along before he rented it out and asked if he'd consider selling.

'You didn't think about living in town and commuting in every day, I mean Stonedale... neither of us could wait to leave.'

'It was different for me, Robin, I got on with both my parents. Anyway, one thing I learnt from travelling, over the years... any regrets you've got, changing your geography doesn't make them go away.'

London did. For a while. On the surface.

He consulted his watch. 'Look... do you fancy takeout pizza?'

Robin lifted her eyebrows.

'We could talk? Really talk,' he added, in a hopeful tone.

She rang Amber whilst he washed their cups, to check she was okay to heat up the evening meal.

'What's this, a Saturday night date?' asked Amber in a strained voice.

'No. I only dropped by the shop as a favour. I can easily come back if you've got too much work on. You've got a deadline.'

'You think I don't know that?' she said abruptly. 'I've got it all under control. And I've finally been given a chance to get to know my own grandmother. I intend to make the most of it, so do what you want.'

She ended the call before Robin could pull her up for the rudeness. She didn't often challenge her over it. Guilt about the divorce held her back and she didn't feel confrontation after confrontation would help rebuild their relationship. It was different with Faye, she'd always been off, and by her teens Robin had realised there was nothing she could do to change that. She went through phases, when she was at junior school, of doing bits of housework – she'd set the table for tea without being asked and would ask Faye about her day – but soon it became clear that her own idea of being a good girl couldn't have been the same as her mother's.

Robin took out her compact mirror and studied her reflection. Her blonde highlights needed re-touching. She studied her curls. Perhaps she wouldn't bother. Robin gave Yul the thumbs-up and he came over to wipe down the staffroom table, then she followed him upstairs, via a door at the back of it. His flat was open plan with a modern, marble-effect kitchen, that couldn't have been more different to the living room with vibrant paintings bearing tropical scenes and a woven wall hanging featuring elephants. On a shelf to the left, as she walked in, lay a collection of stunning bookmarks made from leather, card, and various textiles. She studied them as Yul opened wine. Each came from a different capital like San José, Lima, Bangkok, Quito...

'This wooden cart is lovely,' she said and pointed to an ornament underneath them.

'It's an oxcart,' he replied from the kitchen. 'There's a big tradition of oxherding in Costa Rica.'

She sat down in a mahogany leather armchair, opposite him on the sofa, and he put a bowl of olives and their glasses on the driftwood coffee table between them, next to a pile of magazines. They studied the takeout menu and ordered, not something she'd done since being back in Stonedale. Faye enjoyed fish and chips from the family-run chippy she'd known for years, but would sooner eat Hoover's meals than order in fast food.

'You've really travelled and seen the world. I feel wholly inadequate.'

'You've had responsibilities. For the most part I only needed to look after myself. I was able to go backpacking or do volunteer work, that's all. I've not saved the world.' He told her about the beach cleans he'd led in Thailand and animal monitoring in Ecuador, over the years he'd qualified as a deep sea diver and seen coral reef bleaching first hand.

'Stonedale must seem very tame.'

'I'd rather swim into the path of a white shark than face a booklover whose favourite classic has been given a movie cover.'

She stared at him. 'Yul... why did you ask me to drop by?'

A text on his phone lit up saying that the delivery driver was outside. He came back carrying a stack of flat cardboard boxes and placed them on the magazines, the top title of which read *Save our Rainforests*. They ate in silence and she sipped the wine he'd poured out, and when they'd finished the food he put down his glass.

'I wanted to ask...' He ran a hand over the sofa. 'How did you manage to move on after what happened? Look at you now...'

'I'm divorced, Yul,' she said and lifted her hands in the air. 'And I've just been made redundant. Also Todd's business sank and that left us both broke. Whereas you...' She looked around. 'This place shouts a life lived to the full. And you've followed your environmental passion, opening a secondhand shop.' She took a large gulp of wine. 'You think I'd moved on, just like that, you think I forgot?'

'No, of course not. I didn't mean... Sorry. I've not handled things brilliantly since you got back.'

The frown left Robin's face as he poured her another glass and the fuzziness it produced felt inviting. She talked about going to Tearoom 1960 with Tara yesterday, how they'd had coke floats, though she didn't share what was going on with her parents.

'So when Tara said you went off the rails when you got back... what did she mean, exactly?'

Yul lowered his gaze. 'I'm not proud. I hurt a few people. Did stupid things. But eventually I found a way to navigate the rest of my teens, a coping mechanism that became routine.'

'You've blocked it... us out?'

He looked up. 'How did you know?'

'How do you think?'

'You did too.' He nodded. 'When I've thought back over the years, if something's triggered a memory about that time, I focus on that stage of my life in general terms, like how the eighties were special, all that colour, the rebellion, artists experimenting wildly with image and music, life was eclectic, life was exciting, it felt groundbreaking against the backdrop of Greenpeace and

Cold War warriors... I didn't appreciate any of that enough at the time.'

'Me neither.' She took another mouthful of wine.

'If I try to talk about it with anyone who didn't live through it I sound like a boring old fart,' he said.

Robin gave a small smile.

Yul looked at her intently. 'Is your Uncle Ralph still around?'

'Yes. In a care home, I visit every Sunday.'

'Oh. I'm sorry to hear that, Robin. Dementia?'

'Far from it. He's taken to his new smartphone much quicker than I worked out all the functions of mine. We ring each other a lot... I don't know what I'd have done without him. He's always been there, he's always had my back. I'm surprised you remember him.'

'I couldn't forget anything about that hospital.' He got up and took the empty boxes into the kitchen, returning with a bowl of grapes. 'What about your ex-husband, you must have been able to talk about the good old days with him?'

'I think the predictability of adulthood suits Todd better, and for the most part the routine and reliability of our lives was my saviour, but the last few years it felt... suffocating.' She cleared her throat and reached for a grape.

'I get that feeling. It's one reason I set up my own business. I need that fire in my belly that, well... that you and I both had. I've done the travel. I needed another dream. For so long, I looked for that fire in another country or a new relationship, but have come to realise I'm the only person who can ignite it.'

'Is that why you left me?' Robin said, in a low voice, and put down her glass. 'Did it go out when we landed in London?'

He went over and knelt by her chair, resting his fingers on hers. She wasn't ready for it – seeing him again, touching him, the proximity. She thought back to the tree house and back to the hotel, how Yul kept asking if she was okay, if she was enjoying it, how he rested his head on her chest afterwards and told her she was beautiful, even though she didn't always feel it.

'Robin, no, never think that. I just had to. I didn't have a choice. I... I'm sorry. Really, I am. I never wanted to hurt you. That's one reason I invited you around tonight... to apologise.'

'But why ask me here if you still can't give a proper explanation?'

'I want to tell you, Robin, honestly, but—'

His phone rang and he sighed before standing up. Robin quietly left before he finished the call.

26

As soon as Robin could politely escape from the lounge, she dragged off her biker jacket and collapsed onto the bed. A pitter patter of paws followed her, and Hoover jumped up for her to scratch that patch behind his right ear that she'd come to know as his sweet spot. Her phone rang. Tara? They'd only spoken this morning.

'Are you free on Wednesday night?' She carried on talking but the more Tara spoke, the more vigorously Robin shook her head.

'We can't,' Robin said firmly.

'Why not? It's a charity fundraiser. Sophie has been one of my most loyal clients and this mental health charity is close to her heart. She came in for an appointment this afternoon in a right state, panicking that she's not sold nearly enough tickets, asking if I know anyone who'd be interested in going. I would take Prisha but she can't change her shift at such late notice.'

'But we're too—'

'Don't say it.'

'But we are. You and me, at an eighties fancy dress bash, out clubbing in Manchester like we did over thirty years ago?'

'Why don't you invite Amber?'

'You're joking. She'd never agree to a night out with her mum.'

'How do you know? I'd love to meet her, Robin. You know what youngsters are like, the prospect of free drinks is always a pull.'

It would take a lot more than that.

'And we don't have to dance. I'd be happy to sit and chat and we can leave after a couple of hours. I just thought it would be fun... you'll be gone back to London in a few weeks, I'd like to make the most of you being up here.'

The sense of dejection Robin had felt after seeing Yul diminished as she relished Tara's welcoming sentiment.

'I understand if you don't want to, honestly, Robin, no pressure, I'm going to buy tickets anyway. I can always make up some excuse for not turning up.'

'I'll ask Amber, but I'm not promising anything.'

Robin put down her phone and went onto Facebook. Tara had accepted her friend request and she flicked through her posts and photo albums and the years of her life Robin had missed – the bustling, neon nights of her twenties, the countryside walks and meals out as she got older, the posts about her Reiki, acupuncture and crystal healing. She felt that sense of homesickness inside, for not being there. Wherever Tara was, whatever she was doing, the colourful hairstyle and bold smile of her teen years stayed the same.

Then Robin scrolled through her own page, wondering what Tara would see. Compared to her natural shots, Robin's looked staged with the careful choice of clothes and symmetrical shots of food. She'd always got Amber to smile for the camera and make sure her hair was off her face. Todd would stand with his arm around Robin and in the last few years they'd smile wider for the camera than they ever did for each other. A tide of heat swept across her body, as if she'd somehow let herself down. She'd projected a filtered image of her life that reflected a safety zone she'd escaped into, after the drama of running away. For Todd, that safety zone really was life at its best whereas increasingly, for her, it felt fake. She shuffled on the mattress, finding it harder to get comfortable the more she thought about how she'd never actually explained that to him.

Robin brought up his page, sat more upright and gave a gasp. Hoover butted his head against her, not wanting the scratching to stop. Two days ago, he'd posted a photo of himself with an arm around a woman. She wore a simple anorak, her red hair was windswept and she looked around Robin's age.

She felt a jab of something unpleasant. Did he buy her little gifts? Leave work early so that they could go out?

Months before their divorce, she'd known for sure that Todd could sense her distance. She'd tried so hard when Amber was tiny to keep the magic alive, baking his favourite treats, suggesting early nights, but as the years passed the gestures weren't reciprocated, the flowers, chocolates and love notes all disappeared. It reached the point where he only said *love you* if she said it first, and his ambition to grow his software business often meant cancelling date nights she'd planned. In the end, Robin gave up. He'd carried on as he always had, working all hours, doing odd bits of DIY, half-heartedly watching her favourite dance show, convinced an American Smooth was a type of coffee. But sometimes she knew he could sense her distance. She'd catch him looking at her as if she were a computer programme he no longer understood.

She studied the photo again. Did Amber know? Yes, she'd

liked the photo. She studied Todd. That gilet jacket was new, he looked slimmer, younger. The shadows under his eyes had disappeared and there was a glow about him.

Robin glanced at her watch – it was almost nine o'clock. Uncle Ralph didn't like his lights off much before eleven as he always had trouble dropping off. She shuffled up on the pillows and dialled his number.

'Robin?'

'How are you doing, Uncle Ralph?'

'This is a nice surprise, gal. So tell me, did my little brother beat you with the second clue, on Thursday? Tell me all about it.'

She gave him a cheerful version but whilst Dad might have been good with words, Uncle Ralph had always been gifted for reading behind them.

'It's still so difficult between you and Faye?'

'Could be better,' she said, her voice sounding full.

'How's it going with Yul?'

'Up and down. Him leaving London all those years ago, without an explanation... it's harder to forget than I thought.'

'He was only sixteen. You two were in a right pickle. He seemed like a good lad to me.'

He did? She'd always got the impression her uncle never approved of him.

Hoover stretched, got to his feet and jumped off the bed. After they said goodbye, Robin went over to the curtains and looked out. Uncle Ralph had become more sentimental with age but always had been a man who demonstrated his feelings. Dad was the same, resting his head on her lap if she was watching Saturday morning telly, exhausted from another week laying bricks and plastering but looking as if he couldn't be happier. The brothers' affectionate manner must have come from her grandmother. In her last years, Grandy would phone both Dad and Uncle Ralph every night, simply to say *love you, sleep tight* before ringing off. Faye would wrinkle her nose and Robin understood her reaction better now that she'd told her more about her own mother.

A sense of urgency was growing in Robin. They needed to do all the clues, in the hope that each one would explain more of Faye's past. It was as if, all these years, she and Faye had been playing chess, trying to work out each other's moves but never quite able to, neither of them achieving a checkmate. Yet now Robin was beginning to understand the strategy of her mother's game, where the thinking came from, why she'd defend herself or go on the attack.

And why, so often, what they ended up with was a resentful, painful stalemate. A stalemate that needed to be broken. Robin wanted to start the next clue right this minute because when she'd come up to Stonedale she had never imagined that the trip might result in a different, better relationship with Faye. But now...?

She headed downstairs to make a cup of tea, Faye was holding a pen, texting on her phone. She leant on her magazine.

'Found another mistake?' asked Robin.

'Yes. An obvious one, I'm surprised Julian missed it. A cross-word clue asks what you call a person who stays in hospital whilst being treated... The only word that fits is *impatient*.'

27

Robin and Faye came out of their rooms at the same time. Faye wore the embroidered gloves Robin had bought and the new checked scarf. Robin went to help Faye down the stairs but she shook her head. She studied Amber as they stood in the hallway, trying not to stare at her red, swollen eyes. They had been a regular feature every morning that week. Robin had rung Todd after breakfast, keeping him up-to-date about their daughter's wellbeing. He said he'd call Amber later. Robin took the dog lead as they went outside and stopped by the front gate, where she zipped her jacket up, right to the top. Amber opened the scroll and just the sight of it made Robin forget her concern about the darkening sky.

Amber cleared her throat before reading the clue.

'You can't shop here,
Or stop for a beer,
But you could in the old days,
Before a rebuilding phase.
The secrets beneath me that cure,

Add to my allure.
To shine a light on my shape,
I'm tall, dark and handsome – you might gape.
Give me an answer, do,
I know you've got it in you.

'So the first bit is referring to a shopping area that isn't here any more, right?' Amber's eyebrows knitted together. 'The village centre could do with being bigger, if anything. Why would any of it have been closed down?'

Faye straightened her hat, using her good hand on one side and then the other. She'd not moaned once about the cast since Robin arrived two weeks ago, not a single complaint about how inconvenient it must have been for eating or sleeping. Robin averted her eyes, thinking how good Faye was at hiding things. For the first time she considered that maybe, despite appearances, Faye might not have been happy with their rift.

Faye explained how the village used to be more scattered, with shops and pubs dotted throughout what was now a residential estate to the right, if you turned just before the church. It was hit during an air raid in the Second World War, and that was another reason Stonedale was a Thankful Village, as no one died. The bombs dropped at night onto a cluster of shops and a factory. The couple she and Dad bought the house from told them the whole area was redeveloped in the fifties and that's when the high street was made the focus of the village.

They walked towards the church and Faye smiled at an elderly couple. The man patted Hoover, who tried to tug off his glove as a thank you. Then the three women turned right and eventually came to a modest field with scruffy bushes by the fence and a farm-like smell. Crows flew overhead and settled in a tree near to where a few cows grazed.

On from this was the residential area, Yul's parents had lived there. Robin had skipped along this road many a time, jumping in the air to touch the leaves on overhanging branches. Horses used to roam in that field and she'd sneak out a carrot, feeding it to them with her palm stretched flat just as Yul showed her.

'Do you want to stop for a moment?' Robin asked Faye as they reached the first road and Hoover strained at the lead, sniffing around the bottom of a litter bin.

'Why, are you tired?'

'The answer to this clue is *tall, dark and handsome*,' said Amber, quickly. 'Is there another statue in Stonedale, of a man perhaps?'

Faye shivered as a rumble sounded in the distance. 'No. The war memorial is the only one, nice as it would be to have a handsome statue of someone like Dean Martin. I always thought how debonair he looked in his suits, and smoking. Sadly, there's nothing in Stonedale that fits the riddle's description.'

Hoover gave her a wounded glare, sitting on the pavement in his smart new jumper, a lollipop stick hanging from his mouth.

'So what about *the secrets beneath me that cure*, then, does that make sense?' asked Amber, having swiftly removed Hoover's find. 'The answer to that should lead us to the handsome object.'

Faye stopped, then carried on walking, then stopped once more.

'A long time ago, a few years after your granddad died, the vicar asked if I'd consider making visits to one of his parishioners, Joan. She'd recently lost her husband and used to work as a florist. He knew I once did flower-arranging at the Cathedral and thought we'd have common ground. He said she wasn't as strong as me. I saw through the flattery but decided to do my bit.'

She did?

'Did you become friends?' asked Robin and she pulled Hoover to the side as a woman jogged past.

'Yes, once a week we'd meet in Tearoom 1960 for a scone and cup of tea. The friendship was good for me too. I expect the vicar knew that, crafty so-and-so. But then she got cancer.' She leant on Amber's arm. 'Joan lived a couple of streets away from here. They'd had an extension built once and the builder found loads of old pharmacy bottles underneath their back patio. Other neighbours had found the odd one in their gardens over the years and reckoned several of the houses, along that road, had been built on the grounds of an old pharmacy. When Joan explained all this it reminded me that Alan knew about it, one of his builder friends had built her extension. I wonder if that's what Alan was referring to, in this clue.'

'Well done, Gran, you're acing it!'

Faye and Robin exchanged a little smile.

'What was the name of her road?' Amber continued.

'Highfield Avenue,' replied Faye.

The road after that was Green Lane where Yul used to live and sometimes he and Robin had cut down Highfield Avenue instead and gone around at the bottom, just to make their time together last that bit longer. They had a tiny garden, but his parents had made it into a little corner of heaven, as they called it, with a barbecue area and hammock. Robin and Yul clambered into it together once and the ties snapped. She'd braced herself, waiting for his mum to get angry, but she'd laughed and offered to run Robin's blouse through the wash to get rid of a grass stain.

They turned down Highfield Avenue. The houses along this road weren't as uniform as the rest of Stonedale's terraces, some had porches, others a scrap of front garden, a couple had bay windows and one Georgian. They came to the end and a drop of rain fell against Robin's cheek. She stared at the house on the corner. The garden was large and curved around the side but nothing standout. She didn't know why but the sight of a big tree, in the lawn, made her stop and stare.

'Tall, dark and handsome.' Amber sighed. 'Granddad's got me – unless he's been tricky again. Let's study the words of the clue close up and see if any have a double meaning.'

Robin looked over her shoulder at his writing. '*Shine a light on... you might gape...* How about gape as in its other meaning... Faye, has there ever been a sinkhole appear in this area or... a house knocked down... what about something to do with that air raid, did it leave a crater in the road?' Rain fell lightly now. They needed to get this clue finished.

'No, but shine a light... Alan had used that wording before, as part of a clue about a streetlamp.' She looked back up the street. 'Streetlamps are tall but here they are all standard grey so not dark, and nowt but functional. I wouldn't call them handsome.'

A snapshot from the past cut through Robin and the answer to the clue popped into her head.

She stepped back and her hand flew to her chest, thunder rolled across the sky more loudly.

'What's wrong, Mum?' Amber asked.

'Nothing.'

'Something's clearly the matter.' Faye pushed her glasses up her nose.

Robin rubbed her chest. 'I... I think I've got indigestion. That'll teach me to wolf down breakfast.'

'I didn't think you ate it that quickly,' Faye said in a sharp tone.

'It must be the approaching storm.' Amber glanced at both

of their faces. 'Come on, let's go to Tearoom 1960, I've heard so much about it. Hopefully this will just be a quick shower.'

'You aren't telling us something, Robin,' said Faye stiffly as thunder rumbled again.

'That's rich coming from you,' snapped Robin before she could stop herself. 'Just leave it.' She started walking back up the road.

Faye's mouth fell open. 'Do you think it's been easy for me to share, about my mother, about how hard things were? It's not me holding back, I've opened up.'

Robin ground to a halt.

Faye's arm waved around in the air. 'Perhaps this hunt is a stupid idea.'

Robin faced her. 'Don't say that. It's what Dad wanted.'

'But Alan's six feet under. This hunt should have stayed buried with him. There's no treasure at the end of it, it won't bring him back, all we're looking for is a silly anagram and even then we might not be able to work it out. And God only knows what we're doing out in a storm.' She stalked past Robin. Hoover tugged at the lead, wanting to follow her.

'Wait, I—'

Faye turned around and winced, patches of water soaking through her cape. 'I never asked you to move back to Stonedale.'

'I know it must be hard after all these years to—'

'You've no idea.'

Robin's legs felt shaky. 'It's not been easy for me either.'

'What, catching up with Jason, and now Tara? Maybe that's all you really came up for.' Faye pursed her lips. 'Well, it's an embarrassment, I can tell you, watching a middle-aged woman dress up like she used to decades ago, in that ridiculous leather jacket that's seen better days, in shoulder pads and bright colours that belong firmly to the last millennium.'

Robin flinched as if her words were lightning.

'Look, let's get inside,' said Amber, but Faye didn't seem to hear her.

'It's time you stopped this indulgent behaviour, Robin; you've run away from your marriage and what about your job? Oh yes, Amber mentioned you'd lost it – there you are again, holding back. You've run away just like you did when you were sixteen. I guess you saw me as easy pickings, free lodgings until you showed some mettle and got yourself sorted, is that why you didn't tell me yourself?'

'Gran. That's not fair,' Amber said and hovered between them, appearing unsure of which way to step.

'You don't know the full story about back then or now,' Robin said, trying to keep her voice steady, despite her pulse racing in time with the torrents of rain. Did Faye really think so little of her?

'I know enough, that you believe life owes you something. Well, guess what? That's not true and, if nothing else, I'm grateful for my mother drilling that into me.'

Despite the icy wind, a sense of humiliation burnt through Robin.

Faye shook her head. 'Just go, Robin, leave again, get a job, get your own life!' A clap of thunder reverberated across the estate and she grasped her ribs.

Amber gaped and hesitated a second.

'I'd better follow Gran, this storm's getting worse...' She raised her eyebrows and looked at Robin.

Robin gave an abrupt nod and watched them disappear out of view.

Robin Wilson,
16 Parade Row,
Stonedale,
Greater Manchester
June 1987

Dear Debbie,

MY TEACHER LAUGHED AT ME.

I feel a right idiot. Last week the teacher went around the class asking us what we wanted to do when we left school. When it was my turn I said be a pop star, my best friend and I are always singing our favourite songs in my bedroom, and I reckon we could be just like Pepsi and Shirlie, the backing vocalists for Wham! But she laughed and said that wasn't a proper job. Everyone joined in. The other girls dream of being air hostesses, beauty therapists or veterinary nurses, but I just want to be on Top of the Pops. Am I being stupid?

Robin, age 14

Girl's Scene
41 Gover Street,
London

Dear Robin,

Your teacher shouldn't have laughed at you, Robin, and I suspect your classmates only joined in because they felt they should. But she does have a point. For every singer on television there are hundreds who never make it. You can't expect your mum and dad to help you out with bills whilst you try your luck. Instead, why not think about a job that uses your favourite subject at school? Or you could go on to college.

Carry on singing with your friend, it's good to have hobbies, and who knows, one day you might take it more seriously and get lessons. But keep your feet firmly on the ground until then!

Best wishes,

Debbie

28

Robin burst into Brynner's Books and a customer stopped browsing. The underlying musty smell of secondhand books somehow made her feel safer. Strands of sodden hair stuck to the side of her face as she headed straight past and stood in front of a row of crime books in the next section, knocking over a low display table. The books on it fell over with a loud slap. Death, Lies, Hidden, Secrets, her vision was almost too blurred to read their titles. Footsteps came out of the staff room.

'Robin? I wasn't expecting to see you here.'

A strong arm curled around her shoulders and led her into the staff room and up to Yul's flat. He nudged her to sit down on the sofa before he switched on the kettle. She sat, staring vacantly at his DVD collection.

'Robin?'

He was sitting next to her now. Two steaming drinks and an open packet of biscuits lay on the coffee table. Yul pointed. 'Have one of these. A sugar hit might help.'

Robin ate one. Then another. On her fourth he put his hand over hers.

'I didn't say you should get high.'

She sniffed.

'What's happened? Want to talk about it?'

She shook her head vigorously. Rain flicked across the table's surface. He fetched a clean towel. Robin rubbed her hair half-heartedly.

'Sorry. I didn't know where else to go.' She put down the towel and sipped the coffee. She glanced down at her biker jacket. Faye thought she looked ridiculous. Robin pressed her hand against it, tough, she'd be wearing it tomorrow, and the day after. 'I was beginning to think Faye might have missed me all this time, but now I know for sure she didn't, not even for a second.' And why should she? Robin hadn't missed her; those thoughts in the middle of the night she'd had, over the years, about visiting Stonedale were practically dreams and didn't count. But she *had* missed the idea of a more approachable mother. One she could ring when Amber had colic, or when things with Todd became difficult.

'I never realised how much I missed you until you came back,' Yul said quietly.

'Really?' She croaked. 'Faye can't wait for me to leave.'

'I'm sure that's not true.'

'She thinks I'm a joke. I thought we'd become closer.'

'How?'

'We've shared a few looks, mostly over Amber, little personal exchanges that never used to happen. And I've learnt more about her past. She even ate my quiche.'

Robin caught his eye and couldn't help laughing as she wiped away tears.

He shuffled up and lifted her chin. 'Remember all that Buddhist stuff Tara used to tell us, on mindfulness, acceptance, not attaching to the bad or good? What she said made a lot more sense to me, as I got older. She talked about insults once and how she was able to ignore school bullies instead of getting upset. She said insults are owned by the person giving them, a person who's usually damaged.'

'Faye should have my back, she's my mum.'

'But that's not her whole identity. Talk to her, Robin.'

'But now that I'm a mother myself it's even harder to under-stand the way she rejected me.' Her voice broke. 'There is so much I don't understand about the past, like why my opinions or grades, or the things I did to impress her were never good enough, like why you left me in London after... everything.'

'I never left you in my heart.'

Robin's stomach flipped as he took her hand and led her to... the door. He gave her a hug. The storm had passed.

'Talk to your mum. I'm here for you now, Robin, and I'm not going anywhere.'

She stared into his face, stared at those lips and found herself on tiptoe, unable to fight the urge to press her mouth against his. He jolted a second as her body melted into his. What was she doing? Kissing an ex-boyfriend wasn't going to make anything better. She pulled away and hurried downstairs, past the coffee machine and out into the winter chill, hurrying up the high street before he could catch her up.

Robin went straight upstairs to the spare room, lay on her bed and stared at her phone.

The signal between her and Faye was so poor, that even taking the conversation outside hadn't improved it.

* * *

Someone knocked at her bedroom door. Robin sat up, against the pillows. Amber came in, carrying a plate, and Robin realised how hungry she was, it was mid-afternoon now. Amber put the plate on the bedside table. She sat down on the bed.

'My landlord has got in touch. He's releasing us from our contract. The repairs are going to take much longer than was first thought.'

Robin shifted uneasily.

'And before you reach for your phone, the accommodation office has rung. They've offered me a hotel room again, as a temporary fix. I said I was managing. I've got a viewing this Friday, a room has become available in another house. One of the tenants is going home on Thursday... If I don't like it, I'm going home. If we aren't doing the treasure hunt, there's even less point in me staying in Manchester.' She shrugged. 'After the way Gran's been with you... we could travel back to London together.'

'But you can't... your lectures... you're loving them.'

'Lectures are great – until you find yourself sitting on your own, with no one to go for a coffee with afterwards,' she snapped.

Robin bit the inside of her cheek. *Just listen.*

'I'm this close to leaving right now.' Amber made a circle with her thumb and finger and left a small gap between them. 'Dad rang this afternoon, said you two had spoken and he thinks it's a good idea, me sticking it out as long as I feel able. But I can't promise anything if I don't like this new house.' She folded her arms. 'I told him that too.'

'What did he say?'

'That things have a funny way of working themselves out.'

The two of them exchanged glances. Robin wondered if Amber was thinking the same thing... that Todd's answer hadn't applied to saving their marriage.

'Okay,' said Robin, 'well, there's your friends' party coming up next week. Maybe things will work themselves out, like your dad says.'

'They're just a bunch of people off my course,' Amber muttered. She traced an outline of a flower on the duvet. 'You know... you shouldn't have to put up with the way Gran speaks to you,' she said eventually. 'It was horrible, what she said today. I think your old clothes really suit you.'

Robin's chest glowed.

'Look, think about it, Mum. We've both got jobs to find. We both need to get on with our futures. I'm sure you could arrange for a carer to come in. I'm really liking it, getting to know Gran, she... she's kind of funny, you know, and easy to talk to, but when it comes to you and her... maybe some things just aren't meant to be.' She stood up. 'If it's any consolation she isn't talking, a guilty conscience, I reckon.'

Robin ate whilst sitting on her bed. She'd heard crying coming from the loft the previous night when she'd got up to go to the bathroom. It had taken all her strength not to go up the ladder, not to wrap Amber in her arms. Yet despite the sense Amber must have been feeling, of her life falling apart, right now she had sounded so... together. And she'd made sure Faye got home, had prepared food, and Robin had noticed all the little ways she'd tried to divert disagreements between her and her mother.

Amber was a beautiful, strong, capable woman – and Robin was her mum. Robin sat up taller.

After the meal she untangled her hair and sat looking in the oval dressing table mirror. Robin owed it to Dad to make sure this treasure hunt was completed, and to Amber who might just stay around longer with her granddad's clues to fathom out, and Robin couldn't face waking up to a bad atmosphere tomorrow, that wouldn't be fair on anyone. She sighed. Faye was right, she'd started to open up, Robin owed her the same.

Robin strode into the lounge and Amber took her plate into the kitchen. She sat on the chaise longue. Faye looked all of her seventy-eight years, her small frame sitting lost in the armchair.

'You're right,' Robin said. 'I'm sorry, for our argument. I do want things to be better, easier, between us.'

Faye didn't look at her.

'We can work out this clue, all together. You see, the thing I recalled, I haven't thought about it for years but—'

'I think it's best we just leave things as they are,' Faye said, without looking at Robin. 'But... I am sorry about raising my voice. Walking off. I shouldn't have behaved like that.'

Faye turned the television up.

29

'Are you sure you want to come?' Robin looked at her watch, it was seven o'clock. They'd agreed to meet Tara at nine, at Piccadilly station.

'Yes, I'm hoping to strike lucky, there's nothing I like more than a guy in a fluorescent headband and legwarmers.' Amber stood in front of the wardrobe. She'd already thrown a silver sequinned jacket on the bed. 'And I haven't got uni tomorrow. Now the hunt's off, I'll have the whole day to recover and get my studies done.' Her voice took on an edge. 'If that's what you're worried about, perhaps I should stay in.'

'That hadn't crossed my mind,' said Robin, talking to the back of Amber's head. 'I've been so impressed, love, with how you've gone about your course. I'm not sure I'd have got the work-relax balance right at your age. I told your dad as much, this morning.'

'You rang him again?'

Robin couldn't help herself, curious to see if he'd mention his new girlfriend. He didn't.

Amber continued to tug out various items of clothing and lay them on the bed, a green blouse with tassles, a black vinyl coat and long pencil skirt, also, a white mini dress with shoulder pads, sheer polka dot sleeves and luminous splashes across the front. They rummaged amongst the old accessories and found long sleeved white evening gloves and a faux leather corset belt. Everything in the eighties was oversized, from jackets to hair and necklaces, in direct contrast to Robin's minimalist style since leaving Manchester and Amber's no-nonsense clothes.

'I can't wear the black vinyl coat over an outfit, Tara would accuse me of chickening out.'

Despite herself, Amber grinned, daring Robin to wear the fishnet tights.

'We could get a taxi to Piccadilly, if you wanted to avoid the train. Tara would never know.'

'But *I would*,' Robin said, she stripped off and fitted on the mini dress and put on the wide corset belt, not expecting it to fit. Amber helped her do it up. The front buckles still did up thanks to her years of a strict gym routine. Amber hung a chunky gold chain around Robin's neck and insisted a large bow would look perfect in her hair. She gazed, open-mouthed, as Robin back-combed it first.

'That's going to kill its condition, Mum.'

'Just you wait until I spray it,' she said. 'My dad used to pop in to borrow my can if he and Faye were going out, wanting to look his best.'

'He really loved Gran, didn't he?'

'Yes.'

'Then she can't be all bad,' said Amber and pulled on the tassled green top.

Robin misdirected the spray and rubbed her eyes.

Amber slipped into the silver sequinned jacket, then she and Robin made up each other's faces with pearlised lipstick and shimmery eyeshadow. So different to Amber's usual look when she got all dressed up, with the subtle shades of brown and beige and cheek highlighter Robin wouldn't have known how to use at her age. Amber found a small crossbody handbag, Robin swooped upon a mini rucksack. They went into the lounge to say goodbye.

'Have you got everything you need?' Robin asked.

Faye studied the two of them. 'I'll be fine. Don't forget your key, I sleep poorly enough as it is, without having to get up to let you in.' During the last two days Faye had started to talk to Robin again. She'd even apologised once more, saying her comment about Robin being an embarrassment was said in the heat of the moment, that it was nice to see her dress up in bright colours.

During the train journey, people stared at the clothes and big hair. Robin thought Amber might not want to be seen going on a night out with her mum, but she realised she'd under-estimated her self-assured daughter who strolled to the carriage's doors as they pulled into Piccadilly. Tara was easy to spot, walking towards them in a gold bodice with a cone bra, and tight black, ripped jeans. For a split second they were back in 1989, covered in goose bumps in the middle of winter, not wanting thick anoraks to hide their fashionable outfits, Robin excited for an evening away from talk of O levels and jobs, from growing up and responsibilities. A moment of awkwardness hung in the air before they hugged.

'This is Amber,' Robin said.

'I've already heard so much about you,' said Tara.

Amber gave Robin a sideways look. 'Is that good?'

'If your maths is as brilliant as your mum says, I need you to do my books.'

Despite the November chill they headed to Deansgate on foot. It only took twenty minutes and meant Robin and Tara could reminisce about favourite haunts along the way, like the gaudy fashion shop that sold everything for five pounds and the burger bar that used a tasty dill pickle. Several bars already had Christmas trees up and fairy lights in the windows, they'd have been so excited years ago, looking forward to the festive pop videos. Amber also pointed out places she'd visited with friends and couldn't believe going out for Lattes wasn't a thing in their day. They walked past an escape room she'd been to with her housemates, right at the beginning when she was hoping they'd become best friends.

Finally, they reached the club and the beat of disco music led them to the queue. They stood in line underneath a banner advertising the mental health charity Tara's client supported. Robin relaxed as they merged with the crowd who wore Michael Jackson military jackets, neon tights and T-shirts, sweat bands or Crocodile Dundee hats. She spotted Freddie Mercury moustaches and Elton John glasses. The people waiting to get in were of all ages. The ticket sales must have been better than Tara had predicted.

Gratefully Robin entered the warm club. There were mirrors everywhere that complemented the silver metal decor, vintage film set spotlights hung across the ceiling and shot out purple hues. She bumped into a man wearing a punk Mohican wig and walking unsteadily. Tara waved to Sophie, the client she'd bought tickets from, and went over for a quick chat.

Tara came back and suggested they get a drink. They waited for ages behind a couple of rows of people, the smell of cologne and hairspray everywhere, until Amber stepped forwards and waved at the barman. Robin was about to order three pina coladas when an old favourite stood out on the nearby themed drinks menu. A fuzzy navel – a cocktail of peach schnaps and orange juice. They found one of the high round bar tables unoccupied by the far wall under a piece of art, a painted pair of purple lips. They put down their drinks before clambering up onto the bar stools. Robin had fallen off one, once, and Yul had had to give her a piggyback out of the club.

'Are we suffering a midlife crisis?' Robin asked and raised her glass.

'It's called fun,' said Amber.

'Spot on,' said Tara, 'and that's important.'

Robin stared at the orange liquid. 'Okay, so how about down in one?'

Amber glanced her way, as if she were a stranger.

They removed the straws. Robin glugged it back and they sucked on the orange wedge from the rim afterwards, just like they always used to. A Culture Club song came on. Tara grabbed her hand, and Robin clutched Amber's. The two of them led Robin onto the dance floor and the DJ shouted about sexy sounds, she felt ridiculous and simply side-stepped her feet, one two, one two, marvelling at the way Amber twisted and turned. Yet eventually, with the dim lights, the bustling bodies and the psychedelic floor colours, with the music's beat pulsating through her chest, as the second verse played out an unexpected surge of energy infused her. She began to stop thinking about everyone else, hips twisting, arms criss-crossing, and by the time they got to the second chorus, she and Tara were mirroring each other, as they always did. Duran Duran took over and Robin and Tara sang along, Robin's voice and body remembering words and moves she thought she'd forgotten a long time ago.

They went to the bar and ordered another round of fuzzy navels.

Tara pulled a face after a sip. 'If I'm being honest, this is disgusting, like those coke floats – why did we used to order these?'

'Because schnapps sounded exotic and we thought drinking this made us look cultured.'

'Funny, isn't it, I couldn't give a pig's arse about people's opinion of me, these days. That's one huge advantage to getting older, isn't it?'

Robin sucked harder.

'Right?'

'I'm not sure. Since I left I've spent so long trying to... you're going to think me pathetic.' Her voice petered out and the two others both stopped drinking.

Tara put down her glass. 'I promise not to laugh.'

'Me too,' said Amber.

'I've tried to be upstanding, to fit in, because I thought that would make life easier, happier, because me being me, in the end... it didn't work out so well, did it?'

'Oh, chickie... that wasn't you, it was life,' said Tara. 'Shit happens to everyone and it doesn't make you a bad person. You were amazing, blazing, a beacon of light in the dull school day. I think that's why it hurt so much when you left, there was no one around to take your place. The cliques were full of clones, you were never like them, you never aspired to be in with the popular girls and that gave me the strength to follow my own path.'

Robin noticed that Amber was looking at Tara intently, listening to every word.

'But that's how I felt about you, with your beliefs, your

incense and healing crystals, your views on spirituality... you made me want to be a better person.'

Apart from with Faye. Tara said sometimes kindness towards others could harm you and with her mother it always did. Once she bought Faye a bunch of daffodils in the village. She'd seen a mum and daughter sitting in Tearoom 1960, sharing an ice cream, and felt overwhelmed by a sense of longing. But when she gave them to her, Faye had just asked what Robin had done wrong now.

'I've lived with Gran for just a matter of days,' said Amber. 'I've seen what she's like with you. I think Tara's right.' She took the orange wedge from the rim of her glass and sucked. 'I don't know how I would have managed if I'd had a mum like that.'

Robin gave her a slight nod. She gave one back. The Human League came on and Tara pulled Robin off the stool, they shouted the lyrics at each other as they headed back to the dance floor with Amber. A romantic ballad came on next, Robin closed her eyes and swayed, living for nothing but the moment. *It felt right, it felt like... me.* When she opened them three young men were dancing alongside them. Robin was twice their age, and she immediately thought it wasn't appropriate.

But appropriate for what? Her old life, that's what, where the most important words were *should* and *ought*. Her confidence grew as another funky track came on. Who was she to complain if good-looking blokes wanted to dance? They started clapping, their hands in time to a Wham! song and one of the men, in a black trilby, grabbed Robin's hand and twirled her around. She hadn't expected that.

'Mum, let me buy you two a more modern cocktail that's actually drinkable,' Amber suggested, shouting over the noise.

'A mother and daughter combo? Lay-deez, pleased to meet you,' said the man Robin had been dancing with and he put his arms around both their shoulders. Before she had a chance to reply Amber told him to get lost and guided Robin away from the dance floor.

'Is that why you agreed to this night out?' she hissed. 'To find a toyboy?'

30

'I'll get the drinks,' said Tara and she strutted off in time to the music, still clapping her hands, in her flamboyant outfit. Robin and Amber sat down at a quieter area, near the toilets. Why had she deprived herself of so much freedom since running away from Stonedale?

'If you're that embarrassed, Amber, we can pretend we don't know each other, although I don't understand what the big deal is. I was only dancing.'

'Sure you wouldn't have shagged him?' asked Amber, starting to slur a little.

Robin gasped. 'Don't speak to me like that.'

Amber rolled her eyes and her shoulders sank.

'Is it so difficult to believe that your old mum just wanted to let her hair down for once? It's been such a hard couple of years, and the last few weeks haven't been easy either.'

'But you got what you wanted. You felt your marriage was over, but didn't have the guts to end it, Dad had to do it.' Amber's voice wavered. 'You spoilt everything.'

Robin looked at her daughter, the evening's fun having evaporated. Amber looked less in control and more like a confused teenager. Robin's tone became softer. 'Yes, one day I might meet someone else. I'm sorry, but your father and I aren't going to get back together. And he was right to end things.'

'You still can't give me any real explanation? You can still only say that the two of you grew apart?'

Robin gave a jolt, realising Amber must have felt like she did about Yul, him not explaining why he left London. So she thought hard, forming the words.

'I think... when the marriage became more... routine, over the years, when the initial romance and passion waned, I... it made me feel... that lack of attention... it sounds stupid but...'

Amber sat up straight. 'It reminded you of how your mum made you feel?' Robin bit her lip and nodded. Amber stared, her frown disappearing.

Tara arrived, breaking the intense atmosphere, with three cosmopolitans and a round of extra vodka shots. Amber's hand hovered over the table for a moment and then she slid over one of the shot glasses to Robin, who knocked it back. They talked about the letters of the treasure hunt worked out so far, and how Faye was refusing to continue.

'G and I... let's guess what the six-letter word would have been,' said Amber and she hiccoughed, not knowing that Robin secretly knew what the next letter was as well. 'How about... *guilty*. Perhaps the hunt holds a dark secret.'

Robin took a large mouthful of the cosmopolitan. She hadn't considered that the hunt might have revealed something she'd regret discovering about her mother or even her dad.

The 'Birdie Song' came on, and a tipsy Amber followed the others' moves, before spotting one of the girls who'd invited her to the party in halls. After hesitating, she headed off to say hello, whilst Robin sat down with Tara. She gave a big yawn. It was almost one. Had Faye managed to change into her nightdress on her own?

'Glad you came?' Tara asked.

'I've lost my hearing, ricked my back and that vodka has numbed my taste buds.' She gave a thumbs-up. 'I've had a great night.'

'Never forget, Robin, your needs are important,' Tara said, deadly serious, one word running into another as she swayed on her stool. 'How often, over the years, have you put yourself first?'

'Plenty of times, I mean… I'd get Todd to babysit whilst I went to the gym or out on a works do.'

Tara leant forwards. 'Babysit? He's her dad.'

'I did lay the groundwork for our marriage to end.'

'That's all you can think of?' Tara looked more awake for a moment.

'I've felt guilty enough about that.'

'Shit happens. You learn from it and move on.'

Robin had thought moving into her own flat would help her do that.

'Thanks, for still caring,' said Robin, head swimming now. 'I wish I could wave a magic wand and make things right between you and your dad.'

'That really would take a spell. He's coming into Manchester tomorrow on business, suggested we meet for coffee.' Tara gave a start as she almost slipped off her seat. 'Now and again, if he's in town, he texts to meet up. We don't get into a deep conversation. I reckon he only does it for Mum. I was upset when he said Prisha couldn't go to their party, but I'm over that.' In slow motion she punched the air. 'It's his problem, not mine, and no reflection on who I am.'

Robin digested this.

'So I'll be dropping by the party, just for an hour, to give

Mum and Dad their present. But afterwards, I'm going to sit them both down for a chat and tell them I won't be going to any more family events unless Prisha is invited.'

'Yul was only saying the other day how you've always been wise.'

'Please no, that makes me sound so boring, like our old maths teacher, what was he called?'

'Mr Noballs,' said Robin. She caught Tara's eye and they giggled.

'Ah yes, good old Nobles.' Tara fiddled with a drinks mat. 'Buddhists don't believe in good or bad behaviour, you know, they say we are either skilful or unskilful. So when Dad insults me... yes... *that*...' She shook herself. 'Am I making sense?'

'Please don't stop.' Robin needed to hear this.

'It really helps for me to think of Dad as being unskilful, rather than a bad person.'

What if Robin thought of Faye as unskilful instead? Suddenly those nasty comments, in the rain, didn't hurt quite so deeply.

Tara pushed the mat away too hard, and it shot off the edge of the table and onto the floor. A passing man in ripped jeans picked it up and gave it to Tara and winked. She and Robin giggled again as he walked off.

'Where was I...? Yes... I've thought more about your dad as I've got older,' said Tara. 'He handled things so well. He was...' She burped. 'Super skilful.'

A super dad.

'I'm sorry we haven't chatted more, the last few hours have flown,' Robin said, feeling woozy as the room spun a little. 'It's just that me and Amber—'

'I understand. I hope tonight helped.'

Robin eyed her closely. 'The turnout *was* excellent. Your

client must have somehow sold a lot of tickets at the very last minute.'

Tara looked at her phone. 'Is that the time?'

'You planned this, didn't you, a chance to get me and Amber talking?'

'You've drunk too much, lady, and now it's taxi time.' She slipped off the stool to go and find Amber, but Robin took her hand and squeezed it.

Feeling more awake in the cold air, Robin paced up and down by the taxi rank. Gratefully, she clambered into the next one that pulled up. She woke up in Parade Row after nodding off on Amber, who'd already paid the fare. Robin slammed the door shut as she climbed out, got caught off-balance and tripped over as the taxi drove away. Amber hauled her up and the harder they tried to be quiet the louder their laughs got. A light flicked on across the street in an upstairs bedroom. Someone stared out, and Robin took a bow. Amber was fiddling with the key in the lock and finally the door opened. A yapping and set of paws flew down the stairs.

'Shhh!' Robin said to Hoover and she carefully took him upstairs, switched on the landing light and shooed him back onto Faye's bed. She didn't wake up, the lace collar of her nightdress visible around her neck. Robin went back downstairs, welcomed into the kitchen by the steam of the kettle and the smell of the stew Faye would have heated up.

Amber slumped in a chair, eyes closed, cheek on top of her hands, on the tabletop.

'Sorry for being a bitch,' she slurred.

Robin bent over and kissed her head.

Robin Wilson,
16 Parade Row,
Stonedale,
Greater Manchester
September 1987

Dear Debbie,

   MY BOYFRIEND DOESN'T LIKE SPORT.

   I know your magazine is for girls but I'm hoping you don't mind me writing about a problem my boyfriend has. He doesn't like sport and the other boys are mean because he'd rather read in the library with me, at lunch, than kick a ball around. He says he doesn't care what they think but it must hurt him. My dad says we're all different and that he should just do what makes him happy, but the captain of the football team is in our class and the other day called him a poofter. I got so angry and swore at him but my boyfriend just rolled his eyes and called him an idiot. How can I make these nasty comments stop?

   Robin, age 15

Girl's Scene
41 Gover Street,
London

Dear Robin,

   That's excellent advice from your dad, Robin! At times we all feel as if we have to fit in, but the most important thing is to be yourself, like your boyfriend is. And some of those boys playing football outside, in the winter, would probably rather be indoors with you two!

It's great that you're so caring but it sounds as if your boyfriend's coping okay with the unkind comments, and that this might be more of a problem for you. Why don't you both have a chat with your teacher, or the librarian, about setting up a lunchtime reading club? That way he'll make lots of friends with the same interests and those football boys might just wish they knew more about books!

Best wishes,

Debbie

31

They sat in the kitchen in front of two black coffees, Amber's back to the cooker, Robin by the door. Robin had overslept and hurried into Faye's to help get her dressed but she was already downstairs in her slacks and jumper, so Robin went back to bed. It was almost ten and they'd both just woken up, after Hoover barked when Faye opened the front door to the postman. She came in and took out a frying pan. It clattered as she placed it on the hob and Amber and Robin both flinched.

'I'll make us all toast in a minute, Faye, if you like,' Robin said.

'Pfft. I ate two hours ago, and forget toast – fried kippers are what you both need.'

Amber pulled a face and took a large gulp of coffee. 'No offence, Gran, you're a star, but the thought of that makes me feel sick.'

Faye ducked her face and turned to the stove. Perhaps she hadn't heard. She held onto the oven door handle for a moment and Robin wondered if she still felt unsteady after her fall.

'No arguments,' Faye said. 'If it was good enough for your

granddad after a night on the town, it's good enough for you. I bet you've never even tried them.'

'I don't remember Dad ever getting drunk,' said Robin.

'You're right. He really enjoyed a pint or two and that was enough. But this one time his workmates laced his pint with vodka. I've never seen him so ill. So, kippers it is,' she said.

Robin exchanged a horrified look with Amber. She'd bought them for Faye and Blanche.

'But can you manage?' Robin asked. 'Honestly, toast will do.' Although after the storm, after everything Faye had said, Faye wanting to cook Robin's breakfast was progress.

'Very well, thank you,' she said crisply. 'It's time I started doing more for myself.'

'Right, so... are you sure you don't want to do the next clue... it is Thursday today?' Surely the fish represented a truce or was it nothing but a red herring?

Faye bristled and the pan clattered again.

Robin sighed to herself and gazed out of the window, head pounding. Full clouds hung low in the sky. The smell of melted butter rose into the air and the back of her throat constricted. It had been so long since she'd had a fried breakfast, it wasn't part of the regime she followed in London. Robin shook her head.

'What?' asked Amber, bits of hair sticking out, just like when she was a little girl and would stumble down to breakfast to wolf her bowl of cereal that she'd insist on eating dry, with a glass of milk on the side.

'Just thinking about those fuzzy navels. I'm glad you got to meet Tara.'

'I liked her.'

'How are you feeling now?'

'As if the Birdie Dance is taking place in my head.'

'Me too,' said Robin and she took another mouthful of coffee.

Faye dished up and put down two plates, along with several slices of white bread, and scrambled eggs on the side. Then she went to a kitchen drawer, rummaged for a moment and pulled out a small blue cardboard packet. Whilst she struggled to open it with one hand in plaster, Robin resisted the urge to ask if she needed help. Finally, she pulled out the silver contents and pushed out four tablets. She paused before putting two down in front of each of them.

Robin stared at the white discs. Paracetamol? Faye never used to help her recover after a night out as a teenager. She'd call upstairs that breakfast was ready at the usual eight o'clock and tell Robin off for slouching at the table. Robin knocked the tablets back with coffee and, following Amber's cue, tried a forkful of kipper. It tasted much better than it smelt. Faye made herself a cup of tea and sat down between them, even smiling when Amber told her about all the cocktails. Robin reached for her purse, which she'd left in her mini rucksack in the kitchen last night.

'Here.' She passed Amber a twenty-pound note. 'For the round you bought.'

'You don't have to—'

'You're a poor student, remember.'

Amber got up and yawned. 'You should have seen Mum fall over when we got out of the taxi, we couldn't stop laughing. Right, I'm going to have a long bath.' She put her empty plate in the sink and disappeared.

The skin around Faye's eyes had come out in red blotches.

'You okay?' Faye's chair scraped back as Robin spoke, but Robin put a hand on her shoulder. 'What is it?'

She gulped and her face crumpled. 'You and me... we never

had a single moment like that, did we? We never laughed together. We were supposed to, weren't we?' Faye pushed herself up and left the kitchen.

Robin stared after her. Yes, they were.

She tidied up and went through to the lounge. Faye was consulting her latest copy of *Word Weekly* and texting, seemingly composed once more.

'Contacting Julian again?'

'Yes, I'm doing the first wordsearch and there's a misleading positioning in the grid, nitpicking has been placed with a *K* in front of it.'

As Robin walked past Faye stretched out her good arm.

A twenty-pound note? 'What's that for?'

'A contribution towards spends last night.'

Robin stood stock still and Faye shook her arm. 'Are you going to take it or not?'

'But I can't—'

'You're not earning at the moment.'

'Um, right, thanks.' Robin reached out. She always used to pay for herself, thanks to a paper round and Dad subbing her earnings so that she could go to burger bars and concerts.

Faye's voice wavered as she spoke, still without meeting Robin's eye. 'I'm sorry that... that things weren't better between us; that... I wasn't more like the kind of mother you are.' She rolled her lips together and started texting Julian again.

* * *

Robin was still in a daze about Faye's apology, about the compliment, when she dropped off Blanche's evening meal later that afternoon. She'd left Amber and Faye once again playing dominoes. Robin went inside, welcomed by the pot pourri smell of her plug-in air freshener. She switched on the lights and drew the lounge curtains. Blanche wore an eggshell blue fleece that swamped her.

'Want me to make a brew before I go?'

'Love a duck, what are you trying to do, keep me on the loo all night?' said Blanche. 'No, just sit down for a minute.' She pointed to the sofa. 'So what's the latest with you and Faye? She cancelled coffee yesterday, said she wasn't in the mood. Is everything all right? Weren't things improving?'

'Oh, nothing, I'm sure it will blow over.'

'Blow over my elbow, now tell me the truth.' She jabbed her finger at the sofa and smiled.

Robin sat down and sighed. 'We had an argument. I didn't want to tell her something. There have been times when it's felt like we've made real progress, but because of the fallout she's declared the treasure hunt's over and won't let me try to explain, she's not bothered.'

'Of course she is, otherwise this wouldn't have happened.' Blanche jabbed her finger at Robin again. 'You need to be firm, flower. If you drift along with life you'll never get what you want, I've learnt that time and time again. You need to take control of the steering wheel.'

Drifting. That was *exactly* it, how Robin would describe the last thirty years, sailing with no ultimate destination, hugging the safety of the coastline; blending in instead of setting off on great adventures. She needed to feel the wind in her hair, the salt on her teeth, the swell of a wave that might throw her to a totally unexpected place...

Blanche flexed her swollen knuckles. 'My husband and I almost separated once. I'd become close to a patient, Ed, taking in his favourite bakes and staying past the end of my shift to read him books. He reminded me of my dad, you see, and I never got a chance to say goodbye to him. I knew something was up when Dennis started to switch off every time I mentioned Ed. What with his job taking him down to London every month, he got paranoid about how exactly I was spending those weekends. Ridiculous, honestly, I'd explained that Ed had dementia, but looking back, Dennis felt hurt. Even so, he should have trusted me.' She leant forwards. 'So I took matters into my own hands.'

'What did you do?'

Blanche had suggested they went out for a pub lunch one weekend and that she'd drive so that he could drink. Then she made out she'd left her purse at work and needed to drop in there on the way. She got him to go in with the excuse that there was a problem with the staffroom sink. Apparently Dennis was very handy with a plunger. As she led him through the building she took him to see Ed and he was confused as to who Blanche was. Once Dennis saw his mistake, she made sure he apologised for doubting her.

'In my job I had to be firm, dealing with confused residents, taking decisions for them, being responsible for their happiness. I knew them best and now and then had to fight their corner with the doctors or care home manager, like pointing out that current medication wasn't working or insisting that a room by the road was distressing because they'd been in a road accident. It's like the Adopt-A-Grannie scheme, I missed having people close to me in my life, so I did something about it.'

Drifting. Robin thought about the last couple of years and how she'd got up each day at exactly the same time and strictly rotated her breakfasts, how she'd gone into work always taking the same route, come home, watched her usual programmes on telly and been in bed by eleven. Her routines had acted like an almighty anchor.

And anchors were necessary when you'd reached your destination, but not before you'd even started your journey.

'Come here.' Blanche beckoned her over. Robin got up and Blanche put one of Robin's hands between hers. Blanche's felt rough and wrinkled but just as comforting as they'd always been. 'I still remember that gutsy young girl, who'd pilfer a warm brownie when she thought I wasn't looking.'

'Guilty as charged,' said Robin, and they smiled at each other.

'But these days you're giving in to Faye's moods and that won't get you anywhere, love, and I don't mean that nastily to your mum. She's a good friend. I... I think the world of her. That's why I want this sorted, for her good as much as yours.' She patted Robin's fingers. 'None of us are getting any younger. Sometimes it's hard for us women to squeeze out of life what we really want, even nowadays. I see it in couples I know, I read the papers. Taking charge, not taking any shit...' She looked Robin straight in the face 'They aren't seen as feminine qualities. Well, bugger that.

'You're an adult now, you make her listen, whatever it takes, you don't have to accept the way she's carrying on. That treasure hunt's all well and good but the important thing is to improve your relationship so that you can build on it in the future, when you're no longer living together. This is your one chance, Robin, to finally make things work with your mother. You need to be focused, with no other distractions. You've only got a few weeks left. Go for it, girl, you *can* make it happen.'

Robin went back to number sixteen and heard music coming from the loft, Amber's favourite K-Pop. She wondered how her student house viewing would go tomorrow. Robin spotted the scroll, discarded on the chaise longue. She picked it up and thought about what Blanche said. Hard as it was, she needed to get her priorities right and that might mean she had to play clever... not to trick Faye, not to deceive her, just to *take control of the steering wheel*. To take charge. Her thoughts raced as she came up with an idea. She turned to Faye.

'No point hanging onto this. Dad wouldn't want us falling out over a silly treasure hunt.' She screwed up the paper, hating seeing his handwriting, his last words to them, crushed into a tight ball, even if it was part of her plan.

32

Fired up by Blanche's words, Robin hadn't fallen asleep until the early hours on Thursday or Friday night. Finally she crawled out of bed Saturday morning to find Amber had gone out for a walk. She'd refused to talk about the house viewing she went on yesterday, just said the room was a good size. She still wasn't back by lunch. Robin resisted texting and decided she'd leave it a couple more hours. After she and Faye had eaten sandwiches, she nipped into the loft bedroom and smiled at Amber's clothes strewn across the floor. It smelt of bodyspray and stale hot chocolate. Robin stared at the Boy George poster and his defiant gaze. He and other eighties stars had inspired her to realise that happiness could lie on the periphery of a crowd, not just in the middle of it. The teenage Robin who'd think nothing of going out sporting The Cure's smeared lipstick look would never have played it safe like she'd done as an adult. With a flourish she pulled her phone out of her trouser pocket.

Hi Yul, I know it's late notice but fancy a meal out, tonight, my treat? Robin X

She put on a pair of her old giant hoop earrings, blew Boy George a kiss and went downstairs. Amber was back, sprawled on the chaise longue, boots still on, Hoover at her feet, tail wagging. She was eating peanut butter out of the jar, with a spoon. Every now and again she stuck her finger in and pointed down, letting Hoover lick it clean.

Faye wasn't even frowning.

'Everything okay?' asked Robin and sat down in the armchair, across from Faye.

Amber and Hoover carried on eating. Finally, she put the jar down in her lap. 'I was just telling Gran – I went over the bridge and for a walk through the woods, just thinking.' She took a deep breath. 'I've tried to be positive but there's no way around it – that house, yesterday, is even further away from the campus and Students' Union, and the three other people aren't freshers, they're in the third year, doing finals. There are rotas on the walls for everything, from emptying the bins to filling the dishwasher.' She sighed. 'They seemed okay but are hardly going to want to go out socialising and...' Her voice caught. 'We're not even doing the hunt, are we?'

'Your mother threw it out,' said Faye.

'Would it make any difference if I hadn't?' Robin said calmly.

Amber's shoulders sagged. 'It's just as well, then, that I've decided that I'm speaking to my personal tutor on Monday. I'm going to drop out.'

Robin looked down at her wrist and studied her watch, followed the long hand going round.

'Hasn't the accommodation office got anything else?'

'No. They said I was lucky to get that chance. There's just no point delaying the inevitable. I'm wasting time, racking up a loan, when I could be getting my job, starting to build a career. I feel like my life's on hold. University just isn't what I expected it to be, I came here as much for the people I'd meet as the studies. Everyone says uni should be about developing your character with the social side, it's not just about lectures. So don't try to change my mind.' Jaw set, she undid her coat. 'In fact, I'm going to start work on my CV this afternoon.'

Robin got up and moved to the chaise longue, next to Amber. 'You're sure about this? Looking back, I... I wish I'd fought harder for my dreams, not settled for working in an office, doing a job I didn't really like. I can see now that I could have worked it out and gone to university to study English, as I'd hoped to.' She paused, bracing herself for a sneer from Faye, but both she and Amber were simply focused on what Robin was saying. 'I couldn't have asked for more in terms of a daughter... and a husband, for most of our marriage, and a good father to you, Amber. But lately, since seeing my old room, I can't help thinking teenage Robin would be disappointed in me. I wouldn't want you to ever feel like that.'

'Mum, I've really thought this through.'

Amber reminded Robin of her sixteen-year-old self who could never have been talked out of running away from Stonedale.

'Okay. But if you ever change your mind, we'll sort it out. You could take a gap year, work during that, then perhaps reassess. Life never is a straight path and there's no shame in taking a diversion. You could always go to uni in the future, if you wanted.'

Amber stopped unbuttoning. 'I hadn't thought about that.'

'I can't say I'm happy, but it's your decision. I'll fully support you, Amber. Just let me know if I can help in any way.'

'Oh. Right.' She tilted her head. 'I mean... it's not like I haven't made an effort.'

'I've seen how tough it's been. And I've seen how tough you are. I'm very proud.'

Amber looked taken aback.

'Are you still going to that party tonight?' Robin asked. Faye hadn't turned the page of her magazine.

'Yes, I mean... I may as well, right?'

'You deserve a bit of fun, love, but if your CV can wait just a little longer, I'd like to visit where Dad's ashes have been scattered. The crematorium is about thirty minutes away, isn't it, Faye? I've not got long left in Stonedale if the consultant's happy to remove your cast in a few weeks. How about we go this afternoon?'

Amber nodded her head vigorously. 'That would be great. At least I'd feel I'd kind of got a little closer to Granddad.'

'What if it starts raining again?' asked Faye.

'There's not a cloud in the sky,' Robin said cheerily, and pointed out of the window.

'I don't visit as often as I'd like, in winter – the bus isn't the warmest and the service to get there is poor at the best of times.'

Wait, she visited regularly?

* * *

After settling Hoover in the lounge, Robin and Faye stood in the hallway. Amber came down and passed Robin a scarlet beret.

'I found this in one of the drawers. It goes with that lipstick of mine you've got on.' Tentatively she held it out. Robin put it on her head and adjusted the angle in the mirror, pulling down one side.

'I'm surprised it's still in one piece,' said Faye. 'You wore that most weekends for a while, said it made you feel French. Shame it didn't help your grades.'

'I got a B for the O level.' By the time her exam results came through she was living with Uncle Ralph. Faye never asked about them.

They stopped on the way to get petrol and pick up flowers. Robin was growing to love the pedestrian aspect of life in Stonedale and didn't miss the car or the buses and underground trains of her other life. The crematorium was at the top of the hill on the outskirts of a neighbouring town, with glossy black painted gates and matching barred metal fence all the way around. She steered up the sweeping gravel drive that seemed more suited to a mansion. She'd forgotten how the grand building, with its Roman pillars, didn't fit the understated look of the Peak District. Huge rhododendron bushes lined the way that must have looked magnificent in the spring. Robin parked up and Amber helped Faye out. They didn't bother with gloves, it was warmer today, and Faye pulled a printed map out of her pocket and gave it to Amber.

'Don't know why I always bring this. I know where Alan is. But you can lead if you want,' she said.

Robin passed the flowers to Faye, carnations like the ones Dad used to give her every week.

'This way,' said Amber as they passed the office. Robin tried not to look at the big chimney. A small group of mourners gathered outside the chapel. Inside the organ played a hymn, one she didn't recognise.

Robin had worn her big numbered T-shirt dress to Dad's funeral, the one he'd asked Maeve to make for her fourteenth birthday. Faye was furious, said it was disrespectful, that she should wear a more sombre outfit. Robin told her she wasn't dressing for the vicar or her friends, she was dressing for Dad, and everyone else and their opinions could do one. Robin glanced sideways as they walked past the gleaming black hearse.

It hadn't struck Robin to change clothes for the sake of her mother. But then why would she? Robin still felt a fleeting stab of rage at the way Faye had behaved, at what she did – or rather didn't.

The thing was... Faye didn't cry.

Not one tear.

Not when they left him cold, in the hospital, nor when the vicar visited, not at the funeral service nor the do afterwards. Her cheeks remained dry. And after the service she'd never looked back at the coffin, nor thought to leave a red rose or kiss the top of it, and she'd got to her feet as soon as the curtains closed, as if Dad's life had been a bad play and she didn't want to stay for an encore. There wasn't so much of a dab of a tissue when she told concerned neighbours at the door, or his colleagues over the phone. Uncle Ralph had cried great big snotty sobs as he'd held Robin tight, even though, at that point, they weren't close.

Instead, Faye worried what people thought of Robin's clothes. Something just as visible would have been more of a talking point. Her lack of tears somehow tarnished Dad. He deserved hair that turned white overnight, swollen eyes, obvious proof that she'd lost the love of her life, but her day-to-day ticked on as if nothing had happened – washing, eating, sleeping, working. If Robin sat at the table crying, during the days that followed, Faye would tell her to blow her nose and pull herself together.

Faye wouldn't talk about him either. Robin would start chatting about the treasure hunts or the car boot sales she and her dad had visited and Faye wouldn't reply. She never recounted anecdotes of her own, nor asked Robin how she was doing. So instead, Robin would sob into Yul's arms and binge on cake with Tara, she'd talk about her dad with them and *their* mothers.

'We turn left here and into the Gardens of Remembrance,' said Amber.

Robin followed them towards a huge, grassed expanse, divided by trees and benches into smaller sections. They walked down a narrow path that cut through an area called Coppice Garden, the borders around its edge filled with shrubs, each accompanied by a plaque.

Doris, much loved Mum and Wife, rest easy, sweetheart, 1924 – 2009.
   George, a friend to everyone, loved by all, 1933 – 1998.
   Sally, a wife missed every minute, every second of every day, 1963 – 2011.

They continued and Amber stopped at a place called Maple Patch. There was a bench by a Japanese maple tree. Robin gave Faye the flowers and she bent down and dropped the bouquet to the right of a plaque. Robin peered over it.

Alan Wilson, 1939–1989.

Anything briefer would have required the services of Alan Turing.

Tears sprung into her eyes and she crouched down, wiping a spray of soil off the metal. She inhaled the woody scent.

'Love you, Dad, miss you so much.' She left Amber and Faye talking and sat on the bench. Robin tugged the flask out of her small rucksack and the others joined her, Faye in the middle. Robin agreed with Amber it was a beautiful resting place, she smiled at an elderly man who limped past.

'Did Granddad like gardening as much as you, Gran?' Amber asked.

'No. But our different interests served us well in the pub quizzes. I knew about textiles because of work, plants, of course, novels and cooking, whereas he was a whizz when it came to antiques, buildings and obscure facts about all sorts of knick-knacks.' Her cheeks plumped up. 'We never ran out of conversation, you know, not like some couples.'

'And he kept up with pop music,' Robin said.

Faye nodded. 'My tastes are stuck in the forties and fifties, whereas Alan moved with the times. I could never understand why he'd watch *Top of the Pops* with you.'

They sat sipping their drinks, enjoying the winter sunshine, Robin finished hers first and stood up in front of them.

'Right...' She cleared her throat. 'That memory I was going to tell you, at the bottom of Highfield Avenue...' She crossed her fingers, hoping her plan came together.

33

Faye shook her head. 'This trip is supposed to be for your dad. I'm not listening to a word.'

'I'm afraid you haven't got much of a choice.' Robin delved into her pocket and pulled out the screwed up scroll and unfurled it. Amber gasped. 'You didn't think I was really going to let Dad down, did you, and throw this away? Like you said, Faye, there's no public transport from here. Go and sit in the office if you want, but I'll still be out here. I'm not leaving, not driving anywhere, not until we've sorted this out and agreed to carry on with the hunt tomorrow, a Sunday, as planned.'

'It can't do any harm just to hear her out, can it?' said Amber eagerly.

'Were you in on this, young lady?' Faye's eyes narrowed.

Amber shook her head. 'Please Gran, and I don't want to be late getting ready for this party and going into Manchester. Mum's ambushed me as much as you.'

For a couple of minutes all they heard was birds chirping.

Faye sighed. 'Fine, I'll do it, if it means that much... to both of you.'

'Right, Yul and I often used to cut down Highfield Avenue on the way to his. A few weeks before Dad died we stopped by that house on the corner. That big tree is a cherry tree, beautiful in the summer, with ripe cherries hanging on it. It would make me think of baubles on a Christmas tree.' Amber perched on the edge of the bench. 'It was early June and Yul picked one with a long stalk and tied it together so it looked like ring, the cherry being a red ruby.'

Faye's top lip twitched. 'Next you'll be telling me the giddy lad proposed.'

Come on, Robin, you can do this.

'Nothing giddy about it. For lots of reasons he *did* ask me to marry him but mainly, he said, because he loved me. He was always a bit of a romantic. When he slipped the ring onto my finger I didn't hesitate in saying yes.'

'What? You got engaged?' asked Amber, eyes wider than Faye's magnified by glasses.

Faye's mouth fell open. 'You aren't serious?'

Robin lifted her chin.

'Romantic?' She snorted. 'What a couple of fools you were. Running away was stupid enough, but actually believing that would make a good start to a marriage...'

'Did anyone know?' asked Amber.

Her stomach tightened. 'I was going to tell Dad.'

'At least you had the sense not to tell me. Whoever heard of anyone proposing with a cherry?' Faye smirked. 'Granted, though, it's absolutely priceless. At least Yul had the sense to end such nonsense, assuming he did. You've never told me why he came back to Stonedale.'

'And you've just demonstrated why I could never talk to you about the little things, let alone the big.' Robin's words burst out and she collapsed onto the bench, next to Amber. 'The times I could have done with your advice about all the things teenagers go through.' She shook her head. 'I had to get my advice from a problem page in a magazine.' Robin recalled what Tara said about being skilful. Breathe, in and out. Faye gripped the bench's arm and her sneer disappeared.

'I... I did my best,' she said, in a small voice. 'I just thought you were... private and didn't like to discuss those things face-to-face.'

'I was a child, Faye,' said Robin, and her posture stiffened.

'I would have helped if you'd talked to me.' Faye fidgeted with a handkerchief she'd pulled out of her handbag.

'No, you wouldn't,' said Robin and threw her hands in the air. 'You'd have made me feel stupid like you did just now, like you always did, with your digs and insults.'

'Maybe we should go,' mumbled Amber.

'I... I'm sorry,' said Faye.

Robin's body loosened.

Faye stared into her lap, at the handkerchief. 'I'm sorry. I am, I never knew anything about being a mother.'

Nor did Robin.

'Mine was just... just this woman I lived with who expected me to look after myself,' Faye half-whispered. 'I thought that's the way it was. I sorted myself out when I started my monthlies.'

'How?' asked Amber.

Faye didn't speak for a moment.

'You don't have to tell us, Gran, if you don't want to,' Amber said and took her hand.

Faye sucked in her cheeks. 'I'd roll up a flannel and stick it in my undies but sometimes it got loose and once the blood came through my school skirt. The whole class saw. The school matron had to show me what I should be doing and gave me the necessary products.'

'Oh, Gran.'

'When you were born, Robin, my mother said what a shame it was, that a boy would have been something to be proud of.'

Robin's own grandmother had said that?

'I always knew she saw me as a nuisance and expected me to fend for myself, to do the chores and not be a burden. I never got invited to other girls' houses, so didn't see that all mothers weren't like that. But over the years I've observed other parents, watched families when I've helped out in church...' Faye stuffed the handkerchief into her slacks' pocket and wandered over to the plaque. 'Your dad used to talk about what good parents robins were. I used to think my mother was more like a cuckoo that, given half the chance, would leave its eggs in other birds' nests. And if I'm honest, I think I used her as an excuse, but... I can't blame everything on my mother. I saw how Alan was with you, Robin, I saw how Tara's mum was. I had role models. I should have tried harder. I let you down.'

Amber got up and gave Faye a hug. Robin remained by the maple tree, unable to move, unsure how to react. A starling emerged from the border, a worm squirming in its beak. When Faye finally turned around it flew off, sunrays catching its irides-cent purplish-green plumage.

'Right,' Faye said and she sniffed. 'This treasure hunt... what's that cherry tree got to do with the words tall, dark and handsome?'

'I'm sorry to hear how hard it was for you, but I'm glad you've told me more about the way things were when you were younger,' Robin said, her tone gentle as she stood up.

'I don't want to speak any more about it.' Faye shivered.

'You look cold,' said Robin. 'I'm cold. Look, let's chat in the car.'

Fifteen minutes later they sat huddled in the back. Robin

explained how Yul had proposed there because of the street-light. There used to be a gothic-style lamppost in front of the cherry tree. It must have been removed since she left Stonedale. It was black, antique – that would fit with the clue's line about something tall and dark. Standing there at night was like being in Paris. He thought it would be perfect.

'I remember it, now,' said Faye. 'Joan told me that the house belonged to an antiques dealer. Whenever he and his wife moved they always took the lamppost with them.' She leant nearer to Robin so that she could read the scroll. '*Give me an answer, do.* Clever Alan, that's almost identical to a line out of the song "Daisy, Daisy". The post was very ornate and had circles of daisies engraved all the way up.'

'I'd forgotten those.'

'That'll be why Granddad said it was handsome. So the answer must be lamppost. That's L. So we now have G, I and L.'

'So... we'll carry on, solving the clues?' asked Robin. 'It's Sunday tomorrow.'

Faye looked Robin straight in the face. 'Yes.'

'Amber? Are you up for this? I know you were going back down south, regardless. And I'll support you if you still want to speak to your tutor on Monday, but now that the treasure hunt is back on... Why don't you continue with the original plan, carry on with the hunt, see if the accommodation office comes up with anything else? Just for a bit longer?' Robin passed her the screwed up scroll.

'You want me to rethink my whole life plan yet again?' Amber sat thinking for several minutes. Then she smoothed out the brown paper. 'Fine. Just for a while longer. But only if you keep me and Hoover supplied with peanut butter.'

Robin Wilson,
16 Parade Row,
Stonedale,
Greater Manchester
February 1988

Dear Debbie,

TAMPON HELL.

I'm really struggling to use tampons, even though I follow the instructions. I've been trying for ages and have bought all the different brands. How on earth am I ever going to be able to have sex, if I can't even push a tampon up there? And I won't ever be able to go swimming on holiday if I get my period. Please don't say to tell my mum or go to the doctor, I'd die of embarrassment.

Robin, age 15

Girl's Scene
41 Gover Street,
London

Dear Robin,

And breathe! Most girls find it tricky to start with, and if you become anxious your muscles tense up and that makes it much more difficult.

Perhaps just use pads for the time being, and try again in a few months. Next time make sure you try with a slender tampon, and wait until your period is moderate to heavy, that will help it slide in more easily.

And if there comes a point when you'd like to talk to someone about it, why not write your mum a note instead?

Best wishes,
Debbie

34

Yul had suggested they go for a pub meal the other side of the common, near Stonedale Primary, but Robin didn't want to leave Faye alone after today. Somehow, she felt closer to her. She wiped her hands on the gingham tea towel and strode into the lounge where Faye sat.

'How about I stay in, instead of eating out?' Robin let Faye assume she was meeting Tara, everything with Yul still felt so awkward, especially after that kiss. 'We could get fish and chips as a treat or—'

'I could do with an early night.' She tickled behind Hoover's ears. 'I've still got that suede jacket. Wear that tonight if you want.'

Faye closed her eyes and rested her head against the side of the chair's back. Robin paused before going up to her mother's bedroom and sifted through the smart trousers and blouses, her tailored wardrobe of old had been replaced with elasticated waists. On the left hung a selection of jackets and she pulled out the farthest away, a brown suede one with tassels down the sleeves and across the back. She took it out and held it in the air.

As soon as Robin had seen it she'd known it wasn't Faye's style even though she'd thanked Dad – he'd just returned from a job in Rochdale and he said it was the height of fashion, the lady in the shop had said so. A friend's fifteenth birthday disco was looming and Robin had swallowed her pride and asked if she could wear it. To her amazement, Faye had actually let her and even said to borrow her perfume.

Amber had already left for her party. So Robin went up to the loft with her laptop and lay on the bed, she smiled at her poster of Andrew Ridgeley even though he'd never asked her to marry him. She didn't want to drift into another meaningless nine-to-five job and skimmed through various job-seeking websites until...

Robin stopped scrolling. Working as a freelance marketing consultant? Could she do that, selecting the clients and products she really believed in, being her own boss...? She stared at the screen for several minutes before starting to make notes, typos becoming more frequent as her fingers tapped faster. Could this be a serious option? Robin would need to set up her own website and research pricing and where to advertise. It would take a while to bring in the income she hoped for so at the beginning she'd have to find another job to run alongside.

For the first time since leaving Todd, she could imagine an exciting life. The job she'd been doing all these years would take on a whole new dimension if she was her own boss, only working on projects she passionately believed in. She turned up her playlist and Kool and the Gang called her to celebrate as she squinted and rubbed her eyes. She stood on her bed, and danced under the window, under the moonlight, slowly at first, then faster and faster, as if her life depended on it.

A life that might, finally, have found a new direction.

She slid down the ladder. Faye had eaten half a plain scone.

Hoover dozed on her lap. She didn't look up when Robin walked in, so Robin texted Yul back, agreeing to call for him at seven. Robin rummaged in her old wardrobe in the loft and found a blouse with shoulder pads and a bow at the neck. It was full on Dynasty, made from a shimmery purple material. She squirted it with perfume to take away the musty smell. Jeans and Faye's jacket completed the ensemble.

'I'm off now. You've got my number if you need anything. I doubt I'll be very late.'

'I used to admire the way you wore what you wanted. You look pretty, tonight, Robin.'

Images popped into her head of the way Faye used to wash her clothes and iron them neatly. Perhaps that was why.

'You'd better get off. He won't wait forever.'

'What?' She focused again. 'Oh. How did you know?'

'You always did want to borrow my favourite perfume before meeting Jason.'

As Robin passed the front window outside, she looked through a gap in the curtains, for some reason disappointed not to see her waving. Maybe she'd phone Faye once she got back to London, perhaps once a week. Would Faye contact Robin as keenly as she did *Word Weekly*'s editor?

Yul stood outside the bookshop in a black evening jacket and tie dye jeans, the top buttons of his shirt undone, with the self-assured air he'd always had. As she approached, he crooked his arm and they strolled towards the river, over the bridge and past the Iron Horse, veering away from the woods and over the common. They continued on the path that led to the other side and the main road where the primary school sat. Robin told him about the crematorium visit, without giving the detail of what Faye said. Years ago she'd have felt no such loyalty. By the time they'd reached the grass's edge his hand was in hers, their fingers interlocked just like they used to be.

She stopped, feeling herself blush. 'Sorry about that kiss.'

He ran his thumb over her palm and heat flickered up her arm. 'Do you regret it?'

She ran her thumb over his.

They chose to eat in the Nag's Head – unlike the White Hart, it hadn't got rid of its snooker table or darts board, and it smelt of stale beer. An understated Christmas tree sat in the corner. They chose a booth away from the noise and as they shared a bottle of wine, Yul told her more about his travels. He'd never been on a package holiday, had never even booked accommodation before his plane landed.

'This night out is just what I need before next week,' he said and stretched. 'I've decided to stop procrastinating and give the café area a lick of paint, I've been putting it off. So Monday night it is.'

'Why don't I help and ask Tara to muck in? Wouldn't it be great to meet up as a three again?' Today was the twenty-first of November; the middle of December and Robin going home was looming.

'It's a lot to ask, Robin, perhaps just us two – if you're sure you don't mind helping, that is.'

'Tara won't mind. Honestly, don't worry, I'm sure she'll jump at the idea.'

As they drank she didn't tell him about her freelance idea. She wanted to hold it close at the moment, to relish the excitement and iron out the details, make sure it was really feasible. The menu boasted scampi and chips, and trifle, it was decidedly retro. On the way back she suggested walking through the woods, lit up by the moon. Their conversation petered out as trees creaked and welcomed them with a damp pine fragrance.

A hedgehog crossed their path, Robin never saw any in London. They both stopped instinctively as a silhouette of the tree house came into view.

'Our special place,' she murmured and leant against the ash tree. 'Do you ever... think about him?' There, she'd said it.

Yul's face clouded over, under the moonlight. 'Of course,' he replied, an edge to his voice. 'You?'

She couldn't speak.

Yul continued, 'Now and then I have to go to London for work, and he's always the first thing on my mind. I was surprised you stayed after it happened.'

'I didn't have a choice,' Robin said flatly. Yul's hand reached for hers. 'Do you think any other couples have ever used it?' she asked, gazing at the treehouse.

He shrugged and pulled her away, they walked further on, fingers interlocked, Robin thinking about London.

'Come in for coffee?' he asked as they reached the bookshop and as a shy look crossed his face something inside her combusted. In her 1980s ruffled blouse and wearing Faye's perfume she felt like a sixteen-year-old again. It has been so long, even longer with him, she could hardly stand still as a young couple walked past laughing. They went up to his flat, he didn't turn on the lights and neither of them said a word as the suede jacket fell to the floor. His hands curved around her waist.

'Are you sure about this?' he murmured.

'You?'

His lips stroked her cheek. 'You're so beautiful, Robin.'

And in that moment, in her old clothes, in his arms, she felt it. The pull to feel his skin against hers felt stronger than gravity as he led her towards his bed and took off his shirt. He undid the top of her blouse and tugged it gently over her head. They faced each other like two teenagers, unsure of the next move. He turned down the bed and they slipped between the covers, staring at each other through the warm glow of the streetlight that sneaked through the window. They edged closer and as they kissed the flames between them quivered more vigorously, then grew taller, grew stronger, she reached down with one hand and his fingers cupped her breast. Their mouths met once more and the movement of their hips synched. As the past became the present her desire ignited and she lost herself in the fire.

35

'What time did you get home last night?' asked Amber as Robin walked in and sat down at the kitchen table.

'Shouldn't I be asking you that?' Robin said lightly. 'How was the party?' Faye passed Robin a cup of tea.

'I was home before you. Your door was open and I saw that the bed was empty.' Her voice was sharp.

'I heard her not long after you, Amber,' said Faye who sat between them. She helped herself to another slice of toast and spread on a thick layer of cherry jam.

A large mouthful of tea burnt Robin's throat. Faye had been asleep when Robin got in, her snores resounding across the landing. Amber looked at them both, then brushed her hands together and picked up the treasure hunt scroll that lay next to her plate.

'So, did you chat to many people from your course? Have you made any other plans?'

Amber's eyes glazed over.

'Sorry,' Robin said quickly. 'None of my business. Right, why don't you read out clue number four?'

'Rub-a-dub-dub,
Ewe need a scrub.
Next, there's no point veering right,
Go to where the last is midnight.
Bend over and look in, before the slope,
You'll see who looks back, I hope.
It's a sight nothing else can upstage,
A right little gem, whatever its age.

'Cryptic as ever. Well, apart from the first bit, even I can work that out and I haven't lived here long,' said Amber.

'Ewe. A female sheep,' said Robin.

'Rub-a-dub-dub, in other words wash,' added Faye.

'Sheepwash River here we come,' said Amber.

Hoover waited impatiently by the front door as they got ready. He often waited there, especially if, like today, weak sunrays managed to break their way through the winter cloud. Amber attached his lead and the three of them braved the air's crispness. As they passed the church the congregation's voices leaked outside.

'Don't you go to the Sunday morning service any more?' Robin asked her mother.

'Of course. And I help organise the coffee and biscuits in the hall afterwards. Once you've gone, I'll get back into my old routine.'

No doubt she was still too tired to attend, and one arm in plaster would be no good for setting out tens of cups and plates. She couldn't be missing it just to spend more time with Robin, surely?

The possibility that she might warmed her insides though.

Faye was walking a little quicker today and Robin hadn't seen her rub her ribs for several days. The bruising had all but disappeared. She managed to dress on her own, apart from tighter tops or fiddly buttons, and today her face powder was more evenly spread than it had been since Robin had arrived up north. Less and less she needed help and Robin should have felt relieved that her time in Stonedale was almost at an end. But instead a heaviness weighed in her chest.

They reached the river.

'Why the big smile?' asked Amber.

'I was just thinking about the line rub-a-dub-dub. Dad used to sing it to me when I was little, at bathtime.'

Amber passed Robin Hoover's lead and read the scroll once more.

'We mustn't turn right but have got to go where the last is midnight.' Amber wanted to know what Faye and Robin meant when they said this clue was worryingly easy.

'Because the last train back from Manchester was midnight, everyone knew that. So we go left and head up to the station.' Faye jerked her head towards the box shaped ticket office in the distance. 'This clue isn't challenging enough for number four.'

'It could be that he's trying to fool us into coming up with the wrong letter for the anagram.' Oh. Robin was talking about Dad in the present. It lifted her spirits yet also caused an ache.

Amber upped her pace whilst the others trailed behind. A cyclist zoomed past on the path and Robin took Faye's elbow, slipping her arm through hers, confused by a mixture of awkwardness and something else... A pleasant feeling.

'She's a lovely girl. You've done a grand job.'

Robin glowed.

They reached the slope, several metres away from the station and a railway bridge overhead. Amber was on her knees, staring into the water, bending over and looking in, just before the slope, as instructed by the clue. Hoover strained to jump in.

Robin passed his lead to Faye who had a firm word with him. The grassy bank was dry and she dropped down next to Amber and stared at a huge sandy coloured stone under the water, it was smooth on the top, ragged around the edges.

Amber looked at Robin as a train pulled in. 'It's a big stone shaped like a bone?' They both stood up.

'Huge, isn't it? Didn't you and Tara have a nickname for it, Robin?' asked Faye.

Robin shrugged. 'I can't remember.'

'A member of the council had a degree in geology,' said Faye. 'He thought it looked very unusual but it turned out not to be anything of note.'

'Well, the word *gem*, in the riddle, certainly fits with the geology theme, so we've found the right object. The answer to this clue could be S for stone...' Amber shrugged. 'It does all seem a little obvious.'

Faye thought for a moment. 'I think the answer might be the nickname you and Tara gave it, Robin. Alan liked to make the clues personal, where possible. So you'd better do what you used to when we got stuck.'

'Ask a friend?'

Faye smiled.

Robin took out her phone. Tara picked up. Their chat was interspersed with silences and then Robin started laughing and nodding before ending the call.

'Of course, we called it Dino after Fred and Wilma Flintstone's pet. We thought those dark bits at the top looked like a pair of eyes on a dinosaur and reckoned it was prehistoric bone.'

'So the answer is D for Dino,' said Amber and she grinned. 'Especially as the sentence *a right little gem, whatever its age* fits something you used to believe was very old.'

'We've worked this out all too quickly, I still think Dad might be playing games with us.' Robin knelt down again and peered over, when a bump from behind caused her to shoot forwards, narrowly missing the stone as she leant to the side and fell in. Spluttering, Robin surfaced and spat out water, she pushed herself up, biker jacket and hair dripping. Robin grabbed her beret from the river's surface just before the current carried it under the railway bridge. A toddler giggled as she clambered onto the bank.

'Hoover got a bit over-excited when you talked about playing games,' Faye said and offered Robin her handkerchief. Hoover poked his innocent-looking face out from behind Faye's legs.

As the three of them walked back, linking arms, Robin's daughter and mother glared at a passer-by who shot her a curious glance. A teenager accidentally bumped into them and the three women moved even closer together. They got chatting and Amber opened up about the party.

'It was the best time I've had since starting university.' She went on to describe several girls who'd asked her to join their study group.

A hopeful smile on her face, Robin caught Faye's eye. She smiled back.

'Although I still couldn't face alcohol after that night out with you and Tara, Mum. But I enjoyed watching the drinking games. Everyone got really competitive playing one called Beer Pong, it was so funny.'

They fell into a comfortable silence until they reached Parade Row, where Faye eyed Robin up and down. 'Honestly, you took your father's rub-a-dub-dub line a bit too seriously, by actually washing yourself in the river,' she teased.

The muddy water may have been wintry, the breeze making Robin shiver, but inside, where it counted, she had never felt toastier.

36

Humming from the hallway indicated that Amber was back after lectures, with her earbuds in. Hoover charged out of the lounge, barking. Shoes were kicked off and she appeared at the doorway with him in her arms, struggling like a toddler. She put him on the floor and turned off her music.

'I've made tea for you and Faye, tonight,' said Robin. 'Mushroom and ham pie.'

Hoover bolted into the kitchen.

Faye put down the duster. She'd been doing more housework lately. 'I meant to tell you, Robin, Amber texted me on her way home, there's been a change of plan. That pie will do us very nicely tomorrow, thank you, but tonight your daughter and I are eating at the White Hart again.'

'I see. Whilst I'm busy painting?' Robin said with a superior air.

'And ordering takeout,' replied Faye. 'Wine as well, probably. You don't fool us.'

Robin hurried into the kitchen and leant on the sink. Banter with her mother? It was uncomfortable, unnerving, bloody brilliant.

'Going anywhere nice?' asked Amber in a stilted tone.

'Around to Yul's to help him paint the shop. Tara's going as well.' Robin called through.

Feet stomped upstairs.

'What time will you be back tonight?' asked Faye, coming into the kitchen.

'Not sure. It's a big room to paint.' Although it wouldn't take long with Tara's help. She hadn't seemed keen but Robin had promised they'd order in her favourite. Chicken Tikka with chips. Some things hadn't changed.

'Amber might have questions again,' said Faye, not looking at her.

'It's too early on to say anything, Yul and I live so far apart and have only just started getting to know each other again. But you've got a point, I should act if things progress.'

Faye turned to look at her and nodded. 'Right, I'd better make myself presentable.'

What had just happened there?

It hadn't been easy telling Amber about the divorce. Robin just couldn't find the right words. She blamed the nature of her work for that; most of her day focused on searching for the perfect phrase to up-sell a product. She'd spent hour after hour crafting the perfect sentence to explain. *This is a brand new start for all three of us. Happier parents make for happier children.* She'd worked on the vocabulary she'd use – *safe, secure, growth*. But in the end Amber's first inkling was overhearing her dad blaming Robin for them splitting. Amber didn't speak to either of them for two long days afterwards.

Robin climbed up the ladder and paused by the bedroom. 'Can I come in?'

Amber opened the door, leaving it half ajar. Robin pushed it wider and sat on the bed.

'Perhaps tomorrow night you and I could do something together, sweetheart?'

Amber stopped buttoning up her top and folded her arms.

'You really like Yul, don't you?'

Robin shrugged. 'It's complicated.'

'Dad's got a girlfriend.'

'Oh... I did wonder... saw a photo on Facebook.'

'I figured he'd tell you when he was ready, although it doesn't really work like that, does it, not in our family?' Amber's arms dropped to her sides.

'And I wish I'd handled things differently, love – explained, earlier, about why the marriage wasn't working. But sometimes I wasn't even sure myself. It's coming back to Stonedale and living with mum again that's given me enough clarity to talk about it.' Her voice caught. 'I can't imagine how challenging the last couple of years have been for you.'

Amber exhaled. 'Except you can. Since I've moved in here... how Gran's been with you at times, stories from the past... and sensing Granddad here by the way you both talk about him, seeing his possessions, doing the treasure hunt... I understand now just how bad it was. Losing him was way harder on you, it changed everything about your family, at least my dad is still around and... even though I couldn't see it at the time I know it wasn't either of your intentions to hurt me as well.'

'It really wasn't, you're the most precious thing to us both.'

Amber picked up her phone. 'Gran and I are leaving in ten minutes. I need to finish getting ready.'

Robin went down to the spare room and quickly changed, she pulled on Faye's suede jacket. She then charged outside and stopped by the gate for a second, breathing in the cold night.

She still thought about Todd, the way he slurped with apprecia-
tion when drinking hot tea, how he never swore – well, only at
football referees. Did this girlfriend bake his favourite tiffin? Did
she do that thing he liked when they kissed? This new relationship of his felt more permanent than any official papers. She
and Todd were over for good. Would this woman hurt him like
Robin had? Hurt her daughter? Or would they all form a new
cosy family that excluded Robin?

She walked down the high street, and her breathing slowed.
She still loved her ex-husband. She did. But not in the way a
wife should. Robin realised that part of the reason she'd felt in
limbo was the guilt and a sense that she had no permission to
move on and feel happy until he did. This new romance was a
big step forwards for him, and for her.

Robin knocked on the glass, impatient to get inside. Yul
pushed the door closed behind her and they stood facing each
other. She didn't know what to do, didn't know what the other
night had meant, only that she'd felt the happiest afterwards
than she had in a long time.

He'd set up for painting, cotton sheets covering the chairs
and tables. They poured paint into plastic trays and she tied up
her curls. She was wearing her London clothes – beige trousers
and a matching top – because it wouldn't matter if they got
ruined. Yul said a friend of his would visit, later in the week, to
draw flower motifs in the corners, near the far window. Yul
wanted to give the room an airier, brighter, conservatory feel.
He'd swap the vase of black roses for dried wildflowers he'd
bought in Manchester, and take down the picture with the skull
in it. He blushed as he confessed he'd originally decorated the
room more to his personal taste, not thinking about his
customers. They started on opposite sides and challenged each
other to finish first, their smiles slicing through the awkward-

ness. A knock at the door sounded and Robin put down her roller.

She waved to Tara who stepped in and shuddered. 'How did we ever use to go out, in the middle of winter, without our coats?'

'Cinzano.'

They went out the back, Tara lagging behind. Yul stood, holding a tin of paint in front of him as if it were a shield.

'I can't believe you two have never bumped into each other since the bookshop opened,' Robin said.

'I don't visit my parents that often.' Tara put her rucksack on one of the sheet-covered tables and rolled up her sleeves. Yul put down the tin and clenched his hands.

Something was off.

'Robin told me how bad it was, down in London,' said Tara to Yul.

'The threat of homelessness and being mugged,' Robin said quickly and gave him a meaningful look.

'I felt sure she'd write to you once settled at her Uncle Ralph's,' he said. 'That's why I didn't explain.'

Robin felt as if she were eavesdropping.

'I'm sorry,' he mumbled. 'For—'

'For being such an idiot back then,' Tara said quietly and held out her arms. He almost fell into them. 'It's okay. I get it now,' she said.

A lump formed in Robin's throat as their eyes closed and they held each other tightly.

Eventually Tara pulled away. 'Right. What's with this wishy washy magnolia? I was thinking bright pink.'

Robin wanted to ask what had happened all those years ago, but the two of them were already joking together. It couldn't have been that important.

Robin Wilson,
16 Parade Row,
Stonedale,
Greater Manchester
May 1988

Dear Debbie,

I NEED MORE DOSH.

After school I want to go to university in Manchester, to study English. I can't wait to leave home and I'm going to move out as soon as I get my A level results. I'll be sharing a flat with my boyfriend and best mate, we've got it all planned. I've saved up from birthdays and my paper round, and sometimes Dad pays me if I clean the car, but I'm desperate to earn more dosh. I can get a Saturday job when I'm in the sixth form, but I need to start saving now so that we'll really be able to enjoy ourselves, throwing parties and going out to night clubs. It's going to be such fun! Have you got any ideas?

Robin, age 15

Girl's Scene
41 Gover Street,
London

Dear Robin,

Hold on, Robin, you haven't even started your A levels or applied to university yet! Whilst I admire your longing to be independent, and even though you'll get a grant, or financial aid from your parents, university is an expensive business, with unexpected bills for books or trips... and that's aside from all the responsibilities you'll face if you choose to live in a flat that isn't being subsidised by your college. Getting your first place isn't all about parties, it's about having a regular income big enough to cover energy supplies, repairs, and so much more.

I don't want to dash your dreams but you need to think this through very carefully.

In the meantime, hats off to your work ethic! How about placing an advert in the local newsagents to offer babysitting or dog walking? What about washing neighbours' cars or mowing lawns? And take a look in newspapers, magazines, and on the back of cereal packets, as winning competitions will boost your savings.

Good luck!

Best wishes,

Debbie

37

'He most certainly was *not* giving me the glad eye, young lady.'

Robin passed Hoover in the lounge, he was sniffing Amber's bag – an old one of hers from the loft – and went on her way into the kitchen. Faye and Amber sat drinking orange juice, both of them already dressed. She'd grown to love their breakfasts together and the hint of harmony that had developed between the three of them. She'd hated breakfast as a teenager, eating as quickly as possible to avoid having to make conversation with Faye. Dad would usually be behind one of his antiques magazines, a moment to himself ahead of a day using concrete and brick to realise the dreams of others.

'Gran, I have no idea what that means, but I'll say it again – the man at the bar last night, wearing that spotted cravat, couldn't stop looking at our table.'

'Perhaps he felt attracted to that cookie dough concoction you insisted I try.'

Robin sat down between them and shook out a bowlful of cornflakes.

'Have you ever dated anyone, since Dad?' asked Robin. 'I... wouldn't blame you, thirty-two years is a long time.'

'No one would ever come close to Alan. He... was my every-thing,' Faye mumbled.

Robin stared at Faye. He was? Then why didn't she show more emotion when Dad left them?

'Well, I'm not dating anyone until I'm at least twenty-five,' declared Amber. 'I need to focus on building a career, I'm an independent woman. I've got better things to think about than how to attract a man. I don't need one.'

Paws padded in.

'Apart from Hoover,' she said and looked down. Her ears turned red. Faye plucked a leaflet out of his mouth headed Student Speed-dating Night.

Amber's phone rang and she left the room. Faye topped up Robin's teacup and she passed Faye the butter. Small gestures, between the two of them, that never seemed to happen when Robin lived at home before. Back then it was usually big ones like slamming doors or lengthy silences.

It hadn't always been like that, not when she was at primary school, in those days she used to hold Faye's hand out walking, proud of a mum who always looked so smart with her beaded necklaces and starched trousers. Robin had forgotten that view she once had of her mother. She'd only remembered since moving back into Parade Row. Perhaps those moments would have been too painful to recall before, because they'd have made her wish even more that things had been different between them as Robin got older. Much of her time, in those days, was spent in a fantasy world of dragons and wishing chairs, or amongst nature, she had vivid close-up memories of furry cater-pillars and glossy ladybirds. But as learning took over, as the days filled with maths and English, as she joined hobby clubs and her days became increasingly structured, her view of home life sharpened and she realised minor missing things were actually major – how Faye never kissed her goodnight, how rarely she paid Robin a compliment.

Amber ran into the kitchen.

'I might go into lectures early today to visit the accommodation office,' she said. 'You see... I didn't want to mention anything in case it never worked out, but one of the girls who invited me to the party, Lucy, she's really nice and mentioned that the student in the room next to her is leaving, something to do with a health problem. Anyway, Lucy suggested I ring the office, ask if I could have her room. They said it didn't work like that, but have discussed it and have just let me know that seeing as my situation is an emergency... I can move in this Saturday if I want, but they'll need the paperwork signing today. They said to go in and they'll be there to answer any questions about it.'

'Oh, Amber. I'm so happy for you,' said Robin.

Amber sat back down. Stared at the phone.

'If it's what you want, love,' she added. 'What do you think?'

'Everyone was really friendly at the party and they've already asked me on another night out. I saw Lucy's room, the layout's great.'

'That Lucy's been a real friend, hasn't she?' said Faye.

Amber looked up from her phone and scratched her ruffled hair. 'You're right. Do you think I should buy her something as a thank you?'

'I'm sure she'd love a small box of chocolates, whatever you decide to do.'

Robin saw what Faye had done there. She'd never done that for Robin. Or didn't Robin ever pay enough attention?

'A group of them who haven't got lectures on Thursday, like me, are going shopping for Christmas decorations. I mean, it *is*

December next week.' Her eyes shone in a way that Robin had only seen on the treasure hunt.

'I think you've made your decision then,' Robin said.

Amber was moving out, back to Manchester. It was the best outcome, everything Robin could have hoped for. As Amber chatted, Robin made encouraging noises, not taking a single detail for granted. The divorce had made her realise that her daughter sharing her life was a precious present.

Not one that Robin had given her own mother. Faye had admitted she should have tried harder – perhaps Robin should have too.

Robin ate her last mouthful of cereal, thinking about the treasure hunt letters they'd worked out: G, I, L and D. Her heart beat faster as she thought about the possibility of never finding out Dad's special word that could have *changed everything*. And she'd miss Amber so much, all the chats they'd had about clothes and fashion, their laughter over Robin's *Girl's Scene* magazines... the superficial conversations that had hidden depths and under the surface had pulled the two of them together again.

'Don't worry,' Amber said.

How did she manage to talk and text at the same time?

'I haven't forgotten the treasure hunt. I know I can't make this Thursday now and they're all cooking a roast together on Sunday...'

'Of course, you must go to that,' said Faye.

'... but you're staying up here until the middle of December, right, Mum?'

'My appointment with the consultant to have the cast removed is on Tuesday the fourteenth – that's exactly three weeks today,' said Faye.

'So we've got bags of time. How about we do clue number

five next Thursday, on the second? That still gives us almost two weeks to fit in the last one.'

Robin didn't need to panic, that would work.

'But don't feel obliged, darling,' said Robin. 'If you can't fit in the treasure hunt any more, we understand, don't we, Mum?'

Robin ducked her chin. Where did *Mum* come from? Luckily no one seemed to have noticed.

'And let you two finish it and take all the glory after I've done most of the hard work?' Amber smiled. 'In any case, the fifth clue has a very intriguing beginning.'

38

Amber arrived at midday and couldn't wait to read the scroll. Robin sat down in the lounge and yawned. She hadn't slept well, she'd been to Yul's for a meal. He was back in her life, back on centre stage, they were the leads in a romance that only had two more weeks to run. Anything after that, grabbed at weekends, might just seem like a series of encores.

Amber pointed to a glittery advent calendar in the bookcase, next to the seaside painting.

'Whose is that?' She picked it up.

'Faye bought it for me.' Robin had opened door number two first thing that morning. When she'd gone down to breakfast yesterday it was leaning against the toast rack. Faye had watched as Robin opened the first door, cheeks as red as the envelope the calendar came in, after the side hug Robin gave her as a thank you. It had always been Dad who'd slide one under Robin's bedroom door on the first day of December. Spurred on by Faye's gesture, Robin had picked up a small Christmas tree from outside the supermarket. Faye said the old decorations in the loft hadn't come down since the year Dad died.

When Amber moved out Robin had prepared herself for more friction between her and Faye, they'd always needed a third person before to smooth things over – Alan, Blanche or Amber. But Robin needn't have worried. Oh, there had been little disagreements, awkward moments, but they'd managed to move past them without someone else helping.

Amber went over to examine the tree, in the far left corner of the lounge, by the front window. She touched a wooden decoration hanging at the front, in capital letters it spelt out the word *family* and was decorated with fake snow and hearts, a couple missing now.

'That was Dad's favourite, he bought it one December whilst away on a job.'

'I always liked the colourful harlequin, I bought that when I worked at Lewis's.'

The tinsel looked tired and the fairy lights didn't work, Robin would replace them both at the weekend. Faye had suggested going into town with her for lunch at Marks & Sparks, her treat. They could also look around the Christmas markets.

Amber took the scroll out of her rucksack and uncurled it, Robin noticing her old friendship bracelets around her daughter's wrist.

'A game of Monopoly to start.

'I told you it had an intriguing beginning.' Amber smiled cheekily before reading on.

'Each of you must play a part.
Don't fiddle with the cards,
So that I can catch you off guard!
At your destination press the brass,

Then head to the beautiful glass,
The answer is within a gold frame,
It's a flower, what's its name?'

'I'd forgotten Dad sometimes included a game,' said Robin. 'We played Cluedo once, at the end.'

'The answer to that clue was the lounge card and, cleverly, the world lounge was the anagram as well,' said Faye. 'He'd hidden chocolates in there to celebrate me being promoted to supervisor.'

'Granddad must have rigged it so that this is a short round of Monopoly otherwise you'd never have completed all six clues in one day.'

Robin's pulse raced. 'You've still got the box, right, Faye?'

'I... oh. No. I'm afraid I got rid. What a nuisance. Most of his things went straight to charity shops in Manchester. They came to pick them up.'

'Are you sure, Gran?' Amber's face fell. 'That means we can't work out this clue.'

'I can't believe it, after all the effort we've put in.' Robin clasped her hands together.

'It's only a silly treasure hunt, we found that scroll by accident,' said Faye and her jaw tightened. 'One more word from Alan isn't going to make a difference to anything.'

'Dad loved Monopoly,' Robin said in a thick voice. 'He always insisted on being the boot, he teased that it reminded him of being a builder, a job that kept him down-to-earth when he won, which he usually did.' She hugged a cushion. 'I loved the hat. And Faye, if you joined us you'd choose the ship token and said one day you'd like to go on a cruise. Faye?'

Faye took off her glasses. 'Alan said to me once that we always had to keep the board games, that we'd pass them down to grandchildren, like those playing cards in the fancy felt-lined wooden box.'

'I remember, they'd belonged to his grandfather,' said Robin.

'You know, I think I did, I did keep all the old boxes – Cluedo, Scrabble and Monopoly. They might be under your bed in the spare room.'

Amber whooped and Hoover raced over, yapping. But it didn't make sense. She'd shown so little emotion when he died, why would she bother honouring such a sentimental wish?

As a teenager, Robin had thought she'd known everything about Faye. Perhaps she'd been wrong.

Amber ran upstairs, Hoover following her heels, and minutes later they both appeared again, out of breath, carrying a worn looking rectangular box. Relief flooded through Robin as they sat at the dining room table and she carefully set up the board. It smelt musty.

'The riddle implies we mustn't shuffle the cards.' Robin lifted them carefully onto their places.

Faye put her glasses back on and sorted through the tokens, for a moment holding the silver boot up in the air. Then she passed Robin the hat and Amber chose the dog. Faye dealt out the money and Robin was in charge of the property cards.

The dice rolled and Robin and Amber argued about the rules, Robin insisting you couldn't buy any houses until you had all the properties in one set. Amber said that was boring. Fifteen minutes in and they started to pick up the Chance and Community Chest cards. Aptly, Faye won a crossword competition, and Amber happily collected a bank error in her favour. Next, she landed on Leicester Square and told Faye about the musicals she, Todd and Robin had seen in theatres there. Robin rolled and yet again missed out on landing on a property and it was her turn to take a Chance card. She turned it over and grimaced at the image of window bars.

'Typical, I have to go directly to... oh.'

'Jail?' asked Amber.

'Dad's crossed that out. It's his handwriting. Instead he's written *church*.' Robin's hand trembled. Little did Dad know that just a few weeks after writing that, she and Faye would be there for his funeral.

* * *

Dressed up warmly, they headed outside, leaving Hoover behind. Faye was worried he'd cause havoc with the hymn books and candles. The birds sang like a choir, not quite in sync, rather each voice rang out clearly, showboating its unique rhythm and pitch. Amber asked Faye about her wedding day. Faye explained how money was tight and afterwards she'd dyed her dress blue to wear dancing. Robin never knew that. She still had the satin white shoes in the loft and no, she didn't mind Amber looking for them. They reached the church.

'*Press the brass*, of course, the brass handle,' said Robin and took a deep breath as she pushed open the big wooden door. It felt cold inside and she pulled on her gloves. Amber went to stand under the twisted spire and looked upwards at the many beams that had been put in to bolster it. She took out the scroll again.

'*Beautiful glass*,' she read out, in a hushed voice.

'A stained-glass window, obviously,' said Faye.

'I had wondered, at the start, if it meant Granddad was going to lead us to a pub. But I think you're right and...' She consulted the scroll. 'We need to look for a flower within a gold frame.'

They walked around the church but all the gold edged windows contained figures, green plants or mosaics.

'Granddad must be pulling a trick again.'

'Have any of the stained windows changed since 1989?' Robin asked.

Faye shook her head.

They sat in a pew and thought for several minutes.

Then Faye stood up and Amber and Robin looked at each other before following her, up to the altar where she turned left and pointed at a window, a circle containing mosaics of blue and red patterns, the whole thing framed in a gold square.

'You see? I just thought of it. The picture may not be in the shape of a flower, but that design is known as rose window,' said Faye.

'So it's R for Rose,' said Amber. 'Ace, we've only one more clue to go now.'

The only word they could think of containing G, I, L, D and R was girdle.

'But often it wasn't obvious and we needed the last letter. I've never forgotten that anagram where we had A, D, R, O and A. We thought we must have got one letter wrong but it turned out the last clue's answer gave us B to make ABROAD. That's when Dad let us know he'd booked that surprise holiday in Spain.'

They sat down on the pews again, Faye in the middle, staring at the marble altar with its white flowers and gold candleholders.

'It was cold, Robin, the last time you and I were here together, at the funeral, even though it was the summer.' Faye's body gave a little shudder.

'I remember shivering even though Uncle Ralph sat with his arm around me.' Robin zipped up her biker jacket higher.

'I miss Alan,' said Faye and her voice caught. Robin watched

Amber hesitate and then take Faye's good hand. 'That's why I didn't want to do this treasure hunt. I thought it would hurt too much.'

Robin squeezed her eyes closed, took a breath and said, 'Then why didn't you cry when he died?' The words tumbled out. 'Not a single tear. You'd just lost your husband.'

Faye stiffened.

'You didn't so much as flinch when we got the phone call.'

'Mum...' Amber muttered.

Robin got to her feet and rubbed her head. 'Sorry. It's probably best left in the past.' Faye's hand grabbed the sleeve of her jacket and pulled. Robin sat down again.

'My own mother...' Faye didn't say anything for a moment, still clutching onto the jacket. 'She believed tears were for babies, that they were justified for food and a nappy change, but not for any other problems because life was hard and once we could fend for ourselves we just had to get on with it. If I fell over she'd tell me to wash my own knee. If a bully called me names she'd simply say I should have answered back. She said people didn't respect tears, they respected a no-nonsense attitude and hard work. A friend of hers told me once how my mother never cried when she heard my dad had died in the trenches.' She looked Robin in the eye and swallowed. 'Her example, it was all I had to go on. Alan wasn't coming back, I just had to get on with it.'

The three of them sat in silence for a moment.

'But it was almost as if you were angry. You couldn't leave the crematorium quickly enough.'

Faye slipped her hand back into Amber's.

'I *was* angry, I suppose,' she croaked. Amber pulled a bottle of water out of her rucksack. Faye took a slug. 'The truth is... I never wanted children. I was quite happy it just being me and Alan.

Wind rattled the church door.

'But Dad would have understood that, surely,' said Robin, her voice sounding full as she fought an unexpected urge to cry. 'Why didn't you tell him before you got married?'

'I did but then I got pregnant accidentally. I... I wanted to end it.'

Robin couldn't believe she'd actually said that to her.

'And if I'm completely honest... I resented it.' Faye stared at the marble floor.

Robin leant back against the hard wood.

'Alan said it would all work out, that he'd be there every step of the way, and he was, but then the teen years became even harder and he left when I most needed him.'

'He couldn't help that!' Robin snapped.

'I know, it doesn't make sense, I... I can't explain it now, but at the time I felt betrayed and gave all his belongings away.' Faye's voice wavered. 'I regretted it after a few years and would do anything, now, to have them back and feel close to him again.' Red blotches appeared around her eyes, eyes that glistened.

Robin's fists curled and she stared at Faye. 'Well, I'll never understand how—'

Amber placed a hand on Robin's arm, darting looks between her and Faye.

'Like I've said before, Mum, you... you and Gran aren't so unalike. I... I don't always tell you stuff, because you try to take over and fix things.'

'What are you talking about?' Robin snapped again, still staring at Faye.

'Like ringing up the university accommodation office, the times you went into school over things all students were struggling with, not just me... and remember that Saturday job I had in the sixth form? You rang up my boss when he couldn't give me the day off so I could go on that trip to Alton Towers with friends. It was so embarrassing. Sometimes I just want you to listen but you always have to do your best to make everything better as if I'm still at primary school. It's... suffocating.'

Robin turned to Amber. 'But you're my daughter...'

'But that's life, Mum. You can't protect me from ever getting hurt. But now I get it, both of you have over-compensated for your childhoods, just in different ways...'

A band of pain tightened around Robin's forehead.

'Gran by not wanting children, you by thinking you had to be a perfect parent. Both of you had the best intentions.'

'I'm nothing like her.' The words spat out. 'Fair enough not wanting to go through with a pregnancy, but to punish the child for it if you decide to go ahead...'

'You've no idea how difficult it was,' said Faye, hugging herself.

The band of pain tightened further. 'You're not the only one who suffered an accidental pregnancy but it didn't make me hardhearted,' Robin whispered.

Amber gave a jolt. 'What?'

Faye sat upright.

Oh, crap, thought Robin. Now the dice were loaded.

'But you and Dad always said I was planned,' stuttered Amber, 'that you couldn't wait to get pregnant after you got married.'

'That... that's all true, love.' Robin got up and paced in front of the altar.

'What, then? Have you both been lying?' Amber pressed a fist to her lips.

Robin sat down and covered her face with her hands. Slowly she lifted her head.

'I was pregnant, when I ran away. That's one reason Yul proposed.'

'*What*? And I never knew?' Faye gaped, a tide of red rising up her neck.

'I imagine a baby grandchild would have felt like a huge burden.' Robin bit the inside of her cheek. 'I... I lost the baby anyway.' Despite the chill, Robin's hands felt clammy.

'You should have told me.' Faye's voice echoed around the nave as she pushed herself up and loosened her scarf.

'You'd have gone ballistic. I had no one to speak to apart from Yul.'

'I'd have listened,' said Faye and sucked in her cheeks.

Amber's fist curled tighter and she shrank into the pew.

'Don't make me laugh,' Robin's voice shook as she strode up to Faye. 'You'd have lost it, told me I was a fool. When the worst happened, Uncle Ralph had to sort me out, he... he was practically a stranger, for God's sake.'

Faye pushed past Robin and headed up the aisle, knocking into the end of pews. A hymn book slapped the floor as it fell. The church door slammed shut behind her.

39

Orange light from streetlamps slipped through the stained glass windows.

'Were you ever going to tell me?'

Robin wiped her eyes, she could barely hear Amber's voice. 'I've wanted to, sweetheart, now that you're older. It's been hard to find the right moment.'

'The baby... was it another girl?'

Robin unzipped the biker jacket so she could slide her hand in and touch Yul's sweatshirt.

'We called him Ash. He would have been thirty-two this year.'

Amber swung her legs, to and fro, against the bottom of the pew. 'I can't take it in. I could have had a brother, almost old enough to be my dad... does Dad know?'

'Yes.'

'And how did he react?'

'Your father was very supportive.'

Amber shuffled up so that their shoulders rubbed. Robin had always admired her daughter's courageousness. She'd dived backwards off a ten-metre board, defended a friend from bullies, interrupted Todd during a season finale of *Line of Duty*. And in the weeks after the separation was decided, but before anyone had moved out, she would drag Todd out of the house for coffee and walks. Robin overheard the conversations, Amber taking charge, Amber caring. And now here she was, repeating that Robin and Faye weren't so different, even though Amber must have known Robin didn't want to hear it.

'That's been the hardest thing for Dad – and me.'

'What?' asked Robin.

'You not opening up about exactly why being married to him wasn't working for you any more. We both felt you hadn't shared the absolute truth. That left Dad feeling in limbo for a long time.'

'I'm so sorry.'

'I know there was probably fault on both sides.' Amber sighed. 'I've thought about it a lot. And since living in Stonedale you've been able to explain more because, as you said, coming back here has given you clarity. I think I understand it a little better now.' Amber fidgeted with one of Robin's old friendship bracelets on her wrist. 'And I'm sorry too. I've given you a hard time. You've had a lot of stuff to deal with over the years but you've kept going, dealing with it by yourself. I phoned Dad the other night. He knew snippets about your past but when I told him exactly how Gran had been... he had no idea just how tough your childhood was.'

'It was easier for me to try to forget.'

'Coming up north again proves you can't forget something like that, Mum, it's like deleting an email from your inbox so that you don't see it every day, but there's always a permanent copy saved somewhere.'

'If today means the treasure hunt is over...'

'I think that's likely,' said Amber and she gave another sigh.

Wind rattled the church's door again.

'How do you feel about your studies?' asked Robin eventually. 'I know solving the anagram was an incentive for staying.'

'It's early days, Mum, but I've got a good feeling about halls, I already feel happier there than I ever did in that student house.' Her voice lifted a little. 'So I'll see out this term and make a decision at Christmas.' She stared at her through the shadows. 'However, I'll stay in Stonedale tonight. I'd better go and see Gran.'

'No, love.' Robin tried to smile. 'You go back into town.'

Amber put her hands on Robin's shoulders. 'How about you and I make a fresh start? From now on you stop trying to be perfect, and accept I'm no longer a child, and me, I'll try to remember that you're hurting in all of this, too. We can just be there for each other, can't we, two women listening, helping where possible, without trying to fix everything?'

Robin gave a small nod, her heart bursting over the woman Amber had become.

'I'm like you and Gran, I'm not made of glass.' Amber gave Robin a brief hug and left.

Robin sat there, on her own. She'd always felt like a one-off, some sort of freak observing life from the outside, asking herself how other people could be so happy. But now Amber was saying the three of them shared traits... Robin blinked in the darkness.

Eventually she left the church, eyes squinting at fairy lights twinkling in a shop. Would their baby have had Yul's black hair and eyes? She'd tried, so hard, to block Ash out too, all these years, but couldn't ignore him on celebratory occasions. Like Easter, she bet he'd have loved making chocolate nests with mini eggs in the middle, as a treat, just like Amber did. And on

Mother's Day she'd feel like that sixteen-year-old again who'd tortured herself with thoughts that perhaps he'd still be here if she'd chosen Stonedale over the drama of fleeing to London.

Robin knocked hard on the bookshop door. Lights flicked on and Yul appeared. He pulled it open and she went inside. They sat down at one of the tables out the back, holding hands. She told him about the church. Faye storming off. Ash.

'Do you remember why we called him that?' she whispered.

'Of course. The wooden house in the ash tree. Our special place.'

'I've thought about him a lot, over the years,' she said quietly.

'Me too. Every July.' That was when they lost him. 'I imagine the birthday celebrations, him playing pass the parcel when he was younger, barbecue parties as he grew, me getting excited about meeting his friends. Silly really.'

He lapsed into thought and Robin studied the face she'd loved so much, once, the firm line of his jaw, the eyebrows that would wiggle with indignation or amusement and make her laugh, oh, so hard.

'What are you thinking?' she asked.

'No, it's all right.'

Robin tilted her head and squeezed his hand.

'Has having your daughter made it easier?' It came out as a whisper.

'Not the pregnancy, that's for sure, I was terrified of losing her. And in the beginning, after she was born, every time she got colic or fell ill, I felt a gnawing inside, that I wasn't up to the job, that losing Ash was nature's way because I'd be a terrible mother.' Todd had been good at reassuring her, listening to every one of her endless worries, supporting her choices over weaning, sleep routines and dummies. It made a real difference and she could see how her pregnant grandmother must have struggled when her husband never came back from the trenches.

'Oh, Robin, I wish I'd been there.' He held her tight, his arms as strong as they always used to be whenever she had a fallout with Faye. He leant back and took her hands. 'I wasn't expecting this... us to...' He swallowed. 'You're only up here for a couple more weeks, so who knows...?'

'Yul?'

'Seeing Tara again, it's made me realise, there are a few things you should know. The reason things were awkward between me and Tara... I tried to kiss her at a party.' He looked away as the words hurried out.

'What?' Robin let go of his hands and sat upright.

'It wasn't long after I got back. I was drunk. I apologised the next day but it ruined our friendship. And this is really hard, but I want you to know... I took a couple of girls to the treehouse during that summer. A few times it went all the way.'

Yul had slept with other girls, there, in the woods? But they'd had an agreement, the ash tree, it was private to them. She sat perfectly still despite the turmoil inside. It shouldn't have mattered decades later, but that place was where they'd made Ash. It felt as if, somehow, Yul's trysts there had let their son down. Robin tried to tell herself that wasn't true but she could hardly breathe.

'Tell me once and for all, Yul... why did you leave me in London? If you could sleep with all these girls so soon after you got back... had I got it wrong? Did you never really love me?'

'No! I did, so very, very much. It's just...' A pained look crossed his face.

Robin threw her hands in the air. 'Silly me, expecting you to finally be honest. Well, I can't live, any more, with hidden truths and secrets.'

She stood up. He did too, eyeliner running down his cheek. Robin walked calmly to the door and pulled it open, relieved it wasn't locked, despite the winter gust. Then she charged up the high street, ignoring Yul calling out her name.

Robin Wilson,
16 Parade Row,
Stonedale,
Greater Manchester
November 1988

Dear Debbie,

MY BEST FRIEND IS ACTING WEIRD.

Since going to a Halloween party last weekend, my best friend has been acting weird. She danced with a boy who she gets on really well with and I saw them kiss. I think it was her first one! But then she ran out of the party and I couldn't find her. I asked what had upset her, the next day. She just said she'd felt ill after too much Cinzano, but I know she isn't telling me the truth, we hardly drank anything. She's stopped coming around to mine after school, and says she feels tired and needs a bit of time to herself.

I feel like asking this boy about it but know she'd go mad. Or maybe I should try to set her up with another guy, if this kiss left her disappointed.

How can I make her tell me what is wrong?

Robin, age 16

Girl's Scene
41 Gover Street,
London

Dear Robin,

She sounds as if she could just do with support rather than pressure to talk about it, or kiss another boy! First kisses can be scary, brilliant, disappointing, all those things, and maybe it wasn't what she expected. Being a good friend is sometimes simply about being there, without trying to fix things or find explanations. Maybe just let her know you are sorry she is feeling bad and that you are there for her if she needs you. If she wants to talk, she probably will in good time, and when that happens try just to listen, without jumping in.

If she's not herself in a few weeks, and you are still worried, perhaps you could have a quiet word with her mum.

Best wishes,

Debbie

40

Robin parked up outside and pushed open the door, stepping on a pile of mail. The flat was waiting for her, calm and tidy. She walked in, her hair full of sleet and shook herself like Hoover. She missed his boisterous welcome. Robin shivered and switched the heating on, and the boiler rumbled into life.

Faye hadn't looked Robin in the eye before she left, didn't say a word when she'd watched her squash Yul's sweatshirt into the kitchen bin. She had left before breakfast, after Amber had left for the train station. Amber told Robin to ring when she got to London, the kind of promise Robin used to make her give. Faye could cook now, dress herself, drink leftover pickle juice. Robin had caught her doing that the last time she'd made lunch. In other words, Faye now had all the prerequisites for a happy single life. She'd manage fine until Robin went back to Stonedale.

If she did.

Right now, she needed to be as far away as possible from Faye, from Yul. Escaping back to London, as quickly as possible, had felt like the only option. It was too hard, too painful, staying close to a mother who'd never wanted her and a (sort of) boyfriend who wouldn't explain himself.

Late last night, she'd rung Tara, who offered to clear her appointments and spend time with her, dropping everything for her friend, just like they used to do for each other. But still, Robin couldn't wait to leave.

Now, on top of the narrow breakfast bar, she unpacked the rucksack of essentials she'd bought at one of the motorway shops – milk, bread, eggs, proper crisps, a large bar of chocolate. The latter two wouldn't have been seen as staples before she'd stayed with Faye, and this week Faye had confessed she'd never eaten so many fruits and vegetables since she and Amber had moved in. Without realising it they'd changed each other in little ways that were inconsequential for others – and perhaps for them too because, in the end, they'd made no difference.

Sleet railed against the window as Robin drew the curtains in her bedroom. She stood and turned three hundred and sixty degrees. Had she really decorated using so many taupes, creams and beiges? The stories the decor told here were simply of shops. A half-price lamp from Marks, a discounted wallpaper from B&Q. She dropped onto the bed and lay on her stomach, surprised the mattress didn't groan – she felt like a dead weight.

Eventually, she dragged herself up, pulled on her dressing gown and snuggled on the sofa with an opened tube of biscuits. She turned on the TV and switched channels every time she wondered if Faye was watching the same programme. Her pumpkin-scented candle released its fragrance and she imagined Faye wrinkling her nose. After her hot chocolate Robin turned off the Friday night chat show and sifted through the mail and put the lease renewal letter for the flat on top of the nearby bookcase. She'd fill that in tomorrow. Her eyes scanned the books and dropped to the bottom shelf. She pulled out a family photo album and sat back down as a train rumbled past.

Amber had had such wavy hair as a toddler. It had straightened out during primary school. She'd love sitting on Todd's shoulders, singing she was the queen of the castle. Swimming in the sea on holiday was a favourite activity of hers, Todd had insisted she start lessons early and took her to the local pool every Sunday morning when he actually took time off work. In the early days he did overtime to fund their breaks abroad, and as the business grew the hours got longer. He said that was to pay for the things he wanted his family to have, like premiere tickets to West End shows and the latest gadgets.

Robin ran a finger over a photo of Todd, recalling how her dad worked all weekends in the run up to Christmas. He'd buy Faye flowers once a week but she never heard him tell her he loved her. Robin had assumed that was only because she wouldn't have appreciated such sentimentality – she knew he loved Faye, he expressed it through his actions constantly. He'd cook at weekends, take her out for lunch, smooth over the arguments between her and Robin. He'd listen to her chat about problems at work. Staying in Stonedale, in the old house, had brought back all these details.

Flicking through the album made Robin realise Todd hadn't been that different. He'd supported her career and the difficult situation with her mother. Had Robin lost sight of the important things he did, day in, day out, that weren't dressed up in the flowers and ribbons she'd wanted? He preferred red wine but drank her favourite white. He always defrosted the freezer, a job she hated. Blankly, she looked at the pages. Her life in London had been created by a teenage girl desperately needing security. She'd told herself that strict routine, that work, work, work, would pull her life back together; that fitting in would advance any career and give her a settled life, no drama. And she'd coupled that with a determination to be the opposite to her mother – a good parent, a caring neighbour and work colleague, an unbeatable homemaker. Her passion, for Todd, in the beginning had been real, but over time got lost, the harder she'd tried to...

Robin closed the photo album and pushed it back into the bookcase.

The harder she'd tried to use him to fill the gap created by an absent mother.

She went into the hall, threw off her dressing gown and pulled on the biker jacket. Despite the clouds she stood in the back garden and looked up at the stars, wondering if her dad might be up there somewhere. It started to sleet again but she didn't budge, not until the streetlamps went out. Hair sodden through, she finally went indoors, switched on the oven and set about baking Uncle Ralph a cake.

41

Robin hurried along to his room and went in. As she closed the door behind her, she took a moment. Ralph wore the waistcoat he kept for special occasions.

'Blimey...' He eyed her up and down.

She rushed over, put the cake tin on the bed and burst into tears. He held her tight, and the smell of his aftershave felt familiar and safe. She sat down on a wooden chair opposite him and unzipped her jacket.

'Alan loved your curls, you know, they're just like our mum's.' He patted the bed next to him. She went over and he held her hand.

'Sorry for getting upset.'

'Nonsense.'

She explained first, about the scene in the church, about how Faye had *never* wanted her; that many women didn't want kids, and why should they? But when it was your own mother and she said it to your face... Uncle Ralph sucked in his cheeks and shook his head.

'I suppose I can't complain, I've always wanted the truth, an explanation but... it hurts.'

'Oh, love.'

Robin told him what Amber had said too. That Robin had always tried to fix things, how most of the time she just wanted her to listen and Robin realised now how good Uncle Ralph had been at that. She retold the argument with Faye, word for word, and he sat, saying nothing, wincing, nodding. When she finally stopped talking, he pulled her towards him and they hugged again.

'How were the two of you getting on, before?'

'Better. I thought we were making real progress. But now I feel as if I don't want to ever go back to Stonedale. It's all so... complicated.'

'Complicated won't get sorted from afar, Missy... and what about this treasure hunt? You've got to finish that. You're so near the end.'

'That's the least of my worries.' Robin waved her hand in the air.

'But you must.'

'Dad wouldn't be bothered, not in light of how bad things are between us.'

'But you could go back for a couple of days, for the hospital appointment, tie the hunt in with one last trip.'

'Why? Why is this so important? I mean, really, does it even matter?'

He fiddled with the tassels of a checked rug on his lap. She waited.

'When I came up on business, that week just before he died and he was about to go to Sheffield on that renovation job, he and I went to the pub that evening... Alan told me that on the last job away he'd suffered chest pains. He went to the local hospital. They ran some tests, said he was to make an appointment with his doctor as soon as possible for a referral, that he'd need to make changes to his diet, but he was putting it off. I did think there was no way he'd cut out cheese and red meat.'

Robin didn't move. Her dad *knew* what might happen?

He gave a sad smile. 'Alan always did ask for seconds of beef. Mum used to say he mooed in his sleep.'

'Did Faye know about the chest pains?' Robin gripped the wooden arm of her chair.

'No. And he made me promise not to say anything. She was worried, having heard rumours that her job was under threat and he always wanted to make life easier for her.'

Robin's knuckles turned white. It all came back now, how Faye had been more irritable than ever in the run up to Dad leaving for Sheffield, worrying about having to leave Lewis's – worries that had turned out to be ill-founded at that time, what with the store not going into administration until a couple of years later. Robin was suffering from morning sickness and one particularly bad morning told her that she had a bug. But Faye had forced her into school saying the symptoms would wear off with fresh air, even though she must have heard Robin throwing up.

'And you had exams. Alan said he could tell you were under a lot of stress.'

Yes, Robin thought. She was pregnant and trying to work out how to tell him.

'He said he'd get around to seeing the doctor when he got back, I could tell the real reason for the delay was that he was scared. If only I'd said something...' Uncle Ralph's face crumpled.

'You can stop that right now. There's no way what happened is your fault.' Robin shook her head. 'Oh, Dad... if only he'd opened up about it, and done what the hospital said, the stupid, stubborn...'

She was beginning to see that the most important thing about family was talking to each other. Properly. Maybe they could all try harder to do that, now... at least she could with Amber and Uncle Ralph.

'It might not have made any difference. I should have told Faye, though, she'd have insisted he go to the doctor.' His voice cracked. 'The only thing left, that we – you – can do for him, is complete that last treasure hunt, as he wanted.'

She told Uncle Ralph about the letters they'd already worked out. A care assistant brought in coffees. The cake tin remained unopened. They talked more about Faye finding out about Robin's pregnancy.

'That's me in the doghouse for sure, then,' he muttered. 'And how's Yul been about all this and you turning up?'

She'd always liked he'd not called Yul *Jason*.

Robin blushed.

'Ah, thought so.'

'So did I, but then I found out he'd... he'd let me down. And our baby.' She pressed her lips together.

He ran a hand over the stubble on his chin. 'That doesn't sound like the lad I met.'

'Really? He ran out on me, in London, without giving any explanation. I'd just lost our child. We had so many plans. We were getting past that but now... I don't think I ever really knew him at all.'

He shuffled in his seat and stared out of the window.

'Ralph?' Robin never called him that. 'Is there something else I don't know?' Her underarms felt damp.

He sighed. 'It was naive of me to think you going up north wouldn't unearth things from the past. You need to know, Robin, I only ever had your interests at heart. When the hospital rang to say my niece had been admitted, my first urge was to call Faye but I wanted to get all my facts straight first. They wouldn't tell me what the matter was. As soon as I saw you and Yul I could see you were both frightened. I'd seen those expressions before on local lads older than me who'd come back from the war, on friends when their close relatives passed. I knew the reason you were in hospital was a matter of life or death.'

'But what's this got to do with Yul going back to Stonedale?'

He carried on talking, focused on the rug's tassels again, bringing it all back, how the hospital had wanted to discharge Robin the next day.

'The pair of you were in no fit state to go back to a landlord threatening to throw you out. So I did what I thought was the kindest thing. I took Yul to one side and told him quite firmly that he was to leave.'

Robin's jaw dropped. She pictured Yul's face in the hospital. The sobs she could tell he was choking back, when he said goodbye.

Her eyes smarted. 'What?'

Uncle Ralph's fingers tightened around a handful of rug. 'I hadn't got the money or room to put up two teenagers and after what had happened, that lad needed his mum.'

'But he just agreed? It doesn't make sense.' The colour drained from her face. 'Didn't put up a fight?'

'Of course he tried to change my mind. You were that lad's everything, anyone could see that. He told me to eff off, that you and he could conquer the world as long as you stayed together, that you were sixteen and there was nothing I could do about it. So I told him that if he really loved you he'd act in your best interests, that, realistically, you'd run out of money within days and that with no exam results a job would be hard to find.'

Thoughts swirled around her mind.

'That would have left you young'uns with just two options: sleeping on the streets or going back to Faye's or his parents. He didn't want either of those things for you and knew I was right when I said you'd never move in with your uncle if your boyfriend was still in the picture.'

Uncle Ralph explained he had bought him a train ticket and taken him out for a meal. Yul had cried into his tea mug when a young mother came in with a baby.

'I wonder why he hasn't told me,' Robin said, her voice quiet, her mind back on the hospital ward again, watching Yul leave, lying there, waiting for him to turn around one last time.

'I reckon he's a loyal lad, he gave me his word he wouldn't say anything.'

Yul had asked how Uncle Ralph was these days. Had he been probing to see if he was still alive, planning to tell her the truth if her uncle had passed?

'Sorry, if you feel I did the wrong thing,' he said in a small voice. 'But at the time I didn't have a choice. I knew how Faye was with you and without Alan around had to follow my gut instinct.'

Robin let out a deep breath. 'With my middle-aged head on, I see now I'd probably have done the same.'

'You and me, we're okay, love?' For a second his eyes looked more hooded, the wrinkles more pronounced. Robin knelt down by his side.

'Of course we are, Uncle Ralph, we're more than okay. I'm so grateful to have always had you in my corner. What would I ever have done without you?'

He caught her hand as she got to her feet. 'It's always been hard for me, the way Faye's acted towards you. But one thing I will say about her – she's a tough cookie. You're your mother's daughter, Robin. You'd have managed one way or another.'

42

A bark shot upstairs and Robin got off the bed. The house had been empty when she'd arrived, even though she'd texted Faye to say what time she'd be back. But then she was a little early, the Sunday traffic had been quiet. The kettle bubbled as she walked into the kitchen. Faye had put out two mugs. Robin placed the cake tin on the table, Faye brewed up and brought over their drinks, then she tugged off the lid. It took her a while with one hand. She stared in, hesitated, and then fetched two plates and a knife. The pink and yellow checked pattern inside had come out all right.

'Why would you make my favourite?'

Robin drank her tea, even though it was far too hot. She could do this. 'It's not that strange, is it?'

'No, it's perfectly normal to make marzipan from scratch, to fiddle with two colours of batter and carefully stack four rectangles of sponge with just enough jam, to transport it over two hundred miles, all for a woman you'd only seen once in three decades.'

Robin pulled her plate nearer, grasping it tightly. 'Maybe I'm hoping we can sit here, drink tea, eat cake, and open up properly to each other. Or don't you care whether we have some kind of relationship?'

Faye looked ruffled.

'And we have to finish that treasure hunt. If nothing else, because it's so important to Uncle Ralph.'

'What do you mean?'

Robin breathed in, breathed out. Slowly she explained how Dad had actually known his heart could pack in at any time, how he'd sworn his brother to secrecy. Their tea became cold, the lines on Faye's forehead deepened. 'It's almost as if he knew he might not return from Sheffield, I think that's why he created an anagram that he said would change everything.'

The teaspoon Faye held started to shake.

'I felt angry too,' Robin said. 'He should have told us, he should have seen the doctor.'

'That was the stupid old fool all over.' Her chin trembled. 'He put off going to see the doctor about pain in his big toe, not long after we got married. It turned out to be an ingrown nail and he had to have surgery and time off.'

'Uncle Ralph said Dad didn't want to worry us. You believed your job was under threat, I had exams.'

Faye jerked back. 'I could have coped.'

'And he'll have known that but... he must have been in denial.' Robin felt queasy but forced down a mouthful of cake. 'So I'm hoping you can be open with me... You say you didn't want children, but... why, Faye, why, despite that, couldn't you try to make it work better between you and me?'

After all these years Uncle Ralph had revealed important secrets about Alan's health and Yul. It had made Robin realise she had to go back to Stonedale, had to find out the things Faye had never told her.

Faye flinched. 'No crime against it, is there, not feeling maternal? I thought you modern women were supposed to respect each other's decisions.'

Robin pushed away her plate. 'That's true, each to their own, everyone's different, but you're my mum. I'm your daughter. I want, I *need* to know, so that I can understand if... you really didn't want a baby or it's more that you weren't sure and I...' Her voice wavered. 'I turned out to be a disappointment.'

Faye stared at her, opened her mouth and closed it. She picked up the blue and white striped teapot but then put it down again. 'I had good reason.'

'I'm listening.'

Her face looked pinched.

'Please.'

Faye took off her glasses and rubbed her eyes, taking a moment. 'I knew I wouldn't be a good parent. Satisfied?' Her voice broke. 'I told Alan I'd be useless but he talked me around, he said I was a brilliant wife and there was no way I wouldn't be as good a mum.'

That rang true. Dad always saw the positives.

A tear trickled down Faye's cheek. 'You think I didn't look at other mothers and daughters too, and think that maybe things should be different? But after the way my mother was with me, I just didn't know how to act towards you, how to be... I tried, Robin, but it was a long labour, a difficult birth, and as those early days passed I didn't feel what I thought I was supposed to.'

Robin's hand pressed against her breastbone.

'Those first few months I was tired all the time. You never stopped crying and whenever my mother visited, which wasn't often, she'd just look at me as if to say *I told you so*. Her favourite phrase was *just you wait*. Just you wait until she starts walking, you'll never get any rest, just you wait until she finds her own voice and disagrees with everything you think. Alan had to go away on a long job when you were just one month old. I felt so alone but didn't feel I could tell anyone. You didn't back then. The neighbours with babies all looked so happy. I was… in a dark place.' She talked about whole days when she never got dressed, and feelings of being a failure when breastfeeding proved difficult. She blamed herself for nappy rash and didn't always get up if Robin cried during the night. It all came gushing out, like water out of a rusty old tap that was finally turned on.

'That whole first year was a blur. I tried to keep jolly for Alan, I couldn't even talk to him. He was so proud and took the pram to the pub, every now and again, to show off how pretty you were. I hated myself most of the time, overwhelmed by the sense that I was a bad person, that I'd let my family down.'

Robin's throat ached as she looked deep into her mother's eyes and felt as if, for the very first time, she really saw her.

'It sounds as if you had postnatal depression, that's what it's called these days. One of my colleagues had to take a further six months off work, after maternity leave, to deal with hers.'

Faye stared back at Robin and her posture relaxed a little. 'Things did seem better for a while, when you were at primary school. I felt as if I got away with not knowing what made a good mother and that took off the pressure.' Faye sniffed. 'But when you hit your teens, I could sense you saw straight through me. I suppose that put me on the defensive and my mother's *I told you so* words kept coming back. I used to tell myself I was a monster,' she whispered. 'But I'm not, Robin, I'm not.'

Robin went around to her side of the table, crouched down and wrapped her arms around Faye, the plaster cast between them. She leant away but Robin firmly pulled her back. After a few minutes, and ever so slowly, Faye's good arm slipped around

Robin. Faye sobbed, big, ugly jerking wrenches and Robin stayed crouched for as long as it took.

After, when Faye calmed down, both of them exhausted, they went into the lounge and sat together on the chaise longue, Hoover next to Faye, his head resting on her navy cords.

'I need to wash my face,' Faye mumbled.

'Has my eyeliner run?'

Faye gulped and looked at her and shook her head. 'I secretly admired that in your Jason. I thought any boy who could wear eyeliner in Stonedale would do all right.'

They gave each other a small smile and heat radiated through Robin's chest.

Faye stroked Hoover. 'How are things going... between you two? I saw you throw his sweatshirt away.'

Robin sighed.

Faye nodded. Just a nod, a little thing, but it meant the world.

'I went up into your old room from time to time, you know,' said Faye. 'Until I found the ladders too difficult. Then recently, I'd just go in when I had to go up there for the duvets.'

That would explain why it wasn't quite as mouldy and dirty as Robin had expected when she'd first discovered it.

'It sounds silly... sometimes I'd talk to you. Try to explain. Often I ended up just lying there, looking at your posters.'

Robin felt like hugging her again.

Perhaps it would have been a good thing if Dad had found the hidden pregnancy stick when he'd shoved his box of paperwork into the bottom of her wardrobe. So much might have been different.

Robin's phone rang; it was Amber. She got up to go into the hallway, to carry on the conversation, but then sat back down. No more secrets. Amber asked how Robin was and, tentatively, whether there was any chance they'd be completing the treasure hunt. Robin said she and her *mum* had talked, that things were now... back on track? She looked at Faye. Faye's eyes filled.

Amber had been studying hard all weekend to meet a deadline and felt she deserved a break, she wanted to catch the train to Stonedale tomorrow. She'd cook them pasta, Blanche could come. Voice bubbling with enthusiasm, Amber couldn't wait to read the last clue again, in preparation for completing the hunt on Thursday.

'Would you be up for that... Mum?' Robin asked.

Faye straightened herself. 'What do you think, Hoover?'

He barked his approval.

Robin Wilson,
16 Parade Row,
Stonedale,
Greater Manchester
January 1989

Dear Debbie,

   WHAT'S LOSING YOUR VIRGINITY SUPPOSED TO BE LIKE?

   I overhead some girls at school talking about losing their virginity and they said it was amazing, just like in the movies. Is it supposed to be like that?

   Robin, age 16

Girl's Scene
41 Gover Street,
London

Dear Robin,

   Like the movies? No, and I wouldn't believe all these girls say! They were probably just trying to impress each other. It's different for everyone, for some it can be great, for others it may feel uncomfortable and awkward. However, all of that improves as time goes by. When the moment comes, the important thing is to relax, and to have a partner who really cares for you and is happy to go at your own pace.

   Just remember – even actors don't get the scene right first time!

   Best wishes,

   Debbie

43

'You and I need a chat later,' said Blanche in a low voice, and gave Robin a pointed look. She and Faye sat in the lounge enjoying a pre-dinner gin. Faye was looking at her phone.

Amber and Robin went up into the loft. Pleading a student budget too small to buy what Uncle Ralph would call fripperies, Amber wanted to root through Robin's old accessories again. She was especially taken with a pair of gold and black dangly earrings. Robin wanted their time together to last forever as Amber laughed at the dramatic, primary-coloured pieces she spotted. She also found a pair of fingerless black lace gloves and insisted they each fit one on, as well as sliding banana clips into their hair, eighties fashion at its best and so different to the plain hair ties Amber normally used. They sat on the bed and talked about how excited they were at the prospect of working out the last of Alan's clues.

Amber cleared her throat. 'I've decided, Mum – I'm definitely returning to university after Christmas. I'm loving halls and have already made a few new friends.'

'Oh, sweetheart. It's great that you've reached a decision you're happy with.' Robin held her tightly. Amber let her.

Robin mentioned her own news, how she was going to set up as a freelance marketing consultant. Two emails had arrived, offering her interviews for the jobs she'd applied for. Confident of her new direction, she turned them down. Amber thought it was fucking fantastic. It didn't feel like the time to have a word with her about swearing.

'Your dad and I, there were lots of good moments, you know, he... he's a good man,' said Robin quietly. 'But I always felt like... like something was missing. Perhaps that's been a satisfying job.'

Amber paused and gave a small nod. 'Or... perhaps it's not been a something – perhaps it's been a *someone*.' She waved her hand around the room. 'All this. The real you.'

* * *

Later, Amber set down the bowls of pasta and the four of them sat around the table accompanied by the aroma of basil and tomato.

'Which meat did you use?' asked Blanche, studying the sauce.

'Beef tomatoes.'

After they finished, Faye insisted on helping Amber in the kitchen, Robin left her drying dishes, Amber putting them away, as if it were a Morecambe and Wise routine the two of them had mastered over years. Blanche relaxed in the armchair, Robin sat on the floor next to her.

'Things seem better with you and Faye, now,' said Blanche and adjusted the hot water bottle wedged behind her shoulder.

'Oh... yes. And my trip to London helped me work out a few things – about my ex-husband too.'

'So is your life feeling more... complete?'

'Amber and I are back on track, I'm talking with Mum. This is more than I could ever have hoped for.' And as she said it, Robin realised this was true.

'I can already see a difference in Faye, she seems... less apologetic.' Blanche smiled.

'I've used a lot of adjectives to describe her, over the years, but never that one.'

'It's why she's been on the defence the whole time, 'tis often the way with folk, what seems like an attack is actually the opposite.' She pulled up her blanket. 'I saw it in the care home, the most aggressive residents were the most afraid. Your mum's always been on edge if strangers have asked about whether she has children.'

'But afraid of what?' Robin asked.

'Anything that made her face the truth, I suppose – that her relationship with you wasn't... wasn't what a stranger might expect of a mother and daughter.'

'Why do you think you and Mum have got on so well, all these years, despite being quite different?' Robin had been wanting to ask Blanche this for a while.

Blanche thought for a moment. 'It's the passing of time that brings you together, flower, however much money or children you've got, or fancy school certificates, the feelings are the same around loss, around all the aches and pains of getting older. And we all ask ourselves the same questions that won't go away in the early hours about whether we've done everything we should have with our years.'

Questions Robin had asked herself in London.

She patted Robin's hand. 'Of course, the reason we needed this chat – you haven't mentioned the one problem you've got left.'

'You don't hold back do you, Blanche?' Robin couldn't help grinning.

'Life's short, you don't realise that until you've burnt the wick down to the wax. What's going on with Jason?' Gently she tickled Robin's side with her toes. 'I spotted him in the village yesterday. He looked bloomin' miserable.'

'We fell out over stuff that goes back years.' Robin looked away. She understood now why he left her in London, but after what he told her about other girls in the treehouse she still couldn't help feeling he'd let down their son, Ash. It was a smaller thing, she felt she should get over it, but in her head it was just getting bigger and bigger.

'You really like him?' Blanche said softly.

Robin rolled her lips together.

'And these things, he was sixteen at the time?'

Robin met her gaze again.

'I know how... fiery things used to be between you and your mum years ago, but you've come back, I've seen you hold your tongue, you've looked after her, and despite the past you've been responsible in a way a younger you wouldn't have been.' Blanche raised her eyebrows.

Robin nodded.

'And I sense she's changed too,' Blanche continued. 'Fallouts in families, it's nothing unusual, frequently I dealt with relatives who hadn't had a good relationship with their parent. But maturity gives us the tools to deal with challenging situations in a different way.'

Robin had seen that with Tara and her dad.

'What are you saying, Blanche?' Robin leant forward.

'Jason seems like a good man. If he did things years ago, that hurt, perhaps you need to ask yourself if it was down to the person he really is, or down to youth. I'm sure you'd act differently if you could go back.'

Maybe.

'What are you going to do about it? It's clearly weighing on your mind.'

'Could you empty the bin, Robin?' called Faye's voice.

Robin jumped up and hurried into the kitchen, relieved to take a break from Blanche's questions. When she came back indoors, the three others were laughing at a comedy show, passing around homemade peppermint creams Blanche had brought.

Robin had had many surprises in her life, good and bad – like the pregnancy, Dad's death, Yul leaving her, like when Todd got down on one knee in their favourite restaurant, like the surprise that Robin had thought she knew everything at sixteen but at forty-eight still hadn't got it worked out. And this warm, good-humoured scene of togetherness with her mum and her daughter... it was right up there with the best of them.

44

Tara had texted Robin.

Call me.

Robin didn't want to talk about Yul, yet didn't want to jeopardise their newfound friendship. Though it was Tara's day off, Robin couldn't face meeting up, so she texted back saying she'd ring soon and added two kisses.

Faye wanted to have a go at making vegetable quiche. Next she'd be asking to borrow Robin's old ra-ra skirt. They were out of eggs and Robin needed to visit the supermarket anyway, to buy Amber's new favourite crisps for lunch in a couple of days, when she came over to do the last treasure hunt clue. As she left, Faye went to Blanche's for coffee, with Hoover, muttering something about needing to pick up the life she'd had before the fall. Robin started thinking about visiting her next year, she could drive up to Stonedale for Easter, birthdays...

Robin tried to ignore Brynner's Books but couldn't miss a huge sign in the window as she approached.

Closed until further notice.

She went up to the glass. The lights were out, the back room was dark. She walked on, turning around twice, down the high street, left at the bottom and into the supermarket. Had something happened? She pictured him wired up to a hospital monitor, like Dad. Robin would never get to say the things she wanted. She bought the eggs and, on automatic, picked up a couple of cream buns. Very occasionally, Faye had bought them, and one would be waiting on a plate, in the kitchen, when she got in from school.

Without reading the total on the card machine, Robin paid. She was glad to get out into the fresh air again. She crossed the high street early telling herself it wasn't an excuse to walk past the bookshop. A flicker of movement in the window caught her eye. Maybe he was in there after all. Her phone rang and, grateful for the distraction, she stopped near the lamppost and faced the road. She answered without seeing who the caller was.

'Why are you putting off speaking to me?'

Tara.

'Where are you, Robin?'

'Out shopping.'

'At least you aren't lying.' Robin turned around. Tara stood in Brynner's window, wearing a thick anorak over dungarees and a bandana in her hair. She opened the door and beckoned her in. Robin put her bag down by the recycling bin and unzipped the top of her jacket, feeling stifled.

'Before you say anything, I told Yul he's a shit for upsetting you. Then he came over to mine last night and we chatted. Yul mentioned something about London, about the treehouse over the bridge… I don't know the details, only that he's desperate to talk to you and has been since you left. You'll find him out the back.'

He was okay? Robin felt the tension in her shoulders loosen a little.

'How about a hot chocolate with marshmallows and cream?'

Robin hesitated. 'I'm not sure.'

Tara folded her arms. 'Talk to him, Robin, if for no other reason than helping me. I've run out of jokes and he's still looking sadder than a sodden dishcloth.'

Tara went back into the kitchen and crockery clattered. Robin walked into the back room. Yul was outside, the sleeves of his black hoodie rolled up, soil all over his jeans. Half the patio slabs had been lifted and turf put down. She opened the door.

'I'm only here because Tara bribed me with the promise of a hot chocolate and all the trimmings.'

He looked up and his spade fell to the ground. A smile crept across his face but rapidly disappeared after meeting her eyes.

'What's all this work in aid of?' Robin asked, not sure what else to say.

'I've decided to make more of the back, make it more pleasant to look out on. Tara's helped me create this small lawn. I've ordered two garden tables, it'll be a reading space for smokers.'

'You could plant a small tree, maybe some plants,' Robin said with a shrug. 'A bookshop with a café, with a nature area.'

'I'm sorry, Robin.' The words spilled out. 'About London. About the other girls. I hated myself every single time I took someone to our place but I couldn't help pressing the fuck-it button. At the time I felt like I had nothing to lose.' He sat on the ground, his back against the wall and bent his legs, resting his chin on his knees. Heart hammering, Robin sat down next to him. A blackbird space-hopped across the new grass as he explained how hard it had been to leave her in London. Still he never let on about his promise to Uncle Ralph.

'I was hurting, Robin. I went a little crazy, sleeping around, desperate to fill the void inside. With each new girl I'd hope to feel something, anything, but never did.' He pressed the balls of his hands into his eyes. 'I'm not proud, I shouldn't have used them like that, and couldn't believe I'd been so stupid with such a good friend as Tara.' His chin quivered. 'I know what happened was shit for you, just the worst thing, but... I lost out too. I'd made so many plans in my head for you, me and Ash. I thought about him all the time and I left a teddy bear by the treehouse once.

Oh Yul.

Robin shuffled up and pulled his hands away from his face, the black liner smudged under his eyes. She leant in close, sensitive to every breath he took, holding tightly onto a handful of his hoodie.

'I'm sorry, I should have trusted your feelings for our son... and your reasons for leaving London.'

'What?'

'Uncle Ralph explained. You did it for me. I should have known.'

Yul closed his eyes and let out a long, shaky breath. 'He really told you? Every time I think back I feel like that young lad again, so angry at him but knowing he was right. I really admired your uncle for taking you in. It's hard to resolve anger against someone you respect.'

All these years she'd thought no one could ever understand the trauma she'd been through but as Yul described his experience he looked like a frightened teenager, and it took her back too. He talked and talked, about how his parents' relief when he went back had swiftly turned to hurt when they discovered he'd not confided in them about the pregnancy, and then outrage that he'd not considered them, sitting by the phone all night, every night, believing he and Robin would both end up on the streets and get into drugs, that they'd end up dead. Then they'd blamed themselves, Yul said that was the worst, Robin took his hand. Once the initial storm ran its course, they decided there should be consequences for him – he had to learn what they'd done was risky.

So they stopped giving him money, gave him endless chores and set him a curfew. Each day of the summer holiday stretched out with no end in sight. Sneaking out to get together with other girls was a distraction. A distraction from the fact that he wasn't getting married, he wasn't going to be a father or live the life they'd dreamed of in London. He was back in Stonedale with no best friends, the subject of gossip wherever he turned. He shoplifted alcohol and got into trouble with the police. And she never wrote. He checked the post every day for months. A pang of guilt swept through Robin but he squeezed her fingers, as if to say, *now I understand*. Eventually his parents persuaded him to get counselling, to get a part-time job. Bit by bit they trusted him again. Slowly he accepted what had happened.

'This weekend, let's go to treehouse and leave flowers,' he said.

'I'd like that,' Robin said, as her phone buzzed.

Everything okay? I'm back from Blanche's. Mum.

Such a simple sentence, such a complex journey to reach it.

'You realise Tara is going to be unbearable now we've started to sort things out,' he said, a spark of light in those ebony eyes.

'Let's get it over with. At least there's hot chocolate.'

45

'I hereby order the last clue be read,' said Amber in an important voice.

Robin couldn't keep still as the three of them and Hoover stood by the gate outside the front of Faye's house. It had been raining but seemed to be holding off now. Amber unfurled the scroll and it flapped in the breeze.

'Think about shapes to take part,
First a circle, last a heart.
Go out and on the left you'll soon see the pump,
Then over we go, mind the hump.
Your destination is opposite the Dancing Queen.
Bingo! My little joke, happy to come clean.
In you go, up you go, look left once more,
Find the contents of the square, lie on the floor.
Here the hunt ends, I hope the memory of it will stay.
Love you so much, my beautiful Robin, my wonderful
Faye.'

Love you so much too, Dad. Robin might have sobbed had Amber not been so excited.

'Circles, hearts, squares, what is Granddad going on about?'

'It sounds like another board game,' Faye said, 'and he always did love ABBA. I'm not surprised he managed to fit in one of their singles. "Dancing Queen" was a particular favourite. He'd play it on repeat.'

'Draught counters are circles but I can't think of a game that uses hearts or squares,' said Robin.

'Should we go to the right or left?' asked Amber. 'There must be some sort of pump in Stonedale village, as the only thing I've seen up the other end of Parade Row is an estate agency.'

Faye and Robin looked at each other.

'An estate agency?' said Robin. 'Years ago, a petrol station stood there, it had a little shop.'

'A huge supermarket on the outskirts took their business,' said Faye. 'About ten years ago it finally closed. A shame because it was handy for picking up milk and bread.'

They turned to the left and headed that way, stepping over puddles. They stopped outside the agency.

Amber pointed to the road. 'A hump! We need to cross over.' Hoover yapped.

Robin took Faye's elbow as they stepped onto the road but she shook her off.

'I need to get used to managing on my own, again... but... thank you.'

Robin felt conflicted by thoughts she'd never entertained before, worries about her mum being on her own.

'Now we have to find the dancing queen. I'm going to Google the lyrics to see if that helps.' Amber took out her phone.

Robin shook her head. 'No need. Thanks to Dad's obsession with that hit we can sing them off by heart, right, Mum?'

'Sing? Out here?' said Faye.

'I'm game if you are,' Robin replied, feeling the part in her rock n' roll biker jacket. 'Or... are you chicken?' She'd never teased Faye before and her body stiffened.

'Go on, Gran, everyone needs to embarrass themselves now and again.'

A neighbour walked past. Faye looked at Robin who gave a thumbs-up and started singing. Robin sang the first lines on her own, then... she did, Faye joined in. Amber cupped her hand to her ear so they raised their voices, Faye's frown disappearing. They sang about Friday nights and tambourines, tentatively at first. Amber knew the chorus and punched the air at the words about having the time of their lives. An elderly man strolled past and tipped his trilby. A pair of teenagers giggled as they veered around them. Hoover was unusually lost for barks. It didn't put them off, each lost in their own world as their voices rang out, louder and louder. Eventually Faye's eyes closed as they linked arms and swayed from side to side, in sync with each other. Faye's voice wobbled as they finished and Robin stared at both of the women before starting to laugh. Faye wiped her eyes and Robin carried on laughing, until she realised Faye wasn't.

'Was that one of those moments?' Faye asked in a muffled voice.

Robin's eyes tingled. 'Yes, Mum, it was. It was.'

'Right, so if the answer is in the lyrics,' said Amber, 'we've sung about lights being low... but all the streetlamps are the same height.'

'If, instead, it's referring to the strength of a light there aren't any places in Stonedale where they are especially dimmed,' said Faye. 'We've never had a nightclub.'

They trawled through the lyrics once more, sentences about getting in the swing – that could refer to a play park. Or looking for a king – there wasn't a pub named after royalty... they dissected the chorus and verses.

'Let's step back and read the whole clue again,' said Robin. '*Your destination is opposite the Dancing Queen. Bingo! My little joke, happy to come clean.* Clean... well, there's no bathroom fitters shop or public showers...'

'Have either of you played bingo?' asked Amber.

'Not for years,' said Faye, and Robin shook her head. 'But you're onto something – Dancing Queen could be one of those nicknames bingo callers use for numbers.'

'The lyrics refer to being seventeen... Dancing Queen, seventeen! Amber, check on your phone,' said Robin, deciding it wasn't cheating if they'd already thought of an answer. And so it was. They walked down to number seventeen. The scroll then said their destination was opposite it. 'Oh. It's your house, Mum.'

'The sly old devil. If we cross back over we'll have walked in a complete *circle*.'

'One of Granddad's tricks again!' said Amber.

They went indoors and took off their coats and shoes in the hallway, Faye muttering how she was sick of her cape and couldn't wait to get her cast off next week. They let Hoover into the back garden as it hadn't been much of a walk and then consulted the scroll. *In you go, up you go, look left once more.* They went upstairs and... into Faye's bedroom. 'Now we have to lie on the floor to look for the contents of a square, that's the answer,' said Robin. 'I can't believe we're so close to finding out the word Dad wanted us to know.' She could hardly breathe.

'Don't worry, Gran. We'll let you off this one.' Amber grinned and lay down, stretching out. She scoured the room but only saw furniture legs, and the bottom of a bin and dirty linen basket. She even lifted the edge of the duvet and looked under the bed.

'The room has changed a lot since Dad died. Mum? Any ideas? Could it have been an album or book, or something we picked up from a car boot sale?'

Amber got up. 'We can't give up now, after all our hard work. We're almost there.'

Faye stood lost in thought. 'I remember now, I used to keep a square storage box under the bed. It used to drive Alan mad, I'd never throw out my old puzzle magazines. I guess I felt proud of all the ones I'd completed. He understood that so bought the box for me.' Faye gave a wry smile. 'I threw them out when he died, Alan was right. They were only clutter.'

'So the last letter is M for magazines!' Amber let out a little cheer and there was silence as each tried to be the first to come up with the hunt's solution.

'G, I, L, D, R, M... it doesn't make sense. I can't think of any word Granddad might have meant.'

'What about changing Dino for Stone, so the letter is S instead?' said Robin.

The anagram still didn't create a word.

'Did this ever used to happen?' asked Amber.

Robin and Faye could only remember once, a clue around the letter C for conker tree. The answer should have actually been H for the tree's proper name, Horse-chestnut.

They drank hot tea in the kitchen and carefully went through all the clues again. G for Greece, there was no doubt about that, it definitely looked like a Greek dance the stone birds were doing. No question about the I for Iron Horse either, if an answer was more than one word they always used to take the letter of the first one. And tall, dark and handsome definitely referred to a lamppost, so that was L. R was correct too, none of the other stained-glass windows in the church had anything to do with a flower in them. The contents of the box too, under the bed, that could only be M for magazines. Their only doubts still pointed at the Dino clue.

'What do you think Dad meant by a circle leading to a heart?

'No idea,' said Faye and she sighed.

'I'll always be wondering what the anagram spelt,' Robin mumbled. 'And I feel like we've let Dad down. I can see myself still trying to work this out when I'm back in London.'

'Doing this treasure hunt is the closest I'll ever get to him.' Amber sounded tearful. 'It would have been ace to end it the way he wanted.'

A sense of panic rose within Robin. 'Let's get our coats on and go into the back garden, it's dark now. Sometimes I... I look up at the night sky and imagine Dad is there, doing that might inspire us.'

They stood under the stars at the bottom of the garden, near the pond, Hoover appeared with one of Faye's gloves in his mouth and dropped it at her feet.

'We've almost got the answer, I can sense it's within our reach,' Robin murmured. It started to spit with rain. 'Just a few minutes longer.'

Help us out, Dad.

'Let's see if we can spot the moon in the water,' said Amber and leant over the dark pond and squinted in the dark. Stars reflected as tiny specks of rippling light. Under the moonlight their faces were just about visible in the water, three generations staring back.

'Fetch the scroll, Amber,' said Faye.

Minutes later, she reappeared, panting.

'Read out clue four again,' said Faye.

Amber stood by the light shining through the kitchen window and read it out loudly.

Faye tilted her head at the last four lines. *Bend over and look in, before the slope, you'll see who looks back, I hope. It's a sight nothing else can upstage, a right little gem, whatever its age.*

'Do you remember, Robin, your dad would call us his pair of little gems?'

'Yes. Usually after his pint or two of Double Diamond ale.'

'I think the answer is staring us in the face, literally. Alan calling us gems, a right little gem, it's you or me, Robin, looking into the water. The answer is our reflection looking back.'

Why didn't they think of that earlier? Robin's stomach fluttered, bigger drops of rain falling now.

'So R for reflection?' asked Amber, pulling out her phone. 'This has been so difficult, I think we should use an online anagram solver...'

The other two nodded.

Amber tapped on the screen but swapping in 'R' didn't bring up anything. Her shoulders slouched. Faye's skin looked blotchy.

Robin started walking up and down. 'We're just so close, it's got to be obvious.' She bent over the pond again. The rain was making her hair curlier than ever. Her head jerked up. 'What about Y for you instead of R for reflection – *you* are looking back? That would fit the riddle as well.'

'Fingers crossed, everyone, Y is our last chance.' Amber tapped on her phone.

Robin's stomach fluttered. GILYRM... The three of them huddled around the lit up screen.

MY GIRL.

'Wow!' said Amber.

'Oh. Two words. Yes, that was sometimes the case, but what

does it mean, how would that answer change everything?' said Robin.

'Could he be talking about Gran? Or you? Why wouldn't he be more specific?'

Robin breathed out heavily. 'Surely we haven't come this far to reach a dead end?'

Faye was very quiet and suddenly hurried inside.

'Leave her,' said Robin gently to Amber. 'This rain is getting worse, and she must be as disappointed as us that the solution isn't clear, let's give her a minute.'

Eventually they went in too, Robin switched on the oven and checked the frozen steaks she'd thawed out for tea. Amber went upstairs but soon came back down.

She shrugged. 'Gran's not here, I can't find her anywhere.'

Robin walked into the hallway and frowned. The front door had been left unlocked.

Robin Wilson,
16 Parade Row,
Stonedale,
Greater Manchester
April 1989

Dear Debbie,

WHY DOES MY MOTHER HATE ME?

I've been so excited about the future, leaving home, university, I've got it all planned. I can't wait to be independent. But I've got to get through my O levels first, in June and Mum really isn't helping. We've never got on, she criticises everything I do. Even the teachers say how important it is to take breaks from study, but she tells me off every time I go out to meet my boyfriend. Dad understands more, but he works away a lot. I can't talk to her about anything. Never have.

I don't know why I'm not good enough for her, even though my grades are high and I don't get into trouble at school. I might be rude sometimes but it's only because she is always nagging. She never asks if I'm okay with exams approaching, never offers advice about stuff like spots or period pains. She doesn't want to hear about my day at school, I have more of a laugh with my best friend's mum. And you'd think, just once, she'd say I look nice, like Dad always does.

Do you think our bad relationship must be my fault?

Robin, age 16

Girl's Scene 41
Gover Street,

London

Dear Robin,

I'm so sorry you are feeling like this and am very sure that your mother doesn't hate you. That you certainly are good enough for her. The teenage years can be challenging for lots of families. Having a baby doesn't come with instructions, either, and when you get older you'll understand that grown-ups don't always have all the answers. It sounds as if your mum just wants you to achieve your best and reach your potential.

Why not chat to her about this or if you can't face that, write her a letter instead? She'll probably be shocked that you feel like this and want to help you with school and personal problems. The fact that you've written to me shows that you aren't happy with the relationship between you and your mum and perhaps want change. Chances are she feels exactly the same, and will do her very best to be there for you from now on, for the big and little things. Don't be afraid, try to open up. I know it's not easy but you can do it, Robin.

Best wishes,

Debbie

46

'I can understand Mum being upset, but why wouldn't she tell us she was going for a walk? And look.' Robin pointed into the corner, by the front door. 'She hasn't taken her umbrella and that cape doesn't have a hood.' She rang Blanche, Faye wasn't there, yes, they'd let Blanche know as soon as she came home, it was probably nothing, not to worry...

Amber took out her phone and turned it onto flashlight mode. 'Perhaps we should look for her. Where do you think she could have gone?'

'Left, up past that estate agency, for a longer walk, or right for the church or further towards the village. She might have gone into the residential area again, where the lamppost used to be or straight past the shops and over Sheepwash Bridge, into the woods, or across the common, towards the Nag's Head...'

'We're going to need a bigger torch,' said Amber.

Robin looked at her watch. 'I'm not sure where we'd start. Maybe give her a little while longer?' Faye wouldn't want a fuss. But Hoover scampered towards them, a glove in his mouth. Robin bent over and gently took it from him. 'This must be the other one, he dropped the first by Mum's feet in the garden, he knew it belonged to her.' She and Amber exchanged glances. 'It might work.'

'Worth a try,' said Amber. 'He's a very intelligent dog, if anyone can track Gran it's him.'

Robin bent down. 'Hoover, do you think we should look for Mum?'

Hoover gave a very decisive bark.

'Can you find her then, boy?' He tilted his head. Robin lifted the glove to her face and sniffed it loudly, then put it to the floor, heart pounding, waiting, waiting, yes, Hoover buried his nose into the wool. Then he picked it up and shook it from side to side. Robin turned off the oven and put Hoover on the lead whilst Amber fetched her umbrella. Hoover ran to the front door, then he looked back into the hallway, past Robin and Amber. His tail stopped wagging. He dropped the glove and sniffed it once more. Robin carried it as they went outside.

Hoover bent down, sniffing the pavement, then he tugged towards the right, leading by his nose, all the way to the junction. Robin crouched down and let him smell the glove again. He strained on the lead, to cross the road.

'Do you think he understands?' asked Amber.

'I don't know.'

Quietly, Robin went into the church. She didn't want to disturb Faye if she'd needed a moment, but she wasn't there. She hurried to catch the others up – they were near the town hall now. Robin grew increasingly concerned as the weather worsened, not understanding why her mum would stay out, she hated the rain and cold. Hoover was barking and wouldn't stop, holding something white in his mouth, tail wagging furiously.

'He found it by that litter bin.' Amber pointed.

Robin bent down and eased the handkerchief from his jaw.

Her breath caught. She held it tightly. 'Look at that pattern around the edge. I think Mum's got one just like this.' He pulled towards the next junction, straining to cross over that road as well. Hoover led the way over Sheepwash Bridge, wet grass squelching as they reached the other side. They stood under the last streetlamp, near the picnic benches, and Amber got ready to direct her flashlight. Hoover sniffed the ground that gave off a woody, fresh smell, due to the evening shower. He moved to the left, then right. He darted forwards, then stepped back.

'Let's try calling for her.' said Amber. 'Gran! Gran, where are you?'

'Mum! Are you there? Let's go home. We'll have a nice hot drink.' Robin hugged her shoulders, chin resting on her chest, pacing to and fro, listening for Faye's voice. Leaves rustled in the breeze, the river babbled and splashed, but no one called back. Robin was about to shout again when Hoover pricked up his ears. He barked and pulled towards the right. Robin gave Amber a sideways glance before they both headed that way.

'Mum, is that you?' Robin narrowed her eyes as they approached the Iron Horse.

'I'm here...' She was leaning against the memorial, hair and cape sodden. 'I'm sorry if... I've worried you.'

Robin let out a huge breath and wrapped her arms tightly around Faye, thinking again how small she was now. Amber put up her umbrella and held it over her gran.

'I just needed to find some courage,' she mumbled. 'I knew I'd get it here.' Faye ran a finger over the engraved war dates. 'This memorial always made me think of Alan. He was my hero and I was always very thankful to have him. He bravely took me on, knowing about my... difficult upbringing. And the last hunt, the last anagram, I understand now, he's asking me to be brave enough to reveal what MY GIRL means.'

'*You know*?' asked Amber.

'And will it change everything?' Robin stuttered.

Faye sneezed.

'Come on, we can talk about this back in Parade Row, after we've warmed up.' Robin texted Blanche as they started walking.

* * *

'He's a very clever boy. He found you, Gran,' Amber said and stroked Hoover. She lay on her front, on the carpet, hair dry now.

Hot water bottle at her side, Faye sat in her armchair by the fire. She put down her mug. 'Right, let me explain…'

'Finish that drink first,' said Robin. Faye gave a little smile.

'You deserve a reward, don't you, boy?' said Amber, in a low voice, and tickled Hoover's ears. 'You really saved the day when the stakes might have been high.'

He cocked his head and disappeared into the kitchen. They heard a chair fall over, followed by paws padding back into the lounge.

Hoover stood in the middle of the room, a thawed-out steak hanging from his mouth.

47

Amber and Robin joined Faye at the dining room table. She'd lifted a box out of the cabinet by her armchair. It was made from cardboard and had a lid, like a stationery storage box.

'Wow. I never thought we'd end up with a real treasure chest, Gran.' Amber's eyes narrowed as she read a small label on the front. '*My Girl*...?'

Robin sat up and looked at Faye and back at the handwritten label.

'I used to keep this box at the back of my wardrobe,' Faye said, her voice sounding nervous.

'It must be very private then,' said Robin. Faye's hands trembled as she lay them on top of it. 'Are you sure you want to show us inside?'

Please say yes, Robin thought, her fingers crossed.

Faye lifted the lid.

Robin gasped. 'But there's Dad's robin, the one we got from the car boot sale.' She took it out, studying the gold streaks and detailed feathering of the wings, as she passed it to Amber she noticed the chip on the beak.

'May I?'

Faye nodded at Robin who picked out some sort of brochure. 'The programme for that Fourth Form play I was in, Charley's Aunt?' said Robin and she rubbed her forehead. 'But you never went.'

'I stood at the back. I was late. You were so good. So funny. I was going to tell you when you got home from the after party but you wouldn't speak to me.'

Robin had put her fingers in her ears when she'd tried to explain why she wasn't sitting next to her dad, so Faye sent her straight to bed.

Amber flicked through the programme and pointed out a photo of Robin on stage, and Tara too. Then she picked out a small box the size of a matchbox and slid it open. A curl of brown hair. Faye said Robin was born with it, she and Alan had called it her duck's tail.

'But you had such a difficult birth, Mum,' said Robin. 'Such horrendous early months... Why would you want to keep this?'

Faye ran a finger over the hair. 'I have such a clear memory of when they gave you to me to hold, that very first time, the wrinkles in your skin, the puckered lips, it didn't last long but I felt such a clear connection. And then... life got in between us.'

Robin hurried into the kitchen and fetched a glass of water, drinking the first mouthfuls leant against the sink. When she came back Faye was holding a sponsorship form from the charity walk Robin had done with Tara.

'I couldn't tell you I was proud. I was scared of making you stop grafting, stop trying to fulfil your potential. My mother never praised me and feeling that I was never good enough always made me strive to do better. But since I've seen the way you are with Amber I... I can see there's another way.'

Amber gave Faye a hug.

They sifted through Mother's Day cards and drawings Robin had done of people looking like circles with sticks for limbs. And Faye had kept a tiny pair of baby satin shoes from her christening. Robin downed the rest of the water, willing herself not to cry. Amber studied a report card. Faye said it was the first time Robin had got an A in Maths. There was also a crisp packet, red and white and OXO-flavoured.

'Why keep that, Gran?'

'My favourite flavour, it was hard to come by in Stonedale. Robin bought this packet for me once, in Manchester.'

'But you didn't even seem bothered, I never saw you open the packet.' Now and then, very rarely, Robin would want to do something nice for her, but she'd always thought her gestures failed. 'And you kept all these old scrolls...' Robin pulled out balls of screwed up tea-stained paper and shook her head.

Faye cleared her throat. 'I'd discreetly pull them out of the bins, after we threw them away. They reminded me of the rare times you and I had fun together. It wasn't true, what I said, that we only did the hunts because you were a child, to entertain you. Somehow those hunts eased the way you and I were together.' She looked at Robin.

Robin nodded. 'I always felt that too.'

She stared at the last thing in the box. A bundle of envelopes with an elastic band around them. The hairs stood up on the back of her neck. Robin looked at Faye whose chin quivered. Robin picked them up and slid off the band. She didn't need to pull out the letters inside that had clearly been read.

Robin's eyes widened. 'I don't understand.'

'You left them to be posted in the hallway, said you were entering *Girl's Scene* competitions...' Her voice faltered. 'But I knew what Dear Debbie on the front meant.'

Robin felt dizzy for a moment.

'Now and then I'd go into your room and read the latest issue, to check the content was suitable.'

Robin had done the same with Amber's.

'But... but these letters were private.' Robin held onto the bundle tightly. And yet she'd been prepared for them to be published publicly.

Faye clasped her hands together. 'But the first one I ever read, about you hating your short haircut, I felt such a strong pang of... regret, and guilt. It should have been *me* answering such questions, I felt such a failure. So... I figured I'd try to answer your problem the best I could. And then they kept coming.' Her voice wavered.

Amber stared at the letters. 'These are all the letters you wrote to that agony aunt? That's mad. But wait... the postmarks are from London.'

Faye nodded. 'Blanche helped me. I... I didn't have much of a clue, not to start with, how best to answer. We read some of the magazines together, to get a feel for how Dear Debbie responded. We both thought her answers were spot on. And... he never knew about the content, but Blanche's husband, Dennis, he went down to London every month with work, he agreed to post them for me.'

Robin couldn't let go of the letters. She sifted through them. Her mum had cared enough to go to all that effort. She'd wanted to help Robin with her problems.

'All those years you were giving me the advice I needed, I just didn't know it...' Still holding the bundle, Robin got to her feet and paced up and down by the kitchen door, a lightness in her chest quite unlike one she'd ever experienced.

'You aren't angry?'

'I think it's fucking brilliant,' said Amber, tears in her eyes.

Robin stood still and her eyes scanned one of the letters

before she shook it in the air. 'I remember this one, I wrote it not long before running away, saying my mum hated me.' She glanced at it again. 'Debbie... *you*, said you were sorry I felt like that...' Her mum had apologised back then?

'And I was. I wanted to say something to you, in person, but didn't know how to start... I'm sorry, Robin, I encouraged you to open up but didn't have the courage myself.' Faye's voice wavered. 'And then I was worried about my job, Alan died, I felt so angry about everything, and then you left... I didn't show Blanche that letter, you know. I felt so ashamed, seeing the state of our relationship written down, clear words I couldn't escape.'

'When I read this reply from Debbie... from you...' Robin still could hardly believe it. 'I did think about approaching you, but like you, I didn't know where to begin... and then I found out I was pregnant.'

'Was that the last letter you wrote to *Dear Debbie*?' asked Amber.

'No. There was one more... about the pregnancy.' Robin sat down again. 'Of course, it all makes sense now. I didn't leave it in the hallway, it was too risky. I posted it myself, I found a packet of stamps in a kitchen drawer. And when it came back, I was surprised with the embossed notepaper that looked so much more formal than before.'

Robin examined more of the letters, memories coming back about hair removal and boobs, about spots and tampons and money. It was getting late and Amber disappeared into the kitchen to prepare the food. Faye put everything back, the envelopes, the sponsorship form, the cards, the play programme, the duck's tail box and screwed up scrolls, last of all she placed the robin on top. Then she lifted it out again and placed it on the bookcase, next to the seaside painting.

'Your dad said this clue would start with a circle and end

with a heart.' She put a hand on her chest. 'I felt compelled to keep all these little things. Your dad said it was proof of... how much I loved you.'

Robin placed her hand on top of Faye's. Faye turned her hand around, palm up and it shook as she squeezed Robin's fingers. 'And I did love you, Robin. In my own way. Still do.'

'Did he know about the Dear Debbie letters?' she asked, in a hoarse voice.

'No. I felt those were something between women. A mother daughter thing. I'd never been good at that relationship, and Blanche had never had children. We just hoped that, between us, we helped.'

'You did,' Robin croaked.

When Amber announced that tea was almost ready, recovered from her walk out, Faye rushed into the kitchen. A while later she returned carrying a large white jug. She placed it on the table and shot Robin a tentative smile, before pushing it towards her.

'OXO beef gravy, there's nothing better with chips. Help yourself.'

Robin had always hated gravy, but she understood the gesture and smiled. 'Yes, please, Mum, that would be lovely.'

* * *

They tidied up and when the last plate had been dried Robin turned off the light and stood in the middle of the other two. They gazed out of the kitchen window, staring up at the sky, the three of them, side by side.

We did it, Dad, Robin thought, remembering how he'd sweep them both up into his arms at the end of every treasure hunt.

Despite Hoover running after a hare, the lamppost no longer

being there, and the detour to the crematorium; despite Robin ending up in the stream, the fallout in the church and the estate agency replacing the petrol station. Mother, daughter, granddaughter, they'd worked through the challenges together.

Would Robin have appreciated Faye's box back in 1989, and any sort of apology? As far as she was concerned, without Dad, Robin's life in Stonedale was over. Yet she'd always felt he was hanging around, a little voice in her head and, when the time was right, he'd led her to the box – and back to her mum.

And now that voice was talking about how the loft room could be converted into the perfect office for a freelance marketing consultant.

They stood in the dark and watched a satellite overhead. Robin glanced left, at Amber, wearing a pair of her old dangly earrings. It was funny how that secret room in the loft hadn't changed one bit, yet it had changed so much. Amber tucked her arm through Robin's and shuffled closer. The rain had stopped and the moon shone brightly, its reflection bobbing on the pond. Robin was about to suggest going into the lounge as it was getting cold, when, from the right, a hand slid into hers. Faye still stared straight up, but her fingers held on, ever so tight, as if Robin were a little girl again.

Paws padded in and Hoover dropped a wooden object at their feet. He sat expectantly. Robin picked it up and all three of them looked. It was Dad's favourite Christmas tree decoration, the one that spelt out FAMILY.

Robin Wilson,
16 Parade Row,
Stonedale,
Greater Manchester
June 1989

Dear Debbie,

PREGNANT AND RUNNING AWAY.

I'm pregnant, about two months I think, and my boyfriend has asked me to marry him. We can't wait to have the baby and are going to run away to London. There's no way I'm staying with my mum, I won't have her treat a child of mine the horrible way she's always treated me. She's even harder to talk to since my dad died suddenly. I miss him so much and cry myself to sleep every night. If he was alive I'd stay, he'd make an awesome granddad. I was about to tell him but now I can't and there's no one else to turn to. It's all such a mess. I'm scared about leaving home, all my plans have had to change, but excited as well. Do you think everything will work out? My boyfriend and I love each other so much.

Robin, age 16

GIRL'S SCENE
BRITAIN'S TOP TEEN MAGAZINE!
41 Gover Street,
London

Dear Robin,

I'm sending you this personal reply as quickly as I can. What a difficult situation you are in, and I'm so sorry about your dad's passing. Are you sure there isn't another adult you can talk to? What about an aunt or teacher or your boyfriend's parents? A youth club leader? Or the doctor, you should see one as soon as possible, now you are pregnant.

The two of you may love each other very much, but that alone won't pay the bills, and at sixteen it's not going to be easy finding jobs and a new home. How will you manage once the baby is born and half your joint income disappears? I can tell you'd want to do the best for your child and that's why you need to accept that running away isn't the best option and could even be dangerous. You have to be practical.

Why not sit down with your mum and your boyfriend's parents together? Or ask the doctor if they can be there. Lots of families fall out during the teenage years. Your mum might be angry at first but that won't last forever.

You never know, a grandchild might even bring you closer.

All sorts of options might be discussed. Just remember, you don't have to do anything you aren't comfortable with. It's your body. I've included a list of organisations that can help regarding the pregnancy, if you go to London. I hope you don't.

Good luck, Robin. You'll get through this.

And never forget, talk is a great healer — whether that's now or in the future.

All the very best,

Debbie

ACKNOWLEDGMENTS

For many reasons Under One Roof is special to me. It looks back on the 1980s, a period I remember fondly, the concerts I attended, the colourful clothes, the carefree nights out dancing around my handbag when, just for that moment in time, nothing else mattered. This book also heralds a further shift in a direction I've been taking for a while that is uplifting, with humour, but with depths I've enjoyed exploring. Like Robin, I wonder what the teenage me would think of the person I've become. It's been a joy to write from the heart and thanks to all the wonderful readers who have stuck with me during my author journey – and to those new readers who join me now.

Huge thanks to my brand new publisher, Boldwood. I am incredibly excited to be working with this dynamic, forward thinking company that has had such incredible success over the last two years. I appreciate your understanding and enthusiasm for how my writing is organically changing. Thanks to my hard-working, efficient editor, Tara Loder, for helping make this novel the very best it can be – and to the rest of the Boldwood team. I look forward to getting to know you all.

This story wouldn't exist without the tireless support and input from my agent, Clare Wallace, from the Darley Anderson Agency. Thanks, Clare, for helping me take the initial kernel of an idea and create something which is now very close to my heart. I'm always grateful for you pulling me back from my wackier ideas, and pushing me to be more bold when I need to be.

The process of writing this book has been unique. Firstly, it took place during lockdown and secondly, my inspiring, perceptive daughter acted as beta reader. Real life imitated art as we studied 1980s teenage magazine annuals together, chuckling at the features and how times have changed – just like Robin and Amber do in the story. It made the whole process so memorable. Thanks, Immy, for your keen eye and encouragement, for the laughter and love, and for helping to make the character of Amber and her dialogue more realistic.

I can't go without thanking Chris Kavanagh. The stories of the high jinks her beloved Schnauzer, Lottie, and her canine friends get up to, were invaluable when it came to creating cheeky French bulldog, Hoover! As were the anecdotes from Sarah Lucas who lived in Manchester as a teenager, during the 1980s – they really helped me get the detail right for how Robin and her best friend, Tara, might have lived it up!

I like to think of a story as a star with five points, each one of them helping it shine more brightly – author, publisher, agent, reader and blogger – and as my career progresses, and each book comes out, I'm more grateful than ever. They say it takes a village to raise a child... well, it takes a tremendous amount of energy to launch a star and help it rise as high as it can. Heartfelt thanks to you all xx

MORE FROM SAMANTHA TONGE

We hope you enjoyed reading *Under One Roof*. If you did, please leave a review.

If you'd like to gift a copy, this book is also available as an ebook, digital audio download and audiobook CD.

Sign up to Samantha Tonge's mailing list for news, competitions and updates on future books.

https://bit.ly/SamanthaTongeNews

Discover another uplifting story from Samantha Tonge.

ABOUT THE AUTHOR

Samantha Tonge is the bestselling and award-winning author of over fifteen romantic fiction titles. Her first book for Boldwood, *Under One Roof*, was published in February 2022 and marks a broadening of her writing into multi-generational women's fiction. She lives in Manchester with her family.

Visit Samantha's Website: http://samanthatonge.co.uk/

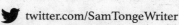 twitter.com/SamTongeWriter

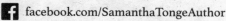 facebook.com/SamanthaTongeAuthor

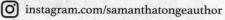 instagram.com/samanthatongeauthor

Boldwood

Boldwood Books is an award-winning fiction publishing company seeking out the best stories from around the world.

Find out more at www.boldwoodbooks.com

Join our reader community for brilliant books, competitions and offers!

Follow us
@BoldwoodBooks
@BookandTonic

Sign up to our weekly deals newsletter

https://bit.ly/BoldwoodBNewsletter